JENNY BUNTING

Editing: Lopt & Cropt Editing

Proofreading: Horus Proofreading

Cover: Kari March Designs

BOOKS BY JENNY BUNTING

Here in Lillyvale

Here (Zoey and Jonathan)

Hustle (Taylor and Malcolm)

Home (Addison and Kirk)

Hubby (Makenna and Dan)

Stuck in Love

Please Be Seated (Erin and Landon)

In Case of Emergency (Cassie and Smith)

For Your Safety (Raegan and Henry)

Finch Family

Fool's Gold (Annie and Cameron)

This book is dedicated to the fur loves of my life who crossed the rainbow bridge too soon.
Woody and Annie, I miss you everyday.

A NOTE FROM JENNY

Thank you so much for reading *Fool's Gold*! I hope you enjoy it.

While this book is overall light and low angst, there is brief mention of an unexpected pet death that is non-violent. If you are sensitive, please take care of yourself.

1

CAMERON

"Emily, the raccoons are back."

I escape inside the sliding glass door and shut it quickly. My sister may be cool with raccoons on her deck, but I doubt she wants one running through the house.

I press my body against the wall, maintaining eye contact with the fatter of the two, currently chowing down on the cat food.

"Go away," I yell at them through the glass. The little fucker keeps eye contact as he dips the dry cat food in water with its creepy hands and stuffs its face.

We don't even have a cat.

My large mug with a C on it sits by a hissing pot of coffee. I pour some liquid gold, trying to ignore the beady eyes and my constant questions of why my sister has sympathy for trash pandas.

The first sip scalds my tongue. "Fuck," I say as I set it down. My eight-year-old niece, Olive, turns the corner into kitchen at the exact time.

"Hi, Olive. You didn't hear that…"

"Hear what?" she asks, pushing her brown hair out of her face.

"Exactly. So, the raccoons are eating the cat food again," I say, pointing as I blow on my coffee.

Distraction is key.

Olive's face lights up. "That's Thelma and Louise."

I blink rapidly. "What?"

"Mommy named them," Olive says, pointing to each raccoon.

"Is Mommy okay with them on the deck?"

Olive shrugs again. She sits in her usual spot, folding her hands like she demands service. That's my cue. I drape a towel over my forearm and walk to Olive's side, doing our usual morning schtick as her mother, my sister, gets ready.

"What can I get you, madam?" I ask in my bad British accent that always makes Olive laugh.

Today, she is stone-faced as she sticks her nose in the air.

"Cheerios, please, with half of a banana."

"Does the lady prefer plain or Honey Nut?"

"Surprise me." Her tiny nose goes higher.

"And what would madam care to drink?"

"Orange juice, please."

"At your service," I say, bowing, and that finally gets a giggle.

I'm glad my back is to her when she says, "Uncle Cam, why was there a lady leaving your house last night?"

Oh fuck. Usually, I get away with it.

There are pluses and minuses to living on my sister's property in my tiny home. It's cheap as hell. Since the structure is paid off, I can live off of very little. I kick in for groceries and electricity, but most of the money I make goes into my bank account. The tiny home is all about freedom—

freedom to live the way I want without worrying about money or another person.

The big fat negative is I have to deal with constant judgment from my sister and her daughter about my...habits.

I like women. I like them a lot.

"That wasn't a lady. It was a raccoon," I say, finding the Honey Nut Cheerios and Olive's favorite bowl, a bright pink one.

"Uncle Cam, get real," Olive says.

I wince. I taught her that phrase. Pouring some cashew milk over her cereal and cutting half a banana, I turn and place it in front of her with flair. She puts her elbows on the table to shovel the cereal into her mouth. Emily would usually tell her to get her elbows off the table, but I let it slide.

I pour the orange juice in a plastic goblet Emily used for drunk crawls when she was in college.

My niece uses two hands to drink, and it's the cutest thing ever.

"She's a friend," I say, biting into the other half of the banana.

Olive looks up, her spoon hovering over her cereal. "What's her favorite color?"

"Purple," I blurt out. I have no idea. I'm not even sure of her first name.

"Will she be your girlfriend?" Olive asks.

I choke on the banana piece and cover my mouth to avoid spewing fruit shrapnel.

"I'm content as I am, Martini," I say, using a nickname Emily hates but Olive loves. "I don't want a girlfriend."

"Aren't you getting older?"

Wow, really stick in my gut. I nod. "Yes, I am. Just like you."

"You're *way* older, Uncle Cam."

I swallow again and my neck prickles with heat. "Yes. That is true."

"You need a girlfriend. Get serious," she says, spooning Cheerios into her mouth.

I sip the coffee, but it does nothing for the dry mouth. At our last family dinner, I overheard my sister discussing my love life with my mom. I've lived on my sister's property for seven years, and I've gotten more brazen with the women I've brought home.

"I'm just wondering if he's ever going to grow up," Emily had said to our mother, like the traitor she is. "It was fine when he was in his twenties..."

"Cameron has always been a barrel of fun. He can't be serious. That's the way he is, Emily Jean," my mom had said.

Can't be serious.

That eats at me, like the raccoons chomping on cat kibble.

Emily tears into the kitchen in a panic, ping-ponging from her child to the counter to the fridge, pulling her own brown hair into a ponytail.

"Oh good, she's eating," Emily says. "We have to leave in five minutes."

"You're more anxious than usual," I say, sipping my coffee.

"Dan's coming today," Emily says. She looks me up and down. "We need to stop on the way over there to get coffee and the spread."

"Oh f—," I say, my lips buzzing as I trail off.

"You forgot," Emily says.

"No, of course I didn't."

Yeah, I absolutely forgot.

Emily leans in and sniffs, her nose wrinkling. "Put on a

different shirt. Maybe one that doesn't smell like an entire Bath and Body Works store."

"Maybe that's my natural musk," I say as I walk to the sliding glass door. The raccoons are gone. I point to the empty cat dish. "The raccoons are back. Why did you put out cat food? Did you get cat food just for those f—" My lips buzz again as I catch my almost-curse.

I'm getting better.

"Thelma and Louise!" Olive says, lifting her spoon in the air.

"It's fine," Emily says, vibrating with nervous energy.

"I'll be back," I say in my best Arnold Schwarzenegger impression. It always makes Olive giggle, and I see a smile on her face before I turn around.

"Five minutes," Emily yells at me as I take my coffee back to my tiny house.

Ten minutes later, we're in my sister's SUV, the tires crunching on the gravel road. Olive bounces in the backseat, her nose stuck in a book.

"You'll have to tuck and roll, honey," Emily says. Olive barely responds as we pull in front of Goldheart Elementary. The dropoff line is sparse, but Emily barely stops the car before Olive gets out and pulls her backpack onto her shoulders.

"Bye, baby," Emily says with a wave.

"Remember, Olive..." I start.

"Shaken, not stirred," Olive finishes, becoming a different child, swinging her arms and shaking her hips.

Emily glares at me. "I can't believe you."

"What?" I ask as we pull away from the curb. "You're welcome for entertaining your child. Feeding your child. Fighting off the raccoons so they don't tear off the face of your child."

"Raccoons are misunderstood creatures," Emily says. "You're running into Gold Roast."

"What?" I say, the blood draining from my face. My ex-hookup, Tara, owns Gold Roast. She moved to town a few months ago, and I was part of her welcoming committee. Well, my dick was.

After I asked her to leave after acrobatic sex against my ladder, she told me to "eat shit and die" and slammed the door loud enough to awaken the raccoons.

I have sensible reasons for not letting women sleep over. The mattress in the tiny house barely fits me; I'm six-five and I love to do the starfish. Another human can't sleep with me up in my tiny loft bed because I tend to travel. My giant feet would end up in her hair.

I own a tiny home so women don't get ideas. I can't be tamed. After two pseudo-relationships in high school, one that ended with me in the ER with a concussion and a gash on my skull, I haven't dated anyone longer than a week. My dick loves wild women, who usually launch hard items at my head when I inevitably piss them off. Women think they want me as a boyfriend, but I would be the worst. I stopped trying to make things work I'm not good at a long time ago.

Tara didn't tell me she was looking for everlasting love, so I thought it was okay to ask her to leave after we were done.

It was not. I've avoided Gold Roast long enough. Still, my hand hesitates at the door handle.

Emily sniffs out my reluctance like a raccoon finds left-over Chinese.

"Oh God, you slept with her, too? Cam!"

"Blame it on the tequila!"

"Well, time to face the horndog music," Emily says with

a point. "That wasn't the woman who I saw leaving your house last night?"

She wasn't, but *fuuuuuuccccccckkkkkk*. Of course I couldn't get that past my way-too-smart sister.

"Why were you up? Your favorite episode of *Law and Order* on again?" I ask.

"I had orders to fill," Emily says, rubbing her face. One of the reasons my sister can afford her beautiful piece of land is because of her kickass jewelry business on Etsy.

Emily shakes her head. "I feel like Dan's going to drop the hammer at any moment."

I roll my eyes. Dan is an angel investor in our family's business, Woody Finch Brewery. Our dad almost bankrupted us, and it would've gone under if it wasn't for Dan Price. With Dan's guidance and investment, we've been able to rebrand, hone our business to build up the brewery experience, and get out of my father's money-pit of a distribution plan.

My dad wanted the glory of being in grocery stores, where the margins are super tight, and neglected the taproom for years. Dan suggested we focus on a taproom model and look at distribution far in the future.

At least, that's what I think he did. I've zoned out at most of the meetings and doodled instead.

Because of Dan, we recently refurbished a barn that had been vacant for some time into a new taproom and are getting decent foot traffic on the weekends. Still, not a lot of people know of us in surrounding areas, and obscurity is our biggest obstacle.

Since our beer is phenomenal.

It finally feels like we're making headway. Dan is ecstatic with us. Still, my sister and mother love to look for worry that's not there.

"Dan is a great guy. He'll understand."

"I hope so," Emily says, gripping the steering wheel.

"Everything's going to be okay," I say. "Relax."

"Oh, thank you so much for that advice. I've never thought of that!" my sister says sarcastically.

My sister needs to take my approach to life. Easy. Carefree. Low stakes.

Emily turns onto Main Street, passing one of many historical landmarks, the church, where prospectors came to pray for a gold mine discovery. Further down the road, Gold Roast Coffee shares space with other small businesses in what used to be the town's bank. Goldheart was founded on California's gold rush, and it's sprinkled with reminders of a time gone by. Lately, the city council's been working on revitalizing the downtown, bringing in tourists and crowding us locals.

Our town refuses to let big-name stores in, so Gold Roast is one of the few coffee options in town. You have to go one town over to get Starbucks, one of the biggest gripes of our tourists. While I see new faces on the street all the time, other Goldheart residents know all about my reputation of drinking at the Swift and bedding as many willing ladies as possible. Jokes are made constantly about me, but I let them slide.

I still wouldn't want to live anywhere else.

We pull into an angled parking spot in front of the coffee shop, and I open the car door. "Your usual?"

"Please," Emily says, smacking her cheeks to wake herself up.

"You got it."

I enter the hallway of the building and duck into the first door. The air inside Gold Roast is warm and sugar-scented. Three people hover by the pickup counter, studying their phones. I tentatively walk up to the counter to find Tara, my ex-date.

Absolutely pissed to see me.

"Cameron," Tara says.

"Tara," I say, crossing my arms. "I have an order for the brewery to pick up. I think it was paid already. And I need a large almond milk latte, two sugars."

Tara flicks an eyebrow as she stabs the cash register like she wants to stab my eyes.

"That will be eight dollars and six cents."

My eyes bulge. "There's no fucking way."

"That's the price," she says.

I don't know why she's so mad. I was upfront, honest. It's common knowledge I don't do relationships and I just like to have fun. She must've forgotten about the three orgasms I delivered that one night after home-cooked Italian food and some really nice wine.

I don't fight it, pulling out my wallet to find a ten. I hand it to her, and she opens the cash register, placing the bill in and closing it, without counting change.

"Aren't you going to get me my change?" I ask.

"Um...no," Tara says.

I sigh. "It's for my sister, so please don't spit in it," I say as she walks away to make the order.

"Harsh," I hear behind me. Turning around, I find Annie Stewart, wearing her work's forest green polo shirt and a teasing smile.

The Annie Stewart. Quartz High School's mathlete legend, and my former math tutor. Looking beautiful as always.

We've run into each other over the years, and seeing her is always like finding a twenty you forgot about in your jeans. It puts me in a great mood for the rest of the day.

I also love hugging her every chance I get.

"Hey Annie," I say, opening my arms. Her arms are always strong and comforting around me.

Annie and I have known each other since we were kids. She's six feet tall, so we always got stuck together in the back row of classroom pictures. Her red hair, the color of amber beer, is in a ponytail, and her face is free of makeup.

She looks stunning. But she always does.

When I let her go, I cross my arms. "Were you here this whole time?"

"I saw most of it," she says. "Lovers' quarrel?" She peers around me to look at Tara.

"*Former* lovers' quarrel," I say.

Her malt-colored eyes gleam. "Breaking hearts everywhere like usual, I see, Cam."

"It's what I do."

"What are you up to today?"

"We have a big meeting with our investor this morning. Emily is freaking out," I say, shoving my hands in my pockets.

"I'm sure it will be great," Annie says.

I can't help but grin at that. "Thanks," I reply.

Annie and I have always been friendly, although we had zero in common growing up. She was the yearbook editor and class president, and graduated as valedictorian. I got caught fucking a cheerleader under the bleachers, got ejected from one too many football games for pushing a kid talking shit, and went to summer school every summer to make up for bad grades.

Annie is the only reason I got my diploma. She saved my ass when it was do-or-die for math, and I almost kissed her in the library when I got a C-plus on the final my junior year.

Almost.

We saw each other once and a while senior year, but what little magic we had seemed to have evaporated.

Annie punches me in the arm. "Thank you so much again for setting up Raegan's engagement. I really appreciate it."

"No problem," I say, looking at the ground.

Her sister Raegan and her fiancé Henry came to the first trivia night we hosted at the brewery three months ago. Henry wanted to propose to Raegan through a series of trivia questions about roller coasters and Miley Cyrus, which I thought was weird at first. Then, I heard the story of how they got stuck on a roller coaster during their first date.

Henry proposed to Raegan after dating her for three months.

Stuff like that gives me heart palpitations. I'm not built like that at all. I rarely make it to a third date.

"Annie!" Tara yells from behind the counter.

"Well, it was good seeing you," Annie says, leaving my side. Tara hands her a tray of coffees and a bag. When she passes me, I smell her scent, something tropical with coconut. She turns back and smiles genuinely. "Good luck on your meeting."

"Thanks," I say, as she breezes past me and out the door.

Do not check out her legs, do not check out her legs, sensible me says.

It's such a nice pair of legs, though, horndog me says.

She's the only person who thought I was more than my large dick or athletic ability. I can't ruin her image of me even if I really, really want to stick my dick inside of her.

I'll settle for those sexy-as-fuck hugs.

I breathe as a sigh as Tara slams down the coffee.

"Fuckhead," she says.

"That's me," I say, taking it with a smile.

I watch Annie walk to her Jeep, putting sunglasses on before she climbs in.

Man, whoever she ends up with is some lucky guy.

2

ANNIE

"Raegan, you just got engaged. Don't you think July is quick?" I say, my phone pinned between my shoulder and my ear.

July is exactly four months away. That little time to plan a wedding makes me nauseous. Never mind I'm an event planner and it seems tight. I need much longer to be sure of someone than my sister does, apparently.

Raegan always jumps in, feet first. Meanwhile, I need a detailed pros and cons list just to decide to take a vacation.

"They had an opening, and I had to jump on it," my baby sister Raegan coos. A deep ache settles in my chest. Seeing Raegan so happy and in love reminds me of my own heartache.

"Maybe enjoy being engaged. Why not wait till next year?" I ask as I pull open the door to the Banning Cellars, balancing the coffees and pastries I brought on my forearm. The coffee tray teeters in my hand, and I catch it, sacrificing my phone to the ground.

The phone lands squarely on the shoe of my ex-boyfriend.

Jason Banning, my employer's son. I'm not even sure he's technically an ex-boyfriend. We were never official, and he hid me like a porn collection. It's been two months since we ended it and I still cry randomly throughout the day. I'm so angry I'm still wickedly attracted to him.

In my twelve years working for his family, I always thought Jason was so handsome, with his wave of golden hair and sparkle in his blue eyes. His bravado pulled me in and I felt special that a man like Jason liked me. Boring, anal me.

The first kiss between us was electric and every interaction super-charged. As we snuck around, the thrill of the secret awakened something in me. I could be wild. I could be daring.

I loved the way I felt when I was with him.

I just wasn't special enough to date out in the open, I guess.

Jason squats down to pick up my phone.

"Hi," I say as my purse drops from my shoulder, causing white mocha to slosh down the front of my polo shirt.

"Do you need a hand?" Jason asks.

"No, I like to struggle," I say.

"Here, let me," he says, taking the tray.

I walk through the lobby, past the custom pottery on display from a local artist, down the hallway to my office and Jason follows me.

Setting down the bag of pastries, I take a deep breath with closed eyes. I turn around to face him when I don't feel like screaming. Seeing Jason is not how I want to start my week.

Jason drops my phone on the desk. "Can we talk?" he asks.

I grab my phone to see a text from Raegan.

Raegan: School is about to start. TTYL.

I point to my phone. "Sorry, I was talking to my sister."

"How's she doing?"

My cheeks lift at his interest in my family. He rarely asked about them before.

"She just got engaged, but she's thinking about July. Crazy, right?" I say.

Jason's face falls, and I'm not sure why.

I open my palm toward him. "How are you? I haven't seen you around the winery much lately."

Like you're avoiding me.

Jason's blue eyes pierce my gaze, and I liquefy like the winery's award-winning jalapeno jelly.

"I wanted to give you some space. I know I hurt you, and seeing you..."

"It's fine," I say with a fake smile and hand flip. He doesn't need to know about the crying, the cartons of ice cream I've blacked out eating, or how my nose got so raw from tissues, I had to sleep covered in ointment.

"It hurt me, too," Jason says.

"It did?"

"Absolutely. We had something special."

"We did?" I ask. Most of my crying is because I feel so stupid. No man has never made me feel like this before. Going over to his house was as thrilling as bungee jumping —I shook with excitement. Our talks ripped me open, and I saw parts of Jason not many people see. I understood why he didn't want us to go public with our relationship. His father expected so much from him, and he had a lot on the line. A relationship with an employee would look bad. I used to nod with his reasoning, although a little voice inside of me kept saying it didn't make sense, if he truly cared about me.

"I want to make sure this is forever before I let them know," he'd told me. "Once I tell them, I'm marrying you."

When he said that, I excused myself to the bathroom and screamed into a towel, I was so excited.

Then, one night, two months ago, he broke it off. With zero warning.

"I don't feel like the way I *should* feel," Jason said. "You deserve everything, and I can't give it to you."

He convinced me to sleep over since I was so emotional and I gave in, crying into my pillow while he snored.

Now, he stands in front of me, with his dimple and his forearms, and I'm putty in his hands again.

Jason leans onto my desk. "I have something to tell you."

My breath catches in my throat. *He misses me! He's changed his mind. Be nonchalant when he tells you.* I cross my arms and sit down, leaning onto the arm. Do I look casual?

"I'm engaged," Jason says.

Wait, what?

My mouth drops, and my head grows light. A shaky breath leaves my lips, and I cannot swallow the huge lump of emotion in my throat. A swig of coffee doesn't do anything, and I shuffle papers on my desk.

"She's wonderful. I can't wait for you to meet her," Jason says, dropping into one of my visitor chairs.

My head is full of helium. I can't think straight. It's been two months since we broke up because he wasn't sure about his feelings for me, but he's sure enough about *her* to propose?

What if we overlapped?

The room spins. This can't be happening.

"Who is she?"

Jason is quiet. I already know who it is.

"Is it Morgan?" I ask.

When he nods, my spirit crumples within me. He dated Morgan before me. Swore up and down that he was over her, that she was a crazy bitch, and that I had nothing to worry about.

Apparently I did.

"How?" I ask numbly.

"It just happened," he says.

I nod like I'm a school counselor hearing a student's outlandish dreams. Relaxing my face, I hope it masks the decimation of my heart.

The silence is as loud as a monster truck show.

"That's great," I say, holding back a sob. "I'm so happy for you."

"I wanted to let you know first, Annie. Before it was announced," Jason says. "So it didn't catch you off guard."

I swallow. "When is it getting announced?"

"In an hour. At the morning staff meeting," Jason says.

"Thank you for telling me," I say, staring at the wood grain pattern on my desk. Although my heart just shattered again into a million pieces, at least he told me. Gave me the courtesy of not being blindsided.

"I'm so relieved," Jason says, grabbing his chest. He exhales a long sigh. "I was so nervous to tell you. I don't know why I was so worried. You're the best."

He stands up and extends his arms. I stand up, walk around my desk, and hug him. I hold my breath so I don't get wrapped up in his scent. Jason rubs my back and squeezes me before releasing me and walking to my door.

Turning around, he says, "We're having an engagement party here this weekend. It's great that we got that cancellation last minute."

If you call a groom calling off a wedding last week and leaving his bride in tears great.

My stomach clenches. "Who's planning it?"

"See," he says, tapping his temple. "Morgan hired an outside event planner. You don't have to do a thing. I know you're amazing, and you would do it if I asked, but I assumed it would be awkward. For you."

Morgan hired an outside event planner. Morgan.

Does she know about me? I feel like a forgotten footnote in their love story.

"I mean, you don't have to come if you don't want to. But you're really special to me, Annie. I want you there," he says.

I hold back the tears like a Dr. Phil guest. "I'll see if I can make it."

"Great," he says as he opens the door. "Have a great day, Annie."

"Thanks," I say. "Can you shut the door when you leave?"

"No problem," he says.

The door closes. I wait a few beats, listening for his footsteps to grow fainter and fainter. Once I'm sure he's gone, I drop my head to my desk. My forehead bangs against the wood, and searing pain rips through my skull.

"Ow," I say with a whine and my hand on my head.

I hyperventilate through the sobs. Memories replay in my mind.

He told me he loved me once. Only once. I had slaved all day on my one day off to make an exquisite birthday dinner for him, complete with a homemade carrot cake. Afterwards, I gave him the best blow job of my life, and as I wiped my mouth, swallowing his cum, he said, "I love you."

I spent the next few months trying to get those words out of him again. Now he's saying it to a woman who didn't have to cook and blow him and be kept a secret.

My chest tightens, and I breathe in and out from my

diaphragm, my deep breaths interrupted by the occasional sob.

We are done crying. You still have to face him.

I try to do a little bit of email-clearing before my phone dings with a five-minute warning of the staff meeting. I take the emergency makeup remover from my desk and fix the smudged mascara and swipe on some tinted lip balm, using my phone as a mirror.

I smile to myself, hoping it's convincing enough. No makeup residue on my face, and my eyes aren't that red. Hopefully, I can fool everyone.

I change into a fresh Banning Cellars polo shirt, one not covered in white mocha, and smooth down my ponytail. Grabbing my pad of paper and my favorite pen to take notes, I take a deep breath.

On the outside, I can be my usual calm, collected self, unshakable and sensible.

Inside, I feel like a decaying corpse.

3

CAMERON

O ur mother is spreading a tablecloth over one of the picnic benches when Emily and I arrive at the brewery with coffee and pastries.

"Oh good, you're here. Is the heat lamp too much? It's a little breezy, but maybe it's *too* warm?"

"Mom, it's fine," I say. "Relax."

She smiles and goes back to nervously straightening a tablecloth that's already straight.

"Where's Dad?"

"Printing off reports with Jackson. He can't figure out the printer to save his life."

Emily and I give each other a look. I love my parents, but they're technology-resistant and always insist one of us kids comes over whenever something goes array. It's one of the many reasons the first couple years of Woody Finch was *bumpy.*

Jackson, my oldest brother, just moved back from Seattle and hasn't set firm boundaries yet, so he's our parents' current tech guru. He went over a couple nights ago to set up Netflix, but my mom still can't figure out how to watch *The Crown*.

Mom places a vase with flowers in the middle.

"Does it look good? We have to make it look good for Dan."

"Dan doesn't care," I say. "He'll probably have holes in his jeans."

"Not anymore," Mom says. "Makenna wouldn't allow it."

I nod once in agreement. Dan's wife did update his wardrobe for him. Still, he's a simple guy at heart. It's why we named the weakest beer in the whole place after him, Dan the Man, a wheat beer with zero IBU, a rating scale to mark the bitterness of a beer.

I personally like a beer that's a punch in the face, but that's me.

Reid comes out with a pint of Dan the Man for Dan, the suds sloshing over the sides of the pint glass. "I saw his car pull up."

Dan told us a long time ago it didn't matter what time of day it was; he invested in a brewery so he could drink during meetings. I think the real reason is he has a soft spot for my dad. Breweries aren't known to be cash cows, but Dan saved us.

Still, he's dead-ass serious about drinking beer at meetings, and it doesn't matter what time it is, we always have one waiting for him. Mom insists we get coffee, just in case. Usually, it's Reid and me drinking it, and we're strung out by two.

"Hello, beautiful people!" Dan says, with his arms outstretched. He always hugs me first, then my mom, then Emily. Dan is quite the character. He's more than a foot shorter than I am, but he carries himself with a bravado and confidence I've never seen in a man his size. I respect the hell out of him because he's successful but doesn't feel the need to flaunt it. If I cared about accruing wealth, I would want to do it like him.

He also recently got married, and he's changed a little bit. He's calmer, happier. Dresses better.

"Hi, Dan," Dad says, followed by Jackson. Dad shakes Dan's hand, and Dan extends his palm to Jackson as well. Jackson's not a hugger.

"Hit me with the figures," Dan says, sitting down at the table. He takes the first sip of beer and lets out a sound of refreshment. He also grabs a scone from our spread to break into pieces and pop into his mouth.

I don't know why my family is so intimidated by him.

Our meeting starts like the others. My family presents the last quarter's numbers and gives Dan an update on our current margins and new beers and products being developed.

Dan nods and listens, sipping his beer. Before only an inch is left, Reid replaces it with a fresh one as my dad sweats more and more, explaining current measures to streamline our brewing process and reduce waste.

Jackson interjects when my dad doesn't know the answer, since Jackson did a thorough review of the finances when he came back home and now keeps a close eye on it.

Reid also chimes in, since he's assistant brewmaster to my dad, and explains the new beers and what our current test markets are saying. My sister gives staffing updates and shows Dan our social media feeds and the engagement and reach.

During these meetings, I usually sit back and daydream, paying little to no attention. My position in my family's brewery is vague and undefined. Since I worked construction before I quit to work for Woody Finch, I led a crew to renovate our current taproom, and I did a damn good job of it. I figured it would earn me at least two years of skating by. While my siblings hate working the taproom, I absolutely love it. I chat, I flirt, I sling beer better than anyone else here. Plus, I'm good at it.

Lately, there's been pressure to host events, and I know it's going to fall on me since the rest of my siblings have so much responsibility already. I feel like I did enough already in planning low-key monthly bar trivia nights. Our last one had twenty teams, and we had a really good night, sales-wise.

Emily slaps me in the bicep, and it startles me.

"I heard the trivia nights have been going well," Dan says louder, like he's repeating himself.

Fuck.

"Yes, we had a proposal during the first one. I worked with the guy, and it went great," I say. I just remember how sad Annie looked that night when her sister got engaged. I wish I knew why.

Man, Annie looked so cute this morning. I love it when she wears her hair up. I can see her creamy neck, lightly dusted with freckles...

"Cam, focus," Mom says, snapping in front of my face.

"Sorry, Dan," I say, smiling. I have no idea why I'm fantasizing about my high school math tutor.

"We're also the title sponsor of the Heart of Gold Half-Marathon, and we're giving out beer at the finish line," Emily says. Oh fuck, I need to put that in my phone. I will forget.

Dan smiles. "Love that we're at the finish line of a half-marathon although I don't get running. The trivia nights are a great start. I like where your head is at, but every other brewery does those. I want people to see the hard work Cameron and his guys did on this beautiful taproom."

I must've given a confused look because Dan glares at me. "Cameron, I want you to plan something new and different on the schedule in two months."

"That's not a lot of time," I say. My mother exhales sharply.

Dan points at me. "You can do it. I know you can."

"I don't know," I say. Behind the bar, shooting the shit with our customers, pouring beer—that's where I want to be. Since I finished the renovation, I haven't been pulling my weight, I know that. But Dan should want anyone but me to plan events.

"Two months," Dan says. He looks me dead in the eye and says, "It's time to get serious."

Olive's words from this morning ring in my ears. The universe is being too on the nose today.

Reid laughs under his breath, and I throw him a scowl.

I lock eyes with Dan. I have too much respect for him not to try. "I'll figure it out."

Dan sips his beer. "Next meeting, I want an idea. Or five. And Cameron will plan it."

"Dan, I'm not sure that's a good..." Emily says, and Dan throws up his hand.

"It's a great idea."

I nod and write down *Event* in bold, blocky letters. We end the meeting with pulling samples of the new beers we have, which is wasted since Dan only likes beer like Coors Light.

"Cameron, is this beer good?" he asks with a pinched face, lifting a sampler glass to me of our new hazy New England-style IPA called Gold Dust.

I nod. "It's a popular flavor profile for our customers in

the summer. It has just enough citrus undertones to balance the bitterness of the hops."

Dan nods once. He gets overwhelmed with the technicality of beer making, so he always asks me because I explain it simply. Reid or my dad start detailing recipes and the nuance of the flavor and Dan's eyes glaze over like a doughnut.

Dan stands. "I need to be sober enough to get back down the hill." He walks by and smacks me on the chest. "Two months. An event to get bodies into this taproom. Bring Goldheart together."

"Sure thing, Dan."

After Dan leaves, Emily corners me in our mini breakroom.

"What?" I ask, dropping my phone as I checked the sports news for the day.

"This is really important," Emily says, crossing her arms and leaning against my door frame.

"I understand," I say.

"You need to come up with something good," Emily says. "We need you to be serious about this."

"I can be serious," I reply. "It'll fall into place. I know it."

"You can't goof off, Cam. Our business depends on it. Dad's dream depends on this. Please brainstorm ideas."

"I will," I promise.

I spend the rest of the morning staring into space and Googling "Fun Events to Have at Breweries." The internet brings me nothing, so I wander out right before we open at eleven to do what I do best.

Interact with customers.

It's a Tuesday so it's slow, a group of people here or there to get a beer. I sell a hoodie and a hat, and even drink a beer myself when the place empties out.

I study the space, wondering what kind of event would work. The taproom is large, with high tops and tables for patrons to drink at. Our outdoor space in front is massive as well. My dad insisted on a mini stage for music, if we got bands or artists to come. I just stand on it for trivia for now.

What should we plan?

When my replacement shows up, I leave after I say goodbye to Reid and Emily. I need a stiffer drink than what they have at the brewery.

This can be figured out. I know a semi-decent answer to my problem will come to me eventually.

I just didn't expect the universe to bring me Annie Stewart for the second time today, this time crying into a banana split at the Swift at four-thirty in the afternoon.

4

ANNIE

Once I stop crying after Jason's visit, I make it my full workday dry-eyed.

However, the minute I park my car behind Town Square, the tears flow like a fire hose. The last time I cried like this in a car, I was eight and my sperm donor of a dad didn't show for a planned Disneyland vacation.

Okay, that is enough, I tell myself. I wipe tears from my eyes.

I don't have an event tonight, so Ice Dream Ice Cream Shop stands in front of me, like a beacon of hope.

Once a month, I allow myself a banana split. Over the years, I've perfected my order, and all the employees know it by heart.

One scoop of chocolate, one scoop of vanilla, one scoop of strawberry. Chocolate sauce on the chocolate ice cream, pineapple on the vanilla, strawberries on the strawberry. Extra whip cream and double the cherries.

I had one last week, but today is an emergency.

Between my sister's engagement, Jason's engagement,

and a consultation with a very particular bride and an even worse mother, I need it.

"Hey Annie!" Ryder, Ice Dream's teenage employee, greets me brightly.

"The usual," I say, and Ryder nods once. Even the bright walls and cutesy ice cream art can't lift my spirits. I'm grateful Ryder doesn't question my habit because I can't handle one more person pitying me.

Annie, the Amazonian spinster, ordering ice cream.

Eating ice cream alone like she's going to die alone.

Ryder hands me my order, and I tip him ten dollars.

I step out into the warm air and turn to the left. It's only four-thirty, but the Swift is open, with a few motorcycles parked out front.

It's our local watering hole, with men only a little creepy, but not enough to tell off. Carl, the owner, always takes care of me, though, and tells the creepers to leave me alone.

Does bourbon go with ice cream?

We're about to find out.

The air is stale when I walk into the dark bar. Dart board machines glow under different brewery signs, including the local brewery, Woody Finch. I find the smallest table in the most tucked away spot.

Usually, I wipe down tables as gross as this, but instead, I drop into the chair like wet cement and drop my ice cream down with a thud. Ryder hooked me up.

"Can I get you anything, Annie?" Carl asks me from behind the bar.

"Four Roses, neat," I say. He nods once and turns toward his wall of liquor, plucking the amber liquid from the shelf.

I unwrap my dairy therapy as Carl walks out from behind the bar.

"Rough day?" Carl asks as he approaches my table.

"The worst," I say, severing a banana with my plastic spoon, dipping it in the melting ice cream and picking up a piece of pineapple.

Carl sets my drink down. "Hopefully this makes it better. Let me know if you need anything else."

"Thanks, Carl."

The first hit of sugar brings me back to life and buzzes through my veins. The bourbon doesn't really mix well with the ice cream, but I'm so emotionally spent, I alternate sips with bites. Another tear falls down my cheek as I spoon a mound of hot fudge into my mouth.

My phone in my purse calls to me.

I had redownloaded Instagram to my phone after a month-long hiatus, just to look at pictures of Jason and Morgan.

Photos from Jason's surprise proposal almost sent me into a spiral at lunch.

"She said yes!" the caption says, with a ring and heart emoji following it.

Morgan is the exact opposite of me—dark hair cropped in a short bob, bronzed skin, and a tiny frame that perfectly fits in Jason's lap.

At six feet, me sitting in Jason's lap looks like an adult sitting on a child, even though he's one inch taller than me.

I enlarge the photo to inspect her ring. It's nowhere near as big as my sister's ring, but it looks pretty.

Just like something I would want.

Morgan's Instagram is private, so I'm in the middle of creating a fake account when a man's voice startles me. "Hey."

I look up.

Cameron Finch.

This is the second time I've seen him today. This morning, I was in a good mood, feeling like I was getting over the breakup hump, finally healing.

Now, I feel like I'm back in the pit of misery. Seeing Cameron doesn't help.

I fumble my phone and hide it under my purse.

Cameron can't see me like this. Sad, bloated, full of sugar.

I wipe my face, and more mascara comes off. Damn it.

His gleaming white teeth blast me. That smile always makes me fall all over myself.

Me and every other woman in a twenty-mile radius.

He flips a chair around to straddle it, resting his elbows on the back.

"Everything going okay?" Cameron asks.

"Fine," I say. "Couldn't be better."

He points to my cherries, surrounded by melted ice cream. I nod as he plucks one out by its stem. Cameron drops it slowly onto his tongue, and I have to look away.

That's just the way he is. Everything is sexual. I swear he does that thing with the cherry stem to give women ideas of what he can do with his tongue.

The cherry show is not for me. We've known each other since elementary school, but he's never expressed one iota of interest in me. I thought we had a *She's All That* moment once when I tutored him in math at the end of junior year, but I was delusional.

Just like I was with Jason.

Cameron hands me a napkin from the dispenser.

"Now tell me why you're crying into ice cream and drinking whiskey at four-thirty in the afternoon?" Cameron asks.

A wail escapes my mouth.

5

CAMERON

My heart feels like I watched five super depressing SPCA commercials in a row.

Annie Stewart is sobbing.

She's completely different to the woman I saw this morning. Her brown eyes are rimmed with red, her freckled cheeks slick with tears. We're friendly whenever we see each other, but we're not close enough for me to know why she's crying.

I shut down small-town gossip about other people because it annoys the shit out of me.

If a guy is responsible for this, I'm gonna break his fucking kneecaps.

I offer my handkerchief, and she takes it, wiping her eyes. She hovers the cloth over her nose.

"Just blow into it. It would be an honor to have your snot," I say. Her lips curl a little and she blows into it.

It's a juicy one.

She hands it back to me, and I tuck it into my pocket.

"Seriously, why are you crying into ice cream? Especially Ice Dream? That shit is so good."

"No reason." Her nose is still clogged, and it's still red.

"Annie, come on. You're drinking whiskey *with* ice cream. This is serious."

She looks down, taking a pitiful bite of ice cream.

"I've had a terrible day. I'll share first," I say, closing my eyes. "Our investor came, and I have to plan an epic event to bring the whole community of Goldheart together so people will buy my dad's beer and we don't need another loan from him. The end."

"That's a lot of pressure," Annie says, sniffling.

"That's what I'm thinking. I've built houses for most of my adult life, for crissake," I say, smiling.

Annie's gaze is still stuck on the table so I lower my head so we're eye level.

"Spill it. What's the problem?"

Annie doesn't meet my eyes. "I was seeing someone, and it didn't work out."

"Who was it?"

Annie's puffy eyes meet mine. "Promise me you'll keep it a secret and you won't freak out."

"Promise," I say, covering my heart and lifting the other arm in a scout salute. I brace for who I think it is. Doesn't prepare me, though.

"Jason Banning."

I almost fall out of my chair. "That motherfucker?"

"You promised me you wouldn't freak out," Annie says. "I know you don't get along."

"'We don't get along' is an understatement," I say. There was the time we played football in PE, and he clotheslined me and I had a black eye for a month. Or how he constantly called me an idiot in school because I was always the last one to finish a test. He's probably still mad about the time he brought home his girlfriend about a year and a half ago and she ended up breaking up with him so she could spend the rest of the weekend with me.

Now, he squandered the love of Annie Stewart, the best woman a man could ask for?

Jason Banning is lower than trash. He's the mold that grows on trash. Even the raccoons wouldn't touch him.

"You just say the word, and I will punch him for you," I say, rubbing my knuckles. "I will beat his ass."

"I appreciate the offer, but it's fine," Annie replies. She plucks the other cherry from her melting banana split. "Here."

I gladly take it. I love those cherries.

"I didn't even know you two were dating."

"He wanted to keep it a secret," she says.

If I dated Annie Stewart, I would take out an advertisement in the paper. And a billboard. Maybe wear a sandwich board around town with a bell.

If I dated Annie, everyone would know she was my woman.

I don't date, but if I did, it would be a woman like her.

"He told me two months ago that he didn't see me as 'the one.' Now he's...he's...."

The tears turn on like a showerhead. After I stand up from my chair, I walk around the table and sit down next to her.

"May I?" I ask, and she nods. I pull her to me and she sobs into my chest. I pet her hair and it's just as silky as I imagined. It also smells like coconut, which makes my dick semi-hard. Anytime Annie gets anywhere near me, I feel things.

Things I shouldn't feel for this wonderful and totally out-of-my-league human.

Her hand on my chest sends goosebumps down my arm.

Her lips are so close to my jaw, my heart races. If she wanted me to hold her the rest of the night, I would gladly let her soak through my shirt.

"Now he's engaged. To this girl named Morgan."

I freeze. Is that the same person...no. It can't be.

I remember every hookup vaguely, and the Morgan I hooked up with had dark hair and licked whipped cream off of my dick. At the time, I didn't know she had been with Jason and broke up with him right before she texted me. It was a weekend that left my dick raw and took a full three days to recover from. She started saying she wanted to move into the tiny home, and that's when I told her it was fun but it was over.

If she's back, I'm scared.

"What does Morgan look like?"

Annie cries harder. "She's so small. So short. Dark hair. I could dunk on her. And I'm not that good at basketball."

It could be the girlfriend I stole, but I can't be certain. That woman was definitely a spinner.

Annie cries harder, and my shirt grows damper by the minute.

"I love that you're tall. You fit in my arms better," I say.

"Oh, stop it," Annie says, sitting up, wiping her cheeks.

"What? It's the truth."

"You're just flirting with me because I have a vagina," she says.

"Who says I'm flirting with you?" I ask.

I'm completely flirting with her. I've flirted with her since she tutored me in the library during our lunch period. Every time. She's never taken my bait, though.

She's too classy for the likes of me.

Her lips quiver again.

I bring up my fingers with an inch space between them. "Okay, maybe a little bit."

"You are?" she asks, her voice full of hope.

"I'm very fond of you, Annie," I say. It's the truth. I respect the hell out of her, and she never treated me like the dumb jock everyone thought I was. No matter how frustrated I got when she tutored me, she never gave up on me. She was more invested in me passing my classes so I could play football than I was at times.

I never tried anything with her. Having sex with a girl was a guaranteed burned bridge for me. Ending it is clean, final. If I slept with Annie, it would never be the same between us, and I would ruin her fondness for me.

"So, what's the plan? Are you going to finally quit and work for us?" I ask. Annie would plan a kickass event. She had already been a lot of help planning the trivia night her sister got engaged at.

She laughs. My family's business, though proceeding in the right direction, is not the pinnacle of job security. Six months ago, we needed to let go of most of our part-time staff, even though it was busy. I work six days a week behind the bar, and we just hired more part-time staff. I know there's not enough money in the budget to hire someone as talented and experienced as Annie.

Annie shakes her head. "I'm just going to suck it up, I guess. Jason isn't making me plan the engagement party or the wedding, at least."

"How is he going to explain that to Pops?"

Theo Banning, Jason's dad, is a cheap motherfucker and scary as hell. I don't know how Annie has worked for him for so long.

"I don't know," Annie says. Her face twists into anguish again. "Oh God, I have to go to this engagement party this weekend and act like everything is fine. Act like my heart isn't being ripped out of my chest."

"Why do you have to go? Can't you skip it?"

"I have to." Annie shakes her head quickly. "Workplace politics."

I can't help it; I lift my hand to massage her shoulder. My chest aches watching her cry. Some men don't know how good they have it until it's gone. Hopefully, Jason will see that.

An idea pops into my head, and I lift my eyebrows at her.

"I have an evil genius plan."

"What?" she asks.

"Let me be your date to the engagement party," I suggest. "Jason fucking hates me. It will drive him crazy. You make him jealous; I piss him off. It will be perfect."

"Are you asking me out on a date?" Annie asks. Her lips press together.

I can't read her look. Does she want me to ask her? Or is she disgusted by it?

The words tumble in my brain, and I just blurt out, "It can be a fake date."

"A fake date?"

"Yeah," I say. "Like that gal who hired a groom and had a fake wedding to make her ex jealous. On a much smaller scale, though. I will just be your arm candy. No need to spend thousands of dollars and hire a photographer."

"No one will believe it, Cam. People will think I'm one of your fuck buddies."

I punctuate the air with a finger. "I will act like I'm madly in love with you. Like I'm a changed man."

Annie's eyes narrow. "What do you want?"

I can't get anything past her. "Well, you're an event guru. I need help."

"What kind of help?"

"Our investor wants us to plan an event, remember? A splashy, fun event to bring the community together. With that sexy, big brain of yours and my pizzazz, we can definitely come up with an event. I make your ex jealous, you help me win with my family so I can coast for a year without any pressure or threat of failure. Everyone wins."

"I don't know," Annie says, looking at me. She hasn't cried in five minutes, so at least we're on the right track.

I grab her hands and hold them between mine. Her palms are soft, and her nails slightly dig into my skin. I wonder what they would feel like raking down my back. "You help me, and I help you."

Annie pulls her hands away and scoops her spoon into her puddle of ice cream, holding her bourbon in the other hand. The sight is sexy as hell.

"Think about it," I say, standing up to go back to my side of the table.

"I don't know how effective it will be," she says, looking up and down. "But thanks, Cam. You made me feel better."

"You're welcome." I lean my elbows on the table, crouching my head down. "Jason doesn't deserve you. If he can't see how great you are, he's not worth it. You deserve a man proud to stand by your side."

Annie blushes. "That's sweet of you to say."

I see her glass is almost empty and point at it. "Do you want another?"

She rubs her head. "I think I'm good. The first one went to my head."

She stands up, opening her arms. I hug her, smelling the coconut on her hair again.

"Think about it," I say, kissing her hair. She freezes in my arms, and when she pulls away, she can't look me in the eye.

"I'll let you know," she says. She walks out.

Carl, the owner, walks over my usual—Jameson over one ice cube. He lightly punches me in the arm.

"Are you going to go after that?" he asks, pointing to the door.

I shake my head. "She's too good for me."

"Yeah, I don't think you could handle her. She's special."

Don't I know it.

6

ANNIE

As I turn onto my street, my feet slipping on the gravel, my arms pumping harder and harder, I cannot get last night out of my brain.

I figured a run would work off some of my feelings, sort them perfectly into their appropriate compartments.

Turns out, four miles can't fix the flutter in my heart I ignore whenever I'm around Cameron Finch.

That man is trouble, and every woman in Goldheart knows it.

He's been a fixture in many a girl's fantasies since middle school. I was one of those girls. Growing up, I was tall with rubber bands for limbs, unruly red hair, and a mouth full of metal. The yearbook and band were my life, while he played football and asked to go to the bathroom every day during history.

Most of his jock friends ignored me or made fun of me. But Cameron always stuck up for me, gave me hugs, and made me secretly swoon. It would crush my heart to see him hang out with our school's petite blonde queen, Alyssa Trammel. He took her to senior prom when she was only a sophomore. Meanwhile, I got stood up by my date, Scott Kimmel, and I cried into a bag of Cheetos, watching reruns of *Dr. Quinn, Medicine Woman* in a puff of blue polyester.

After I moved home from college, Cameron and I floated in and out of each other's lives around Goldheart.

I've watched him go through women faster than toilet paper, but he always arrives alone to community events or surrounded by his family. The only girl who's ever had him wrapped around her finger is his niece, Olive.

Daydreaming about him is unproductive, but here I am, obsessed with the idea of possibly dating him, even if it's for show.

The sun and my exertion made me warm, but thinking about dating Cameron makes me feel hot. How would it feel to walk into a room, on the arm of a man my ex hates? What it would feel like for a second to have Cameron's adoration, even if it was pretend?

Last night, I had to run out before I agreed. I needed time to process. Time to weigh the pros and cons. I'm still not sure if I will say yes. I'm also not sure Cameron was serious.

When I pass my mailbox, I stop my watch and check the time. I haven't run eight-minute miles in over a year, but my average time was 8:32. My legs ache and sweat soaks my shirt, but the fresh air fills my lungs and I feel so much better. My headache from my whiskey and ice cream pity party has subsided, and I feel like I can take on the day.

Today will be a good day. I don't have to go into the winery until later, since I have a private birthday party dinner to host this evening. My free mornings are my favorite. I get to journal at a leisurely pace, drink coffee and read, and clean my place. Heaven.

I walk up the driveway to my bungalow, nestled behind

my landlord's house. It's a small one-bedroom that sits under a canopy of tall trees. I love it, but it's felt pretty bleak to me lately. At thirty-four, with another failed relationship under my belt, I might die here unless my sister's children decide to put me in a home. That's if they like me.

I check my phone. One missed call from Whitney Kilgore. No matter how many times she calls me, it still blows my mind I have my favorite author's phone number.

I've loved romance since I was a kid, and as my experience with boys became more and more disappointing, I sunk further and further to escape into worlds where a happily ever after was guaranteed and the men fought like hell for their loves. My love for romance really escalated when I got an ereader and started interacting with my favorite indie authors, like Whitney.

Whitney writes dark romance novels under the pen name Lila Madden. I discovered her after her first novel was published, and I fell in love with her writing. Her characters and storytelling blew me away, and I instantly reached out, pledging my life to her. I cried when one of her books hit the top one-hundred charts for the first time and sent flowers when her next book hit the top ten. When she finally quit her full-time job, I attended her break-free party in Reno.

To this day, I beta-read every one of her books and provide her critical feedback. I absolutely love her, even though we've only met in person twice.

I just finished an early draft of her latest installment of her mafia romance series, about four brothers revitalizing their dead father's legacy and rising to power because of the support and love of their respective women. The latest book is a second-chance romance that I devoured on my day off, filling fifteen pages of notes for her of what I liked and what I didn't like, and then sent her twenty text messages.

I used to send my feedback in a Google document back to her, but now she calls me to go over them and brainstorm how to make it better. I tap on her name to call her back before my breath even slows.

"Hey, Annie," Whitney says warmly into the phone.

"Hi, Whitney. Still so weird to call you that."

"You're in the inner circle now," she says. Ever since I visited her house, she asked me to call her by her real name, not her pen name. I called her Lila for three years.

"Let me get my notes," I say.

"You sound out of breath," Whitney says.

"I just ran. I...I had some stuff to work through. You know how it is."

Whitney and I also bonded over our love of running. She runs marathons while I just stick to local 5Ks. I would love to do one some day.

"Definitely. I get through writer's block on my runs," she says. "What's going on?"

I find my notebook, but I don't speak right away. Whitney is a great friend, but still, I'm not sure we're at the level yet where I can unload all of my problems on her.

"I don't want to bother you."

"You're not bothering me. Promise," she says. "I can't promise it won't make its way into my books, though."

I tell her all about yesterday. Jason telling me he's engaged, how awful the staff meeting was, how I ended up crying into ice cream and bourbon.

"Then this guy Cameron found me crying," I say.

"Oooh, who's Cameron?"

"Don't get too excited. He's just a friend. Plus he's kind of a man-hoe."

"I *love* friends to lovers. I rarely write it, but I love reading it."

I laugh at the romance lingo. "I don't know if he's a friend so much as someone I've crossed paths with my entire life."

"Oh, okay."

"He suggested I bring him to Jason's engagement party as my fake date to make Jason jealous."

"Something I love more than friends to lovers. Fake dating," Whitney says.

"Right? Does that even work in real life?" I ask, as I flip open to the top for my water bottle. I take a long sip. "I can't."

"What does this guy look like? I assume he's good-looking if he's a man-hoe."

"*So* good-looking." My mouth waters as I picture him. Full head of longish brown hair that falls in his grass-colored eyes. Tall, broad shoulders. A grin that could light up a movie theater marquee. Charm that makes a woman lose her panties in nanoseconds.

"I want to see a photo," she asks.

"Hold on, let me find one." I go to the Woody Finch Brewery site and find a family photo with Cameron standing in the back. I screenshot it and crop it, send it to Whitney.

"Wow. He's cute. I bet he's charming."

"So charming. Like up-to-no-good charming."

"Do you like him?" Whitney asks.

What a loaded question. I bite my lip. Of course I do, along with every other woman in Goldheart. I've always kept my distance, because I know I could lose my head if I let him work his Cameron-ness all over me.

"I've always liked Cameron."

"But...?"

"But I have a tendency to love too hard. I could see myself falling for him, even during a fake date, then being even more hurt than I currently am."

"Well," Whitney says. "I think Jason needs to realize what he's missing. You are spectacular, Annie. I think you deserve a little sweet revenge. Maybe some rebound sex while you're at it."

I laugh out loud. "I doubt Cameron wants to sleep with me."

"Shut your face," Whitney says. "You're gorgeous and smart and you have an amazing heart. I don't think I would've made it through my first year of publishing without your support."

"Men don't want to fuck amazing hearts," I say. Cameron has seen me with braces and glasses, when my body hadn't caught up to my big hands and big feet.

He doesn't want me. He wants tiny women he can spin on his penis.

In some ways, Whitney doesn't get it. She's two years younger than me, childfree by choice, and married to a doctor she loves and who supports her dreams completely. It's been a while since her heart has been smashed.

I still love her to death, but she doesn't get it.

"Well, let's talk about the book," I change the subject.

"Okay, hit me," she says. I go through my notes one by one, how I felt like nostalgia was relied too heavily upon and that the hero needed softening, since he did cruel things on page and needed to show more remorse. Whitney responds with acknowledgments and asks me follow-up questions about specific scenes or lines.

"My biggest thing is Stella deserves the hero to burn the

world for her and he's not there yet," I say about Whitney's heroine.

There's silence before Whitney says, "Annie, this is great feedback. And by the way, you deserve a hero like that too. If that means the look of jealousy in your ex's eyes, I say go for it. I highly recommend sex for sex's sake. It doesn't need to be emotional. Before I got married, I definitely had my share of fun, and I think you should too. Let go of your lists and rules."

"Thanks, Whitney," I say.

"No, thank you. My books are always better because of you."

We say goodbye and hang up.

After showering and getting ready, I wander around my house, straightening blankets that are already straight and going through my catch-all mail basket again. I vacuum and straighten up, even though my apartment is tidy, even by my standards.

Cameron's proposition sneaks its way into my consciousness at every karate chop to puff up my pillows.

It would be pretty great to see Jason lose his mind.

When we dated, Jason grew visibly jealous when he saw another man talking to me, even if it was just Reid, Cameron's brother, who I'm good friends with. Jason's hatred of Cameron is well-known and well-documented. Seeing him with me might make his ears bleed.

I pull up the photo of Jason and Morgan again, and it tugs at my heart.

Why couldn't it be me? Why couldn't Jason love me?

"Really, we're not doing this again," I say to myself as I delete the screenshot.

I don't do my usual pros and cons. I don't weigh my options. I just get in my car and drive.

This time I'm going with my gut.

I end up at his sister Emily's property, outside Cameron's tiny house.

It's Wednesday at nine a.m. and I have no idea if Cameron is even home or awake. I know the brewery doesn't open until eleven, so he could be home.

When no one answers the door, I huff out a breath and turn toward my car, when I hear the door open behind me.

Cameron stands there, shirtless, in low-slung sweatpants. His skin is golden, with a tuft of dark hair on his defined chest, and abs you could wash clothes on if you were a pioneer. His gray sweatpants accentuate an impressive bulge, confirming everything I've heard over the years.

Cameron is hung. Really hung.

Oh, holy hell.

I create a blinder with my hand.

"Well, good morning," Cameron says, leaning against the doorframe. The way he leans makes his biceps look even bigger. I peek past my hand.

"Good morning, Cameron," I say, my tongue fumbling over his full name.

"So formal, Anne," he says. I wince at my legal name, a name I'm never called unless it's by a substitute teacher or a police officer after I've been speeding.

I don't say anything or lower my hand because my face feels like I sat in front of a campfire.

"Are you going to look at me?" Cameron asks with a chortle.

"That depends. Are you going to put your nipples away?"

"Why? The nipples are the eyes of the torso."

"Put a shirt on," I say. He shuffles off and returns. I lower my hands to see him wearing a forest green Woody Finch brewery T-shirt.

Unfortunately, the shirt isn't long enough to cover his... um...pelvis.

"So, what can I help you with on this fine morning?" Cameron asks. "Do you want a cup of coffee?"

"Sure," I say. I didn't sleep much last night.

"Do you want anything in it?"

"Just black."

He disappears and is gone for seconds before he pops his head back out. "Are you going to come in?"

"No, I'll stand out here."

"The bears might get you. Or the raccoons."

"I'll take my chances," I say, wrapping my zip-up sweatshirt around my frame. He walks down the stairs of his home onto his makeshift deck.

"It's brewing," he says, pointing inside with a thumb.

I take a deep breath. "I came over to tell you that I will take your offer. Let's fake date."

His eyes light up. "Awesome," he says.

"And I will help you with your event," I add.

"Perfect," Cameron replies. He walks toward me with his naked arms outstretched. He's always been a hugger. I'm not complaining since he gives the best hugs in the world, but I take a step back. I hold up my pointer finger, and he stops in his tracks.

"We need ground rules. A game plan," I say.

"I would expect nothing less from you," he says. There's that cocky grin again that has spread legs across the county.

It won't be me though. He has zero interest in me, sexually, romantically. We're just friends. Well...kinda.

"What's the plan?" Cameron asks. Something pings from inside the tiny house, and Cameron runs inside and comes back with a mug of hot coffee for me. The steam rises and hits my face. He has his own cup as well. We take sips at the same time, and my eyes close in ecstasy.

"Let's discuss it tomorrow. Moe's Diner. Tomorrow morning before work. Six-thirty sharp."

"I don't usually get up that early, but I will for you, Annie," Cameron says, taking another sip of coffee. "I feel like I should kiss your hand since you're going to be my fake girlfriend and all."

"I'm not the Queen of England," I say. Cameron smiles again. Is he trying to turn my insides into soup?

"I look forward to it. We'll get French toast, and you'll bring those sexy spreadsheets. There will be spreadsheets, right? I know how Excel gets you riled up."

My cheeks heat. I babble *once* about my elaborate Excel spreadsheet for my budget five years ago when we ran into each other at Culver Lanes, the small bowling alley/margarita bar in town, and he's never let me live it down. I know he's not flirting with me. Cameron just doesn't appreciate Excel and all its capabilities.

"I can neither confirm nor deny there will be a Microsoft product," I say. I kick a rock with my sneaker. "Thank you for doing this."

"No problem," Cameron says. His face softens like butter in the microwave. "I'm ready to make your ex so jealous, he'll be begging you to come back."

"Thanks, Cameron," I say. Without thinking, I take another big gulp of coffee and kiss his cheek. I feel the stubble on my lips as I pull away and hand him my mug.

"Tomorrow, six-thirty sharp," I say as I scamper to my car. When I look back, I see Cameron standing there, watching me.

My heart races, and my cheeks heat. Why am I just like

every woman, ridiculously attracted to him, and helpless to that grin?

I am better than this. That's why firm rules and boundaries will help.

My fingers itch to get into a spreadsheet. Maybe a pie chart. We definitely need a mission statement.

I snap my fingers at no one. PowerPoint.

When I close my door and look up, Cameron's door is closed, and I assume he's inside. Deep from inside of me, I let out a squeal. Fake dating Cameron feels like a bucket list item marked off. I get the perks of being with him, without the actual heartbreak.

This is perfect. Jason is going to shit himself.

Getting to pretend like I'm the belle of the ball for once isn't too bad either.

7

CAMERON

W*here are you going? You're never up this early. I know you didn't sleep over at some girl's house.* Emily's text yells at me from my phone.

Meeting a friend who needs me, I type. I look out my truck's windshield as I throw my phone in the back and start the engine. Emily is not at the window or the bottom floor.

How does she always know?

I set five alarms on my phone so I could leave my house on time to get my ass in a Moe's Diner booth by six-thirty. Even with texting my sister, I walk into the small building with a jingle of a bell, exactly on time.

Moe's Diner is a popular breakfast spot in Goldheart, with a jukebox, red booths, and Formica tables. Most of the windows face Town Square so you can watch tourists fighting, my favorite. It's still early, but I spot some old men I see at the Swift sometimes. They're swapping sections of the newspaper, sipping coffee like it's air.

I aspire to be them one day.

Annie sits in a far booth, scribbling something on a yellow pad of paper. There's a war room setup on her table

—a laptop, a huge binder, and a pot of coffee. Her eyes shift to other patrons, but she's tucked away enough and those guys don't give a shit what she's doing. Everyone leaves Annie alone, because Neil, her stepfather, is a scary motherfucker. I've never talked to him at length because his presence makes me want to crap myself.

I'm surprised Jason still has his balls. Neil must not know about him.

From twenty feet away, I can appreciate her attention to detail in our arrangement.

I can be disorganized, so she's the perfect person for my alliance in event planning. She's also not hard on the eyes either.

"I'm early," I say, opening my arms like I'm Gatsby welcoming guests to my party.

"Congratulations," Annie says, looking up. Dark moons dip under her eyes as she takes another aggressive gulp of coffee. After I sit down, I lean onto my elbows and prop my chin on my fists.

"Did you sleep at all last night?" I ask.

She shakes her head, a strand of hair falling in her face.

I want to tuck it behind her ear so bad.

"Did you make a spreadsheet?"

She shakes her head, stabbing the buttons of her keyboard, and turns it around. She tries to shield it, but the old men are arguing about the Giants so they couldn't care less.

"A PowerPoint," I say in awe, sitting back. This woman. *This woman.*

"It was the best way for me to organize my ideas and present my information and guidelines," she says.

The title card says *Operation: Fake Date.* She clicks

another button, and a graphic of a cartoon Prince Charming and Cinderella float onto the screen.

"Wow," I say, my mouth hanging open. "You really went all out."

"Thanks," she says. "I wanted the wow factor."

"It's just me, you know," I say. "I mean, I'm impressed as well, but you could've just told me the time, the place, and how madly in love you want me to be and I'll do it."

"We need a finely executed plan so I don't break into hives," Annie says. She clicks to the next screen with a bold action statement: *To make Jason Banning jealous and apologize for keeping Annie a secret.*

"Done," I say. I'll make damn sure he understands what he lost.

Plus, it will be fun to pretend. Annie has always felt right in my arms.

"We also need guidelines," she says, going to the next slide.

Under the *Allowed* column, there are the following items: side hugs, full-frontal hugs, a kiss on the cheek, lots of compliments.

I see the *Not Allowed* column, and I point with a scoff.

"No kissing on the lips?" I ask. "What's the point of fake dating unless I get to slip some tongue in?"

Delilah walks up to the table. She's been a fixture of this restaurant as long as I've been coming here, and has been married to Moe, the owner, for forty years. She works harder than he does. Annie slaps her laptop closed and covers it with her pad of paper like she's watching porn.

"Hey doll, what can I get you?" She rests her hand on my shoulder.

"How about two eggs, over medium, bacon, and a side of fruit? Just one slice of French toast today, though. I'm trying to keep my figure," I say, slapping my stomach. "And a cup of coffee. Black. Unless you're sharing, Annie."

She shakes her head, moving the pot closer to her.

"I'll get that for you, cutie," she says, squeezing my trapezoid muscle before walking off.

Annie leans in. "Have you, you know, 'been friendly' with her?"

I laugh. "No. You know Delilah. Her and Moe are in love, like really in love. However, I wouldn't say no, if the situation was different."

"Is every woman an opportunity?" she asks, taking another sip of coffee. I've been questioned before, by my family, by folks in town. Annie's question is one of curiosity, not disgust, so I don't mind answering it.

"Not every woman. There has to be chemistry. But I do love women. I just don't do relationships."

"Why not?" Annie asks.

I shrug a shoulder. "I love my freedom. I like to do what I want when I want. If I want to go on a kayaking trip and disappear for two months, I can. Being tethered to someone will cramp my style."

Her eyes narrow like every woman I've disappointed, and I wonder what's going through that big brain of hers.

Something about Annie unlocks a hidden part of myself. I say, "I don't think I would be really good at a relationship. I would just screw it up."

Annie opens a palm to me. "I think you would make a good boyfriend. Once you settle on one woman."

"Really?" I ask.

She nods slowly. Her eyes, the color of brown sugar, focus on me, stripping me of my usual song and dance. "You're caring, fun. I think you could do it. Everyone has the capacity to change. If they want to."

My jaw drops just as Delilah returns with my cup of coffee.

The coffee sits in front of me while Annie re-opens the laptop to the PowerPoint, like she didn't just rock my world.

Think about the fake date, think about the fake date.

"Really, no kiss?" I say. "I promise I'll keep it PG."

She pauses for a moment, swinging the laptop around. Her fingers flutter against the keys and when she turns it around, "one chaste kiss" is now listed under the *Allowed* column.

"Define 'chaste,'" I say.

"No tongue. No lip movement," she says. "Hands only on my torso."

Not my usual style, but okay. I'll take any kiss from Annie Stewart. High School Cameron would've been proud, especially since he chickened out last time.

"I can do that," I agree.

"Perfect." Her gaze flicks over me as she taps her laptop for the next slide.

A purple background with three different fonts pops up. *Concern: How are we going to convince people Cameron has changed his ways and is madly in love?*

There's that mention of change again. My throat feels tight so I tug at my collar. I'm not changing by going on a date with Annie; I'm doing her a favor. Getting my family off of my back for a little bit.

I will still be me when this is all over.

After I grumble, I clap once. "That's easy. People in town know you'd step out with someone only if you were serious about them."

She deflates like a three-day-old birthday balloon. Oh, fuck Jason.

"I'm not saying you weren't serious with Jason."

She glosses over it and leans in. "I mean, you don't date. How are we going to convince people?"

I think about my niece noticing I don't keep women around. My family genuinely nervous that I won't pull my weight for the brewery event, that they'll need to do the bulk of the planning. How it might be worth it to explore what it would be like to date someone like Annie, a forever kind of woman.

"Simple," I say. "If people ask, I'll say it's time to get serious and make a change. That's why I'm dating you. I also can be *very* convincing."

Annie studies me, her lips disappearing in a thin line of thought. "I didn't mean anything earlier about changing. If you're happy, that's great."

"I'm happy as a raccoon in a Taco Bell Dumpster," I say. Why am I so fixated on raccoons now? "I have a great life. Nothing to complain about."

I nod, taking a sip of coffee. It's finally cooled down. "If you help me come up with a great idea, a real showstopper, and give me some pointers to plan it, maybe my family will get off my back. If I pull through, maybe I'll fly under the radar and I can just coast and serve beer."

Annie looks off to an empty space. Striving to be better is how she lives her life. Her days are probably full of planners and to-do lists, while I wake up with my day wide open, full of possibilities. I bet she doesn't do one thing for the hell of it, just because she feels like it.

When she tutored me, she rarely allowed time for jokes or idle chats. She was all business, even though I spent our whole hour trying to make her smile.

The way she kept me on task, how she bossed me around, made me feel hot inside.

"The party is a one-time thing," Annie says. "I've already

checked with the event planner and the guest list. No one will be there who has connections to your family or mine. I don't want your family to know about this."

"Fair," I say. My mom and sister would get so excited if she heard I went out on a date with Annie. It's best not to get their hopes up. However, we live in a small town. No way someone is not going to hear about it. "You really think that party will have people who don't know our families? Get real."

Annie presses a button to a new slide, and it holds half of the guest list, per her heading. I motion for the next slide, and I don't see any other names I recognize or could be dangerous.

"How did you get this?"

"I know the event planner. She's newer and asked me some questions for this party, and I got her to hand over the guest list."

"So, what happens after this event? What's our story?"

Annie hits the button on her laptop, and it goes to the next slide.

After the party, Annie plans to tell everyone she broke Cameron's heart, and Cameron will act devastated.

"I don't have problems being the bad guy," I say. "People are used to it from me anyway."

"It has to me. I have to be the one in power."

I lift an eyebrow. Visions come to me of Annie dressed in leather, flicking a riding crop against my chest.

It's math tutoring all over again.

My dick strains against my zipper, and I shift in my seat.

"I have another request," she says, hitting the next slide.

No sex with other women until two weeks after the party.

"No sex for over two weeks?" I ask for clarification. She nods.

I'll have to break out the nice porn.

"I don't want to be made a fool," Annie says. "Our story won't work if you're caught with some woman at the Swift or having sex with her in the park."

"I'm never going to live that down, am I?" I ask.

Annie shakes her head. "You got caught by Officer Wagner with your pants down and you fell face first in mud. The whole town will never forget."

I shiver when I remember that.

"You were so lucky Officer Wagner thought it was funny and you didn't get written up."

"It's these pearly whites," I say, smiling. Annie looks down at her pad of paper.

I try to read her expression, anything to see if she's affected by me at all. Barely a smile.

"You're not attracted to me, are you?"

"No," Annie says with a laugh. Her pen hovers over the yellow paper.

"You blushed when I had no shirt on yesterday."

"I was surprised, is all," Annie says, looking up. "I'm a redhead. I get flushed easily."

"Nothing whatsoever?" I ask.

She shakes her head. "I wouldn't ask you to do this if I felt something. I know how women get attached to you, and agreeing to this would put me in harm's way if I caught feelings."

Damn. Well. That answers that.

And it explains a lot, actually.

Annie is so out of my league, I can't see her from the stands. She always took advanced courses and read books I've never even heard of. While the teacher called my parents to say I wasn't applying myself, her parents were framing report cards and taking her out to dinner to celebrate. My parents breathed out a sigh of relief when I brought home a D.

It must've been my ego that imagined a moment in the library. When I almost caressed her cheek and kissed her by the reference section. It was just teenage boy delusion, and my cocky ass thinking every girl wanted me. I know I'm not everyone's taste, but I'm pizza.

Many, many people like pizza.

"Well, I'll make this kiss so believable, people will think you're into me."

Annie holds up a finger.

"Absolutely, without a doubt, no tongue."

"Done," I say.

"I mean it, Cameron. If I feel even a lick, I'm biting it."

"It'll be a movie kiss. A fake kiss."

"Exactly," she says, pulling out a piece of paper. She crosses a line out and then prints neat block letters under a section of printed text. Her print looks exactly like Times New Roman.

How her mind works fascinates me. Mine has never moved as fast as hers does.

"What's that?"

"Our contract," she says.

I laugh. Of course there's a contract.

"Contracts are so sexy," I say as I watch her work and read it over again. "If you were attracted to me, I would totally breach your contract."

"Is everything about sex with you?"

"No," I say, contrite. "Sorry."

"It makes me feel better to have a contract," Annie says.

She pushes the contract in front of me.

"Did you make Jason sign one?"

She shakes her head. "He was my real boyfriend. Or at least, I thought he was."

I look it over. It details the guidelines of dos and don'ts. *No kissing on the lips* is crossed out, and above it, in her perfect writing, it says: *One strategic kiss with no tongue and hands only allowed on torso.*

I reach out my hand, and she hands me a pen. After I sign my name and write today's date, I give the paper and the pen back to her. She signs under my name and looks up. She folds the paper slowly, biting her lip.

I want to bite that lip. Hearing she's not interested in me just makes her sexier. I already thought she was beautiful and totally fuckable, but this brings it to a whole new level.

It's going to be a long two-ish weeks.

"I'll make a copy and drop it off," Annie says.

"Perfect," I say.

"Thank you for doing this," she adds.

"Thank you for helping me with the event," I reply.

"I'm happy to help," she says. She tucks the contract in her bag and puts away her laptop. Delilah brings our breakfast, and I dig in. Annie got the oatmeal, a Moe's special, and I wish I was that spoon she's licking the oatmeal off of.

"Do you have any ideas for what kind of event Woody Finch should put on?" she asks, taking another dainty bite.

I have to stop staring at her mouth.

"Well, I would suggest something with dogs, but it's too soon," I say. "Sorry, I took it down a notch."

"Oh, yeah. I'm sorry to hear about Woody. Your dad loved that dog."

I nod. We all loved Woody.

Woody was a German Shepherd my parents rescued six years ago. That dog went everywhere with my dad, constantly watching him, waiting for his direction. When he opened the brewery, there was no question it would be dog-related. We have canine visitors everyday, and there's pictures of Woody and other patrons' dogs on the walls. An outline of Woody still adorns our logo, and I know it hurts my dad.

My parents went on their dream vacation to Portugal and Spain, a trip they wanted to take for their fortieth wedding anniversary. While they were gone, my oldest brother Jackson watched the dog. He had just moved home from Seattle and was staying with my parents.

Woody started vomiting and dry-heaving, running off to hide in pockets of my parents' backyard, and Jackson called us. We all rushed the dog to the emergency vet and discovered that his stomach flipped and turned. We got hold of my parents, and we all agreed that the humane thing was to let Woody go instead of attempting a surgery.

That was three months ago, and sometimes I do catch my dad looking at pictures of Woody and crying. When dogs come into the brewery, my dad seeks them out, pets them, and talks to them.

We're not sure my dad will ever be ready for another dog.

"We'll think of something really good," Annie says. "I know we will. When your family is ready, you can do a great dog event."

We finish our coffee and meals and put on our coats. It's still chilly, and trees are starting to bloom, making my allergies flare up. I'm still planning to walk to the brewery, which is a couple blocks past the main drag of Main Street and town square. Maybe if I show up early, they'll understand I'm committed. I *can* be serious and pull my weight.

For a little while, anyway.

Laura Jensen runs by Moe's window, AirPods in, wearing

tight black leggings and a long-sleeved shirt. I call her when I'm drunk and horny, but not anymore. I am now celibate and committed. I can do this. I've been meaning to delete her number, anyway. The second I get to work, it's gone.

I walk Annie to her car, and she turns around, her hands shoved in her pockets. I open my arms like I always do, and she walks into them.

There's that coconut shampoo again.

She's not into you, I remind myself.

She breaks away first and opens her car door. She turns around.

"Do you think it will work? Making him jealous?"

I think about the rage he had when he found out his girlfriend slept with me the night they broke up and how he threatened to punch me at the pool hall. How he avoided me at the grocery store and how his jaw clenched whenever he saw me.

"It'll work like a charm."

"Good," she says, breathing in and out. "I'll send you the info."

"I'll look so good, you won't be able to resist me."

"Oh, I can resist you." She closes her car door and waves through her window.

I watch her drive off before I head toward the brewery. My mind won't shut up, which is unusual.

If Annie felt even one measly little feeling toward me, I wouldn't have taken it for granted, like Jason did.

8

CAMERON

"Is Cameron here?" I hear the next day at the brewery.

"Hi," I call to Annie, who's standing in our taproom, holding a folded piece of paper. She's talking to my brother Reid, who she's been friends with since we were kids. Reid's been dating a single mom named Callie on and off for three years and, to best of my knowledge, hasn't ever made a move on Annie. I can't be just friends with a woman, but Reid is different.

Reid is smart, capable. There's a lot going on in that noggin. He's the son my parents wished for and tried two times before they got it right with him. Jackson is too broken. I think with my dick too much.

Like right now.

Annie is wearing her usual polo shirt that hugs her breasts, and her red hair is up again so her neck is exposed. I'm so stoked I get to kiss those plump lips in a couple days.

"Here," she says, handing me the piece of paper. I open it and recognize it as the contract I signed at Moe's.

"Thanks," I say. I fold it again and put it in my back pocket.

Reid still stands there. "Hey, Annie, do you have an event on Saturday night? Callie's out of town for a bachelorette party. If not, we can get a pizza, watch a documentary on Netflix..."

She looks at me briefly and then smiles at Reid. "I have a party I need to go to."

"Are you going alone?" Reid asks, his voice animated.

My stomach drops. I want zero people related to me knowing. Too complicated.

Annie shakes her head. "I have a date already."

I fight the urge to yell, *It's me. She picked me!*

Annie looks at me a beat too long. Reid's eyes are wide as he looks at her and then me.

"Are you two going together?"

Annie nods. I cross my arms and blurt out, "It's a friends thing."

Even if fake-dating Annie would up my credibility with my family, I can't chance my family being disappointed in me when it ends.

They're already disappointed me enough as it is.

"Total friends thing," Annie adds. "I can't take you because Callie wouldn't like me inviting you, even as friends. I'm saving you a fight."

Annie is being polite. Everyone knows Reid is dating Callie and it wouldn't have the same effect. Also, Callie would blow a gasket if Reid went to a party as Annie's date. I'm surprised he still has all his fingers and toes for hanging out with Annie for their semi-regular pizza and documentaries nights.

Really glad I didn't fuck Callie when I had a chance five years ago, before she started dating my brother. God bless two-for-one shots of Fireball specials at the Swift around

Tax Day that made me pass out and Thumper had to drag me out. Saved me from myself.

"You're probably right," Reid says, looking at me and then Annie. His expression is tough to read.

"I'll see you Saturday. Six," Annie says.

"I'll pick you up," I say. She waves and leaves. I try not to look at her ass as she walks away. One of our regulars, Drake, walks up to get a refill of Gold Dust, before he goes back to his laptop tucked in the corner. I add it to his tab and as I turn around, Reid crosses his arms and looks at me.

Reid is two years younger than me, but sometimes it feels like he's the older brother.

"How did that come up?" Reid asks.

"What?"

"You. Going with Annie."

I freeze. Annie and I talked about a lot of things, but we didn't discuss what would happen if we were seen together or caught in the lie. Reid is too smart to lie to, so I'll just leave out some details.

"I ran into Annie at the Swift the other day, and she needed a date. Jason Banning got engaged. It's his engagement party."

"Huh," Reid says. "Who's working Saturday?"

"Jackson said he would cover for me. That new guy is working, too."

Reid nods and then looks at me with a laser focus. His intense look unnerves me.

"What?"

"Don't even think of trying anything with her."

Shit. I will be trying something. It's written in the contract in my back pocket.

"She needed a date, and I'm a great dancer. We're friends, Reid."

Reid scoffs and drops some dirty pints into a glass rack for the dishwasher.

"Annie is too good to be yanked around by a guy like you."

Old Me might've fired back defensively, but Reid might have a point. Reid walks to the back with the glasses, and I follow him. He fires up the dishwasher, and the sound of running water overpowers the awkward silence in the room.

I'm seventy-five percent sure Reid never had a thing for Annie. Still, bro code is in effect, especially since he's my actual brother.

"You never had a thing for her, did you?"

"What?" Reid asks, flashing a surprised look.

"It's an honest question. She's great, and I won't judge if you do. Or did."

Reid says nothing as he lines up the crate with the belt so it can be run through to be sanitized.

"No. Annie has always been just my friend. I love Callie."

"Okay," I say, leaning against the wall. "I only want the best for Annie. I can't say much, but it's really important that she doesn't go alone to this."

"I only want the best for her, too," Reid says, walking back out front to two guys standing at the bar.

I'm not sure if Reid is inferring I'm not the best for her or what.

It's only one fake date. We'll kiss, and that'll be it. I can go back to my old life, get some help with planning the event, and impress my family and Dan and everyone else.

Everything will work out fine.

It's time to be serious. I won't let my lust for Annie get the better of me. It won't get me in trouble this time.

9

ANNIE

I flex my hands to release some tension as I walk to my door.

Cameron just knocked and it's showtime.

When I open the door, he looks up, his hands tucked in his pockets. He's wearing a crisp, tailored black suit with an open-at-the-collar white shirt. His square jaw is shaven, and his hair is slicked back.

I may be making Jason jealous tonight, but Cameron might be making every woman in the room jealous of me.

"Hi," I say, letting him in.

"Hi," Cameron replies, walking inside. His eyes flick up and down my body, his lips part, and I'm suddenly not sure how to stand, how to act. Do I look okay? He says nothing, and my stomach drops.

I tried my best. I drove to the mall in Roseville, a good hour away, and bought the most daring dress I could find. It cuts low in the front, giving the illusion of cleavage, and since I'm so tall, the skirt barely covers my ass. I just spent three hours perfecting my hair into effortless beach waves, and rewatched a YouTube tutorial seven times to get a golden smoky eye.

I notice his Adam's apple bob, and I look away before I overanalyze everything.

"Are you ready to go?" I ask, grabbing my sparkly clutch, another impulse purchase from my trip to the mall.

"We can, but I want to tell you something."

I freeze. "What?"

He bites his lip. "That you are a knockout in that dress. Between that and me on your arm, Jason will be beside himself."

"I hope so," I say. My insides glow at his comment.

"You're the same height as me. I'm into it," he says. Tonight, I'm wearing heels. As a *screw you* to Jason and every man who couldn't handle me being taller than him. Cameron and I see each other, eye to eye. It's empowering.

He offers me an arm as we walk out my house and up the driveway to Cameron's blue truck. He opens the car door and presents a hand, one I gladly take.

There's a moment he looks over at me and there's hunger in his eyes. That might just be Cameron, though. I know him. He sees a hint of a boob, and he drools.

He backs out of the driveway and drives down the street to the stop sign.

"Are you nervous for tonight?" Cameron asks.

"A little."

A little means I barely slept the night before and just went over and over again what I would say to Morgan when I inevitably have to interact with her at the party.

I settled on *Congratulations. You two are perfect for each other.*

I calculate I'm about eighty-seven percent over him, but a little part of me wants to ask why her and not me.

"I'm nervous," Cameron says. "I don't have much experience being a boyfriend before."

"It's easy. Just act like you adore me. I'm sure you adore women in the bedroom."

He nods, his eyes not leaving the road. "If the woman does not come first, I didn't do my job properly."

My cheeks flush. I never orgasmed with Jason. A lot of our trysts were in secret, hurried moments in closets or at his apartment in the middle of the night. I always wanted him so bad that it was a fumble of clothing and kisses, and it took me a full ten months to realize that he had never gone down on me and that I constantly gave oral stimulation with no reciprocity.

"I'm sorry, honey, I don't like the way it tastes," he used to say, and I took it as another concession I had to make for him.

I wonder what Cameron would be like between my legs. I wonder if I would be able to enjoy it or if I would get too in my head. Worrying if I'm too hairy down there or if it's too smelly.

"Jason didn't eat your pussy, did he?"

"Cameron!" It feels like a furnace in my cheeks.

"He didn't, did he?" Cameron asks. "Selfish prick."

It was selfish, but it was okay with me. My college boyfriend tried, but I obsessed too much that he gave up after thirty concentrated minutes. I've only ever orgasmed alone, never with a partner.

I wonder if Cameron could make me orgasm.

"Do you like the taste of it?" I whisper.

He chuckles and rubs his tongue against his lips. "I don't mind it."

My core restricts at that information. I shouldn't be so turned on by talk of sex with Cameron since he is not a viable option. I've already had my heart broken by a man who doesn't go down on women. How would it work if I got involved with an emotionally unavailable man with a ready and willing tongue?

If he makes me come, forget it.

All I have to do is make it through one staged kiss and not lose my head. Ever since I lied and said I wasn't interested in him, he hasn't flirted with me at all. Until now. Is this flirting? My radar is broken.

Clear mind, clear. Because all I can think about is his head between my legs.

We arrive too soon at Banning Cellars. Cameron gets out first and walks around the truck, opening my door. I shimmy out to avoid a crotch shot and immediately straighten my skirt.

"Are you going to be okay in those heels?" Cameron asks.

"Of course," I say, just before I stumble and throw my arms out for balance. We have to park down the hill, in the parking lot next to the vineyards. The hill is covered in gravel, slippery, and Cameron offers his arm again so I can balance. We make it up the hill to hear laughter and chatter, loud and bright coming from the tasting room, which doubles as an event space.

Banning Cellars is tucked against a hill, with a deck overlooking a vista. It's a few miles from town, completely intentional on the part of the family. They recently remodeled to a modern, clean look with square angles and cool greys and black accents. The majority of the bottom level is glass, and all it takes is a simple slide to create an indoor-outdoor space. It's not to my taste, but it is a hit with our ideal customers, and it sells events for us.

Dusk has already set in, and the music floats from the open doors. As I enter the warmly lit space, I look for something to do, but I'm reminded I'm the guest, not the event planner. I don't have to worry about the timing of the food, or the flow of the event. I can just sit back and try not to have a breakdown.

"Are you ready?" Cameron asks. We stand apart, our arms at our sides.

"Ready as I'll ever be," I say.

"Good." Without warning, he grabs my hand and laces my fingers with his. There's that familiar jolt I feel when I get a hug from him, or he massages my shoulder.

I'm holding Cameron Finch's hand in a public place. High School Annie would be screaming into a pillow through her headgear right now.

No matter how much I fight it, I've always had a crush on Cameron Finch.

I just hope I can survive tonight with my heart intact.

10

CAMERON

As a rule of thumb, I don't hold hands.

Holding hands signals to the woman that we're more than we are, as innocent as it appears. The only ladies I hold hands with are my mother and my niece. Sometimes my sister when she gets drunk off of one and a half mojitos.

Grabbing Annie's hand is a statement to show the party I'm serious about her, even if this is a huge fake-out.

I also wanted to know if her hand is as soft as I thought it was.

It is.

Eyes are on us as we walk into the space, but all I can focus on is her hand in mine.

It's hard to explain, but it fits.

If I've grabbed a woman's hand during sex, it always feels small and delicate, breakable. Annie's hand in mine calms me but also sends liquid warmth through my arm.

I could hold her hand every day.

This shocks the hell out of me since I *don't do this.*

As we walk deeper into the crowd, people turn and look.

The resident playboy holding hands with the respectable and level-headed Annie Stewart. It's hard to explain, but I feel attitudes toward me shift. It makes me feel like a man, to see how people treat me, now that Annie is fake mine.

"Oh my goodness," Tracy Banning, Jason's mom, says, walking toward us. Annie's hand stiffens in mine, but I rub my thumb against her knuckle.

"You got this," I whisper to Annie. She looks up at me with a smile.

"Hi, Tracy," Annie says, tearing her hand away from mine to hug her.

I want her hand back.

I kiss Tracy on the cheek in greeting. She looks between us and flicks her eyebrows. "Well, this is a nice surprise to see you together."

I snake my arm around Annie's back, pulling her toward me. My palm covers her hip, and my touch flirts with the flesh of her backside. She doesn't freeze with my touch. Goddamn, she feels good.

"I'm obsessed with her," I say, kissing her temple. Annie smiles, since she can't object in front of one of the people we're trying to fool.

I want to fake it with Annie all night.

"I'm so glad." Tracy's eyebrows collapse in suspicion.

I have to sell the shit out of this.

"Annie is the best woman I've ever met," I say. I gaze at her, and when she doesn't look at me, I pinch her hip softly. She jumps, and her gaze catches mine, selling our lie.

"Annie is darling and my favorite employee. Don't tell my children, but I always hoped..."

I watch Annie's lips part, hanging on Tracy's words.

It's clear Tracy hoped that Jason would chose Annie, date Annie, marry Annie.

Instead, he's with a woman I'm pretty sure has had my dick in her mouth semi-recently.

Across the room, I see Jason with a woman, talking to each other, holding glasses of wine.

Oh, that's definitely her.

Fuck me.

She looks in our direction, and her mouth drops. She remembers me too.

I grip Annie tighter to me, which is doing nothing to calm my semi from her body pressed against me and that dress.

I need a drink.

"Baby, I'm going to the bar. Do you want something?" I ask.

Annie nods. "White wine."

"Any specific kind?"

"Sauvignon blanc."

"Sure thing." I kiss her on the head again. If I only get one kiss on the lips, I'm saving it for maximum impact.

I walk away, her skin imprinted on my hand. Shaking it out, I walk up to the bored bartender. He braces himself on the bar top.

"Two sauvignon blancs please," I say, dropping a ten into the tip jar. He nods once and turns to pour the wine.

"Hi," a breathy female voice says. Already?!

"Hi," I say, swallowing, turning to see my one-weekend stand from a little over a year ago.

The last time I saw Morgan, we spent an intense weekend having sex on every surface of my tiny home. When I told her it was a one-time thing, she threw a soda can at my head, dropping me like a sandbag to the floor.

She has stellar aim.

She also has *Fatal Attraction* written all over her. Thank God I don't own a rabbit.

"How are you, darling?" I ask with a smile. *Please don't stab me.*

"I'm great," she says, angling her hand with a ginormous diamond so I can see. "It's good to see you again. Is that your…"

"Girlfriend, yes." Usually, I would gag at the word girlfriend, but when it's attached to Annie, it feels alright.

"Oh, her?" she asks. Her blue eyes flick to Annie, who is still chatting with Tracy. I see the look of dismissal on Morgan's face, and it annoys the fuck out of me.

I can't believe I gave her multiple orgasms.

"Yes, her," I say. "Annie is the best woman I've ever known. Any man would be lucky to have her."

I might not be brilliant, but I know a good woman when I meet one.

This one is not, although she does expert-level things with her tongue.

"I'm glad you found someone," she says, swallowing. "Even though you're an asshole."

She broke up with her boyfriend to come fuck me, but okay.

I don't engage. I made that mistake our night over a year ago, and that's how I ended up in the ER with a mild concussion.

She could slit my throat right now with the daggers in her eyes. "That was a long time ago. We're both happy now, right?"

"Right," she says, her lips cracking a smile. Not sure if it's a genuine smile or a "I'm going to find you and kidnap you and make you love me" smile.

Jason walks up next to her, wrapping his arm possessively around Morgan's waist. He holds her like I want to hold Annie.

I turn back to catch a glimpse of her, and she takes my breath away.

"Finch," Jason says, nodding to me. The bartender puts the glasses of wine down, and I nod. I take one in each hand and turn back to them.

"Banning," I respond.

"I see you're here with Annie," he says, nodding to her.

"Yes. I feel like the luckiest man in the room." *Because I am.*

"I can't believe it. You and Annie. Together," he says, his voice full of venom. It sounds similar to how he sounded when he threatened me at the pool hall after I fucked Morgan.

I had no idea that Jason was dating Morgan. Hand on a bible, no idea.

My arrogance annoys the shit out of him so I quirk a corner of my lip up. "It just happened. I can't believe it. One day, we just clicked, and we've been together ever since. I'm so mad at myself I wasted so much time."

"Just like that?" Jason asks, his voice lowering to eerie calmness. Well, the night is young. I plan to put on a show.

"Just like that. Will you excuse me? I need to get back to my date," I say, walking away. I could feel the waves of fury at my back, but I don't care. Annie fidgets on her heels and smiles when she sees me approaching with wine.

She is so beautiful, and this is so fun, even if it is pretend.

There's a small part of me that wishes it isn't.

11

ANNIE

Watching Cameron talk to Morgan and Jason thrills me to my fingertips.

As I talk to Tracy, narrating my fake love story with Cameron, I sneak glances at Jason and how he's reacting to me being with another man. He clenches a fist at his side, his hand veins protruding. His jaw tightens as he holds onto Morgan like he will float away if he doesn't. Morgan is looking Cameron up and down like he's a soft chocolate chip cookie.

That's strange.

Cameron breaks away with our wine, and seeing him slink toward me with such swagger makes me want to cross my legs. He hands me a chilled glass, and we clink, locking eyes as we sip. Jason and Morgan are still watching us, and I want them to believe we're madly in love. That I've moved on.

I wonder if Jason told Morgan about us.

"It was so lovely to talk to you," Tracy says, giving me a squeeze before moving to the next guest.

As soon as she is gone, Cameron leans into me. His

cologne overpowers me, and I can't help but inhale his woodsy scent. "Did she buy it?"

"One hundred percent," I say, clinking glasses with him again. "What about Jason and Morgan?"

"Fuckface? I can't tell if he's suspicious or jealous."

We both study Jason as he yanks Morgan by the hand away from the bar. They disappear into the backroom.

Seeing Jason hold Morgan's hand brings back the sorrow living rent-free in my heart. I prepared myself for tonight, knowing I would see them together, that he would love her out in public, while he only loved me in private. Still, tears are threatening, and it might not be pretty.

"I'm going to the bathroom," I say.

He takes me into a small embrace and whispers against my hair. "Please don't be sad. You're better off without him," he says. His breath brands my skin. We pull away and my eyes lock with his.

Is the kiss going to happen now? I spent all my time preparing myself for Jason and Morgan, but I spent zero brain power to prepare for Cameron's lips on mine. It would be a great kiss, I'm sure, since he's had enough practice, but I don't know how I'll react.

It's best we wait.

He takes a rebel strand of hair from my face and tucks it behind my ear. I walk away before he can see the redness behind my bronzer.

The bathroom is at the far end of the space, separated from the hallway by a powder room. I stand in front of the ornate mirror and see someone I don't recognize in the reflection.

I'm not the girl who wears sexy dresses to make a man jealous. This much makeup looks better on a woman like

Morgan, not me. Tugging at the dress does not make it more comfortable or make me feel authentic.

I'm just a huge fraud.

Voices from the bathroom drift over the maroon carpet.

"I can't believe Cameron is with *her.* He was holding her hand. I haven't seen him hold a hand ever," the voice says. The voice is familiar, but I can't place it. I should leave. Gossiping about other women only gets uglier. I may be thirty-four-years-old, but mean comments still hurt.

The sick part of me stays because I've never been talked about, envied. It creates a buzz in my belly that people think I'm special enough to tame Cameron Finch, a man who refuses to settle down. That holding his hand makes me exceptional.

I've never felt special or interesting. I hate this makes me feel this good.

"You know we dated briefly in high school and he refused to be affectionate with me in public? Grabbing her hand like that? I mean I'm over it, but *her*?"

That has to be Alyssa Trammel, now Dickey, who was once Cameron's prom date and pseudo-girlfriend. She's married to an attorney who owns a small practice in town, who does legal work for the Bannings sometimes.

Alyssa went with Cameron to prom, while I stayed home, in my dress, eating pizza because my date stood me up.

I have a specific taste, and that's assholes.

Should've seen Jason coming.

Now Alyssa, possibly the most stunning girl at my high school when I went there, is envious of me. *Me.*

I've done my best to live my life under the radar, going with the flow, never ruffling any feathers. A people-pleaser to my core, I prefer to live in the shadows and let others shine. Being with Cameron is the opposite: it's bold, it's exciting.

It shows people that I can loosen up, that I can have fun.

Their comments, though, feel like a punch to the gut. I should leave. The undercurrent of their words reinforces something I've always felt.

Not good enough.

"We shouldn't be talking about this in the bathroom. I think someone is in here," the other woman says. I hear the door open and I'm stuck in the carpet, immobilized by their words. One woman looks back to me, and I recognize her as the owner of Gold Roast, Tara.

Alyssa was on the guest list, but I have no idea how Tara was invited.

She appeared in town six months ago, taking over Gold Roast from the former owners, who picked up and moved to Utah to be closer to their grandkids. Tara's long dark hair is braided over a shoulder, and she's wearing a stunning jumpsuit with gold jewelry. She's the kind of woman who doesn't look like a clown in makeup.

"Hi Annie," Tara says, dipping her hands underwater to wash her hands. Her body language is remorseful, and I can't hold it against her.

"Annie is in here?" Alyssa asks, exploding out of the stall.

"Hi, ladies," I say. No comebacks are on my tongue, but my brain scrambles to think of them.

I'll come up with a great one later tonight, probably at three a.m.

"So, you're with Cameron, huh?" Tara asks, punctuating with a nervous laugh.

"Yes. He's my boyfriend."

Somehow, that doesn't sound weird.

Tara's lips part as she continues to wash her hands. "How long have you dated?"

"A couple weeks," I say. Tara says nothing as she shuts off the water and dries her hands with a paper towel.

"You two look cute together," Alyssa says. "Your height. It makes sense."

Don't say anything. Just smile.

"Yes. It's hard to find a man taller than me," I say, slapping my thigh.

"I like your dress," Tara says, like the compliment stings. "You look really good."

"Thanks," I reply, looking down.

"Just be careful. With Cameron," Alyssa blurts, looking in the mirror so she can look me in the eye. "He acts like he's all in, and then one day he shuts it down. Happened to my friend Melanie."

"Or he doesn't even want to begin when he gets started," Tara says. I remember their interaction in the coffee shop, how she overcharged him for his sister's drink, a murder plot in her brown eyes.

"Thank you," I say. "I trust him, though."

"That's good," they say in unison. I smile and hold up my hand and leave.

When I walk in the open space, I scan for Cameron. He's easy to spot since he's practically a head taller than everyone else.

When he sees me, his lips break into a full grin.

Old Me would be convinced that meant something was there. He felt something more for me than a ruse, a fake-out to make my ex jealous.

New Me is more careful, cautious. I've been burned by Jason, taken advantage of, hidden. Maybe I'm steering myself to a healthier man, not one who's unattainable and bound to hurt me.

I have my eyes wide open with Cameron. I cannot fall for him. It's just another false promise, and I doubt I'm the woman to change his ways.

I think to that girl who cried into her cheese that night of prom. She had had a crush on Cameron, but it wasn't real.

Anything I feel for him can't be real now.

I swallow hard when I see her.

Annie looks across the room, holding her hands in her front of her. She's a knockout in that dress and I've been stifling a hard-on all night. I wish this was real so I could bury myself inside of her later, making her moan underneath me.

I'm supposed to be acting like I'm infatuated with her, and it's not tough.

Not tough at all.

Her gaze falls on me, and I can't help but smile like a buffoon.

She walks across the room like a Victoria's Secret model, legs for days, that dress hugging every curve of her body. She's just as attractive in her work polo and jeans, her hair in a messy bun on the top of her head. This is just another stunning version of her.

I'm going to need some quality time in my shower tonight. This vision of Annie walking toward me will fuel my solos for a while. I won't need to break out the fancy porn.

"Hi," she says, taking a deep breath.

"Everything go okay?" I ask. I grab for her hand again, and she looks down at it.

"Why are you holding my hand?"

Because I really, really like it. "It just seems like something couples do, right?"

She nods once. She pulls my hand up with hers and extends her pointer finger. "I think the table we want is over there."

I take the lead, pulling her. She smiles at me, and we are walking hand-in-hand to the best table, right next to the hors d'oeuvres. Pulling her seat out first, I hold the back of her chair as she sits down. Her creamy skin brushes against my fingers, and I have to physically restrain myself from touching her. I push her chair in and sit down next to her.

Damn, I want to put my hand on her leg. It's not appropriate, though. Everything we're doing is for show, it's not the impulsive touch of actual lovers. Still, I'm not a guy who's ever affectionate toward women in public, unless it's making out in the corner at the Swift or a handy under the table. It's best when it's behind closed doors. Less chance of the woman getting the wrong idea of what I can offer or where it's leading.

"Anything look good?" I ask, looking behind us to the spread. "There's charcuterie galore. I love that word. Charcuterie."

"Me too. Oh, the salami is in a rose?"

"Too pretty to eat."

"Oh, I will eat it," Annie says with a wink.

I let out a violent cough, taking a sip of water on the table. Envisioning Annie on her knees with my dick in her mouth is not helping my windpipe.

I'm hard as cement and a total asshole.

I'm going to be the cleanest motherfucker ever, since I'm spending however long it takes in my shower tonight after this.

"Have you seen Jason and Morgan again?" Annie asks.

I survey the room. "They ran off, and I haven't seen them since."

Like an ancient spirit summoned by a Ouija board, Morgan and Jason walk out at the front of the room like royals. They wave, and people are already hitting their silverware against their glasses. It's not even a wedding, but they kiss to the clinks. Jason takes the microphone from the DJ.

The more I look at him, the more fury I feel.

"Hello everyone, thank you for coming. Morgan and I are so thankful you all could be here today to celebrate our love."

Gag me with a two-by-four.

The audience coos, and their eyes all focus on Jason as he leans down to kiss Morgan, who barely comes to his shoulder.

I turn to look at Annie. She's looking down at the table, her hands clasped in front of her. My arm instinctively goes around her, and I pull her to me. She melts in my arms, and I hear a tiny sniffle from her nose.

"We have some fabulous snacks for you, the bar is open and it's on us, and we will be starting some dancing shortly. Again, thank you so much for coming. You all mean the world to us."

He hands the microphone back to the DJ and lays another kiss on Morgan. Annie's eyes are squeezed shut, and she lets out a shaky breath.

My fury has developed into blind rage. Jason has always been a tool, but I could snap his neck in fucking half.

How could he yank her along for a year? A year? I don't do that with a woman, ever. I'm crystal clear with them on what we are and never promise something that's not going to happen. All I promise is orgasms—not a relationship or that I'll love them if they just hold on.

Jason pulling Annie along, saying one day they'll be together, and then dumping her and getting back together with Morgan makes him the scum of the earth.

I can't stand to see Annie like this. She loved Jason. I can read it all over her slumped shoulders and slack cheeks, but she's holding it together.

I need to distract her and fast.

The first chords of "Crash into Me" by Dave Matthews Band plays from the speakers. A tear collects in the corner of Annie's eye. I stand up and offer my hand to her.

She looks at my hand and back up at me.

"Let's give them a show," I say.

"There's no one on the dance floor."

"Exactly," I say.

She nods in determination. She puts her tiny purse onto the table and stands up, arranging her skirt down her legs. I grab her hand and lead her again on the dance floor.

I splay my palm on her lower back and pull her to me. My nose takes in her coconut scent. I take her other hand, and I begin our slow sway back and forth.

"Everyone is looking at us," she whispers.

"Let them," I say. When I pull her closer, I can feel her breasts against my chest, her hair on my face. I can't help it; I press my cheek into her temple, like she's the only one for me.

"You're so smooth," she says, looking up at me with a smile.

"I try to be. I like dancing. With you," I say, squeezing

her in my arms. A few other couples have joined us as the song builds and builds. I don't know if it's the music or her body against me, the coconut scent or the drama of the night.

All I know is she's consuming me.

"Is now a good time to kiss you?" I whisper into her ear. Jason and Morgan hover near the food, their eyes fixated on us.

"Okay," she says.

We pull away and look each other. I bring a hand to her cheek, her skin velvet under my fingers.

When my mouth finds hers, it's illegal fireworks, an engine fire, and blast of hot water, all at once. Her lips are soft and wet as I turn my head to fit with hers. Everything falls away, and dammit, it doesn't feel fake. Not at all. I rake my fingers through her hair and pull her closer, deepening the kiss. Her hand goes to the back of my head as our mouths move together, and I want to find the nearest supply closet or bathroom stall and devour her.

It takes all the restraint I have not to explore her mouth further, massage her tongue with mine. My hand stays firmly on her waist, as discussed, gripping the fabric of her dress so it doesn't roam.

She pulls away, and her eyes dart before looking me in the eye. Her chest heaves and her lips part, and I want to kiss her again.

But I'll stick to my word. We agreed to one kiss. Only one.

Now it's over. And I want to do it again. And again.

I've never been able to guess what Annie was thinking. I'm not sure if she liked it or if she's performing. Turning around, I see Jason's red face and Morgan's crossed arms.

"We gave them a show," I whisper to Annie, taking her in my arms again to finish the song.

"We did," she says as she leans into me, her cheek against my cheek again.

I almost say something, but I remember the time at Moe's when she said she wasn't attracted to me.

That kiss sure felt like she was, though.

13

ANNIE

That was a *kiss*.

That was the kiss promised in fairy tales, from princes when they save the princess. He drops his sword and charges his lady, taking her in an embrace and kissing the words out of her.

My limbs feel like live wire, and my lips sting from the collision. I knew Cameron would be a good kisser, just from his track record and conversations.

But that kiss made me forget we're pretending. We're here to make Jason jealous. We're here to show the town that I'm desirable, that I'm wanted. Not the beginning of anything.

"Good job," I say.

Real good, Annie.

"Thanks," he says with a laugh. "Good job to you, too."

Jason and Morgan face each other, arms crossed. It looks like they're arguing.

"Looks like it had the desired effect. They saw it. I made sure of it," Cameron says, pulling me close again. I'm not sure what I'm feeling, but something hard presses against my stomach. I look up at him with lowered eyes.

"What?" he asks.

I lean in to whisper, "You have a hard-on."

"Duh," he says, spinning me.

"From one kiss?"

"That kiss was *hot*," he whispers back to me. "Of course I'm going to get excited."

I don't know why I'm grinning that Cameron has a hard-on because of me.

Because of that kiss.

That absolutely breathtaking kiss.

"Maybe you'll calm down if we discuss the amazing event you'll plan for the brewery."

He rolls his eyes. "Probably."

Another nineties song, "Always Be My Baby" by Mariah Carey, comes on, and I sigh.

"I miss the nineties," I say. Cameron goes rigid.

"What?" I ask. Does he not like Mariah Carey?

"I got it," Cameron says. "Nineties-themed party."

I slap him on the chest. "That's a *great* idea. It's the new decade people are nostalgic for."

Cameron swells with pride. He looked like that when I tutored him and he finally grasped the polynomial functions I tore my hair out explaining to him.

"What about making it a prom? Like every nineties teen movie had a prom," he suggests.

"You're a *genius*," I say. I've never seen Cameron shy before, but he hides his eyes from me. "How much fun would a school dance be if you could drink?"

"I drank at school dances," Cameron says. "I used to put vodka in a water bottle and hide it in the bushes."

"Well, *I* didn't do that."

"You were such a rule-follower," Cameron says.

"Hey!" I say, then pause. "Okay, I have to agree with you."

"It's okay to break rules sometimes," he says. He leans in, and his breath on my cheek sends shivers down my spine. "Like lying about dating me."

He's right. I've lived my life by the rules, always worried about other people and their opinions of me. Concealing my relationship with Jason let him off easy, and now I'm here with a fake date, trying to make him jealous at his own engagement party.

If I think about it too long, I'll beat myself up again.

"Let's flesh out this idea more," I say, changing the subject. "We could have a photo area, a prom king and queen voting. We could do it as a money maker for the brewery, but also we could donate part of the proceeds to a charity. Maybe the rescue your dad got Woody from?"

Cameron pulls me to him as we sway out of time to the music. "That is a great idea. I really like that idea. No, wait, I love that idea."

"Right? I love it. Maybe I'll finally go to a prom."

"Why didn't you go?"

"My date stood me up," I say.

Cameron's face grows serious. "I should've taken you."

I laugh.

"What's so funny?"

He releases me so I can dunk under his arm. "You wouldn't have taken me."

"I admire the hell out of you. It would've been an honor to take you."

Admire. I get that a lot. I'm praised for being good at my job, a good friend, a good neighbor. Still, that doesn't mean someone wants to sleep with you. Or they feel the same sparks you do when you kiss. Or they want to tell your parents you're dating.

"By the way, I saw your senior prom date in the bathroom. Alyssa."

"Oh God." Cameron laughs, deep and throaty. Sexy as sin. "Did she say something to you?"

"No. They're just surprised, is all." *And they told me to be careful with you.* "Tara was with her, too."

"Oh, Jesus," Cameron says. "Whatever they said is lies. Maybe."

That you don't hold hands. That you never bring a woman out in public.

The song ends, and we walk off the dance floor. I glug some wine, hoping to remove the brand of his lips on mine. That kiss was nothing. It meant nothing.

Why do I feel like it did, though?

Jason and Morgan are missing again. I scan the room, but I can't find them. Instead, I find multiple pairs of eyes sneaking glances at us.

"I think it was a success," I say. "Everyone is looking."

"I think so. I saw Jason and Morgan fighting earlier," Cameron says. "I don't see them anywhere."

"Me either. To our mission complete."

"Mission complete," Cameron says. We clink glasses again. His arm settles across the back of my chair, and I wonder what it means. It can't mean anything. Right? Men like Cameron just *lean* on things.

"It was a pleasure to fake date you," he says.

"The pleasure was all mine." I look at him as he clears his throat, taking another sip of wine. A vein pops out from his neck and he can't look at me. He hooks a finger to loosen his collar.

We spend another hour at the party, dancing some

more. I'm beginning to crave his arms around me, so it's a relief when we leave, and his hand doesn't hold mine. We're back to friends, and nothing more.

I don't know what I expect, but he doesn't touch me when I get out of his car at my house.

We just say good night, and I look back as I unlock my front door.

Cameron is watching from his car to make sure I make it to my place.

Once the door is closed, I slide down it to the floor, my skirt around my hips and my legs splayed.

I'll need to do lots of journaling to deconstruct what happened tonight.

14

CAMERON

"Hello, my dear Finch family," Miriam Oliver says as we're setting up our station. The Heart of Gold Half-Marathon pulls in people from all over the area, including folks from the Sacramento and Bay areas. Our downtown fills with the event, and our local restaurants—and hopefully our brewery—will see a nice boost. I've heard people like to run it because it meanders through trees and some of our trails and parks, but it's not too rural.

That's what the woman I banged last year after she got her first sub-two-hour time said, anyway.

The first half-marathon finishers are still a half hour out, so the town square is sparse, with a few spectators and vendors twiddling their thumbs. I've been moving kegs so I'm sweating like I participated.

Now that Miriam Oliver is here, I'm sweating more.

Miriam is one of Goldheart's biggest mouths, and if you want gossip, you go to her. For some reason people tell her things and trust her to keep it a secret. It's best not to get on her bad side. She publicly outed Emily and told everyone she was pregnant before she decided what she was going to do.

Emily had shouted at Miriam in the Goldheart Neighborhood Market after Miriam pressed Emily about Olive's father and why he disappeared, before she knew she was pregnant. Mom told Miriam about Emily's pregnancy in confidence, and then Miriam couldn't keep her trap shut.

Bottom line—I hate that woman, but we're polite because she could make our lives and the brewery's life a living hell.

"Hi, Miriam," my mother greets. "What are you up to today?"

"My daughter is running so we're here in support. I have no idea why people run thirteen miles on purpose."

She has a point, but she's still the worst.

Miriam rubs her lips together. "So, I was at Jason Banning's engagement party last night."

I freeze. Where was she? If I had seen her, I would've aborted the mission. I didn't see her on the guest list. Did she lurk in the rafters?

"I saw you there, Cameron." *Don't say it, don't say it.* "You were cozy with Annie Stewart. It was surprising."

The blood drains from my body.

Mom lifts an eyebrow and looks at me. Miriam gives me a similar look, and her lip quirks up. My eyes close slowly as Miriam says, "I saw you kiss her. It looked spicy."

It *was* spicy. So spicy, I came home and spent some quality time with my hand in the shower. Our deal is almost over, so I *could* bring a lady home soon, but I don't want to. Thumper, my best friend, texted me at two a.m. to ask if I wanted to double-date with a new girl he's seeing and her "open-minded" friend, but I turned it down.

I kiss Annie with no tongue once, and now I don't want to fuck other women? What the hell.

"It was a harmless kiss," I say.

"*You* kiss people. Annie does not," Miriam says. "She's a good girl, and you're..."

Fuck you, Miriam. Fuck. You.

Emily walks back from the car and behind the stand, dropping the box of merch on the ground.

"Hi, Miriam," she says sweetly, but I know she hates her as much as I do.

"Your brother kissed Annie Stewart at Jason Banning's engagement party," Miriam tells her without returning the hello.

I see Reid walking toward us, and I'm praying Miriam leaves. That, somehow, Reid doesn't hear that I kissed his friend, after I promised him I wasn't pursuing her.

Which I'm not. Maybe I am? I can't, though? It's complicated.

"What?" Emily asks, her eyes large and mouth gaping.

"Cameron also held her hand," Miriam says with delight, acting like she didn't make my sister cry for two days straight.

My sister whips her head to me. "Excuse me, you *held* her *hand*?"

"You act like I had sex with her on the dance floor," I say, averting my gaze. I can't tell them Annie's secret, especially with that woman standing there. I'm surprised Miriam didn't know about Jason and Annie.

"Well, I hope your daughter has a wonderful time. Running for no reason and all," I say, loud enough that Miriam gets the hint I'm dismissing her.

Miriam's pencil-thin eyebrows raise, and I give her a hard look, daring her to say anything else. She's gossiped enough about me that I have wrath deep in every crevice of my soul, but my parents raised me to be polite, even when the person doesn't deserve it.

Miriam lets out a huff and readjusts her purse on her shoulder. "Well, say hello to Randy for me, Kit. You must be enjoying having your whole family back in Goldheart. Jackson needed to come home."

"Thank you, Miriam. I hope you have a lovely day!" Mom shouts. My mom is smiling, but there's wishes of bodily harm behind her eyes.

Miriam waves and walks away.

"That *woman*," Mom spits out, pulling out the swag from the box Emily brought.

"You don't hold hands. You've *never* held a girlfriend's hand," Emily says.

"He would have to have a girlfriend to hold her hand," my mom says. Her eyes widen. "Is Annie your girlfriend?"

"Would you two stop?" I say, slicing my hands through the air like a referee.

"Tell us what is going on, now that busybody is gone. If you tell me you're dating Annie Stewart, I am going to lose my mind."

"In a good way, or a 'I need to check you into the hospital' way?"

"Good way," she says. "Please tell me. Please make one of my dreams come true."

"What's going on?" Reid asks, finally joining us behind the table.

I wait for the explosion. Might as well clench my butt cheeks now.

"Your brother kissed Annie at Jason Banning's engagement party. Did you know about this?"

Reid looks at me, betrayal in his eyes. Then, he says quietly, "I thought you were just friends."

I shrug.

"Really," Mom says. "Who knows? Annie could be your sister one day!"

"Let's not go that far," I say.

"I could punch you right now, but Dad says we need to represent the brand," Reid says. His threats are harmless.

"No punching," Mom says. "Reid, you have a beautiful girlfriend."

"Not anymore," Reid blurts out. Emily and Mom turn to him, eyes large as moons.

"What?" I ask.

"We broke up," Reid says. "We realized we're more friends than romantic."

"Well," Emily says, taking a sip of water, "you don't mind if Cam dates Annie?"

I run my hand down my face. I want to sprint out of this parking lot and leave. My hands shake, and I regret the two pots of coffee I consumed this morning.

This is exactly what I was afraid of.

"Everyone, enough," I say. I'm sweating and feel light-headed. "We did kiss. One time. It doesn't mean grandbabies. It doesn't mean I will *finally* settle down. Lay off it."

My mother and sister scowl, but they know when to stop questioning me. Reid still looks like he wants to skewer me alive.

The crowd nearby begins cheering as we see the first male finisher run past us to the chute of the finish line. Our beer service is imminent. It's time to shut this down.

"I came up with a great idea for the event for the brewery," I say. "Annie is helping me with it."

"That's nice of her," Mom says. My mom's lip quivers and I know she wants to ask if that's how we got together.

"I'm intrigued," Emily says.

A good way to distract the Finches is to talk about business. I lean in, and my brother, sister, and mother do the same.

"We thought an adult prom with a nineties theme. People buy tickets. We have a photo op. Prom king and queen. Costume contest. Dancing, punch. Drink tickets for two beers."

"That's a great idea," Emily says, lighting up. "The nineties are our childhood. I love it."

Reid is quiet before he grumbles out, "That is a pretty good idea."

"An adult prom with a nineties theme. I just love it," Mom says. She squeezes my forearm, and pride swells in my chest.

"Dan will love it, too," Emily says with a clap. "I'm going to have to plan my costume. Maybe Olive and I can go as Thelma and Louise."

"The raccoons?"

"No, that 1990 classic starring Geena Davis and Susan Sarandon, duh," Emily says.

"We also discussed doing a charity aspect for it," I add. "We could turn a profit, of course, but maybe a silent auction for the German Shepherd rescue. Or leukemia."

Mom shakes her head. "Jackson won't go for that. Please don't mention it. But your dad will be touched to donate to the rescue."

Emily slaps me on the back. "Good job, Cameron. Really."

"I'll have your dad call Dan," Mom says, slapping her hands together in a single clap.

"Annie said she could stop by and go over everything with us," I say.

Emily and Mom look at each other, doing that feminine telepathy thing they do. I thought I lied pretty well about us not being together and creating a distraction from the news about the kiss, but they look like they're not buying it.

"Invite her this week to the brewery so she can see the space," Mom suggests. "I have the best feeling about this."

Finally getting a 'good job' from my family makes me feel like Rocky Balboa.

I have to tell Annie.

We serve hundreds of people. Every time I turn around, there's a new sweaty person, wanting to celebrate with our beer. We get a few inquiries on where people can find us and compliments on our Gold Dust IPA, and GSD, our signature golden ale. In between waves of participants getting beer, I pull Reid aside.

"Dude, I'm sorry about Annie," I say. "It just happened."

"It's fine," Reid grumbles. "She's my friend. I just don't want her to get hurt."

I clamp his shoulder with my hand. "I get that. I don't want to hurt her either."

"Good. We're on the same page, then," he says, walking away.

After I hug my family and get in my car, I end up at the bungalow where I was two nights previously.

"You will not kiss her. You will not have dirty fantasies about her," I say to myself as I walk up the driveway by the main house to her studio bungalow in the back. I hear laughing inside and consider not knocking. It sounds like she's busy. My fist hovers over the door, and I shake my head.

What am I doing at Annie's house? We agreed we were done with the fake dating.

However, that kiss. That *kiss*.

I'm walking down the driveway to my truck when I hear, "Cam?"

I turn around, and Annie's standing there in a long-sleeved shirt, with no bra, her nipples poking through her shirt. Sports shorts sit low on her hips, a sliver of taut stomach peeking through. I want to run my tongue along it. Her posture is nonchalant, but my dick is on high alert.

Thank God she has company so I'm not tempted.

"I'm sorry if I'm bothering you. I—"

"It's okay. It's just the TV," Annie says.

Oh, no. I stay glued to my position. If I get closer and smell the coconut on her hair, things might happen.

"I wanted to tell you my family loved your idea. Loved it." I could explode from excitement. Since I'm a hugger, I want to wrap my arms around her in celebration, but it's not a good idea. That looks like some thin fabric, and I can't predict what will happen if I feel her tits against my chest.

Annie claps, and her eyes brighten. "That's wonderful."

"They want you to swing by the brewery this week. If you still want to help."

She leans against the doorframe. "I can be there Tuesday morning. Will that work?"

"Yes, that would be great."

"You know, Cam, you could've called me."

"I know. But I wanted to see your face when I told you."

Annie places her hand over her heart. "Aw, that's sweet."

I clasp my hands together in front of me. Should I tell her? I don't think it's a big deal, but Miriam's gossip spreads faster than wildfire in the foothills. It's probably best from me to tell her.

"So, funny thing," I say, running my hand through my hair. "Miriam Oliver saw us at the party. She saw our kiss."

"Oh God, I was afraid of this. Tracy always invites

people randomly," she says. "Was she hiding? I didn't see her."

"Right?" I say. "My family got really excited. About us."

"Oh?" Annie asks. She crosses her arms, lifting her breasts higher, her nipples taunting me. I want to slip one between my lips badly.

Maybe both at once.

"I didn't want to say anything. In case it got back to Jason."

Annie takes a step toward me and I wonder how quick I could get her shirt off.

"How excited were they? About us?"

"My mom was ecstatic. Thrilled. Emily was excited too. Reid was...weird," I say as my face tenses.

"Huh," Annie says, shaking her head. Her braless breasts jiggle a smidge. I need to get out of here.

"So, the meeting. They might think we're together. Or interested in each other."

She looks like she wants to say something but doesn't. Her pale cheeks warm, matching the color of her freckles. "Let them."

My mouth falls open. "What?"

Annie shrugs one shoulder. "We don't have to put on a show like we did at Jason's party, but if it helps with the consistency of our story, then, let's just go with it."

My brain short-circuits because I say, "Can we kiss again? This time with tongue?"

"Good night Cameron," she shouts, walking back inside of her house.

"Tuesday at nine-thirty work?" I ask.

"I think so. I'll let you know if it doesn't." Annie closes the door. I walk away, my hands in my pockets.

She wants to neither confirm, nor deny our fake relationship? To my family?

I was about to tell them we're just friends, there's nothing to get excited about. Now, they will get all sorts of excited.

Me too. I'm my-dick-is-rock-hard-and-I-could-hammer-a-nail-with-it excited.

I might get to kiss her again. I might get to hold her hand.

I want to lay her on a table and feast on her. I doubt she'll let me do that in front of everyone, but a guy can dream.

It's more than sex. It's the way her mind works, so quickly, and how kind she is, willing to help me out for the umpteenth time. How she's game to keep this going, on the fly, after it took a PowerPoint to conceptualize the first round of fake dating.

Maybe it's not fake anymore. Maybe I really am into her.

15

ANNIE

I don't know why I put on makeup this morning. Why I spent extra time curling my hair and picking out my best jeans. I have one pair of J Brand denim I bought in San Francisco with Raegan. She talked me into buying the ridiculously expensive pair because my ass looked great in them.

Now, I'm showing up at the Woody Finch Brewery, looking like I'm trying too hard in my Banning Cellars polo shirt. Planning to play along on our fake dating ruse when it was supposed to be one night.

I bring my binders with my vendor contacts and my laptop. I was bored last night so I created a Pinterest board with possible aesthetic inspiration for our nineties-themed prom. My breath is shaky as I try to pull the door to the brewery.

It's not opening.

Reid Finch appears in front of the door with a grin. The lock turns, and the door opens. Ever since Cameron mentioned Reid's odd reaction to our kiss at the party, I've cycled through memories of us. It's only ever been friendly with him; I've never felt more. Still, I don't want to hurt him. He's one of the best men I've ever met.

I decided I would only address it if he does.

"Hey, Annie," Reid says. He takes me in for a one-armed hug and steps away so I can walk past. "Do you need any help?" he asks.

"No, I'm good. Where should we…"

"Over here," he says, ushering me to a table in the middle of the taproom. He's a lot more relaxed since the last time I was here, dropping off the contract to Cameron.

"The idea for the nineties prom is fantastic. Our whole family is really excited about it," Reid says, pushing his hands into his pockets.

"It was Cameron's idea," I say.

"So, is there anything going on? With you and Cameron?"

A low croak leaves my throat. I honestly don't know. Originally, we agreed to one night of pretend…but that kiss. It felt like every romcom first kiss, transformative and transcendent. I feel like I've floated through the last couple days, trying to remind myself that it wasn't real.

Neither confirm, nor deny is our current plan of attack.

"I like your brother very much," I say. As in my body hums whenever I'm around him. I want to kiss him again. The feeling is so delicious, I'm letting everyone think what they want to think.

Reid smiles, but looks sad. "Okay."

I swallow, but my throat feels thick. "Does that bother you?"

"No," he says. "It's surprising, but no."

Cameron appears across the taproom, and my breath catches.

In a simple jeans and the brewery's black polo shirt,

Cameron looks effortlessly handsome. He hasn't shaved, which dial his sexiness up to an eleven out of ten.

I shake myself out of it. It's Cameron, the guy who has chemistry with a light post.

I'm not special. I'm not some exception to the rule. Cameron is a fuckboy, plain and simple. If anyone tames him, it won't be me.

"Hi," Cameron says softly, taking me in for a hug. It's different from Reid's friendly arms. This is a slow press of our bodies against one another. My pelvis presses against his, and his cheek skims my cheek. I feel a whisper of his lips along my hair, and my lips curl involuntarily.

There's heat there. I think.

"Are you okay? Are you warm?" Cameron asks.

Fanning my cheeks, I smile. "It's just hot in here," I say. "I'll be fine."

"I'll get you water," he says, then disappears down the hall. When he returns, he places a cold bottle of water in my hand. After I break the seal, I take a long sip. I have to get it together.

I greet Kit, Cameron's mom, and Emily, who sit on one side of a table. Cameron sits down next to me, so close that I can feel the heat of his body. I take another swig of water.

Kit and Emily watch us and smile at each other. I'm so relieved we're fooling them.

Cameron looks around the taproom. "So, I was thinking we could have the event here"—he points to the front room—"And the DJ booth will be set up there," he says, pointing to the long bar in front of the beer spouts and the refrigerator. "And we'll have snacks on the bar top."

"Did you have a date in mind?"

"You, baby."

My cheeks flame and Emily and Kit snap their heads toward each other.

"A calendar...date," I say, trying not to cough.

"Oh that," Cameron says, pulling his phone from his back pocket. "May twenty-first. It's the week after the high school prom. I looked it up."

"I'm really impressed, Cameron," Kit says, her forearms resting on the table. Cameron grins from ear to ear. "Annie, you're being such a good influence on him!"

Don't freak out, don't freak out.

My voice cracks as I add, "May twenty-first is a great choice. We should set that in stone soon and draw up some marketing materials to get the word out, even if we don't have everything set up. That way we can start to get some ticket sales." I flip my planner open and look up.

Cameron's gaze is on me and I can't focus. Emily and Kit are still watching, observing me unravel just because their family member is so stinking charming.

"I can do some marketing mockups," Emily says. "I have an idea for the poster, and I can put it in the newsletter, once we have the ticket sales landing page set up."

"I'll talk to Izzie at the paper," Kit says. "Hopefully they can do a story announcing it."

"It might be a good idea to do some advertising with them," I say. "Maybe Facebook ads as well to get the ball rolling. It can double-dip as marketing for the brewery."

"Are we planning to take over the world?" Cameron says. He nudges me with his elbow, and my mind scrambles.

No, focus, Annie. Event. Not Cameron's delicious forearms and jawline.

"Annie is already a godsend," Emily says, patting my hand. I catch Emily smirking at Cameron, who smiles and looks at me.

An eyelash falls on Cameron's cheek and I rise my thumb to catch it.

Time to make Cameron uncomfortable.

When my thumb touches his cheek, he leans in, slightly, and Emily and Kit gasp collectively.

"Make a wish," I say, balancing the eyelash on my thumb.

He smiles as he closes his eyes, blowing it off of my finger. When he opens it, I see desire in his eyes.

Did he wish for me?

"That's so sexy," Emily whispers. When I look over, I laugh, because her chest rises and falls.

"Stop flirting and back to work," Kit says, grinning as she looks down at her notes.

We brainstorm some more for the event. Randy, Cameron's dad, comes out to say hello, and Jackson waves from behind the bar. Within the hour, we've come up with a basic marketing plan leading up to the event, discussed pricing, how the beer would be distributed, and whose duties would be whose. I take copious notes while Emily jots things down in her phone.

When I look up, I see Cameron's eyes on me. He doesn't look away, and I don't either. Kit, Cameron's mother, is looking, too.

Emily also studies us like we're an abstract painting. Cameron is three feet from me, but my body vibrates with his frequency, my senses heightened now that he's near me, looking at me, breathing the same air.

Cameron pulls out his phone as we're wrapping up. "Reid needs me. Something about one of the tanks. Annie, don't leave until I come back."

His hand covers mine before he disappears and my whole body lights up like a glowstick.

"You and my brother," Emily says. "Wow."

For the millionth time in my life, I wish I wasn't fair-skinned because all my emotions translate to a flush of my cheeks. Again.

"I just haven't seen my brother like this before," Emily says.

I don't know what to say so Emily keeps talking.

"I know my brother has a reputation in town, but he needs someone like you."

"I agree," Kit says, her voice going down a full octave. Her lips purse in pleasure, and my stomach cramps harder. I need to find a bathroom before I shit myself out of nervousness.

"He's wonderful," I say.

"I'm dying," Kit responds.

"Definitely. Did you see the way Cam looked at her?" Emily asks. They both look at me like they're consultants for an MLM, looking for new recruits.

"The way he looks at her is the way Randy looks at me," Kit says.

Aww, I hate lying to them! I need to go. Now.

"Excuse me, I need to use the restroom," I say, sprinting away from them. I race-walk to the bathroom. Before I get there, I see Cameron's face, staring at me from a family photo.

Of course.

After I make it to the bathroom safely and wash my hands, I lean against the wall.

What the hell is happening? It was supposed to be one date and one kiss. Now his family is practically planning our wedding. What a stupid idea not to come clean. Yes, my belly clenches when he looks at me, but he's waving a big red flag like he's an actor in a second-rate performance of *Les Misérables.*

I walk out of the bathroom, and instead of a picture of Cameron, it's the actual Cameron.

All six-five, perfect jawline, grin-that-could-melt-panties Cameron.

"Hi," he says. His proximity makes me want to run to the bathroom again.

"Hi," I say. It sounds so breathy, so turned on, and I swear I'm not.

Okay, maybe I am. Maybe I want him to cage me against this wall and lower his head to mine and kiss me again. For real. With tongue.

"You did great out there. I haven't seen my family that hopeful in a really long time."

"It was my pleasure," I say. *Don't look at him. Don't look him in the eye because you'll be a goner.*

"This event will be epic. I believe in it. I believe in us."

He offers his hand for a high five, and as our hands connect, his fingers weave in between mine for a hold. I shake my hand away because I can't get used to his sexy hand-holding.

"Your family bought it."

"I know," he says. Is he *leaning?* I put my hands on my hips to do something with them.

"What do we do, Cam?" *Please tell me you felt it when we kissed, too.*

Maybe the chemistry in our kiss is entirely in my head.

Cameron loves women. He's an affectionate guy. All this touching means nothing. It's how he communicates; it's natural to him. I am not special.

"I need to get going," I say, taking a step to the left. He

drags his fingers down my arm to stop me, and my heart flutters.

"I was hoping I could buy you lunch," Cameron says. "I know how much you love those sandwiches from Subtown. We could take them out to the lake."

Subtown Sandwiches is my favorite. It's the only place in Goldheart that doesn't let their avocado get brown.

"Don't you have to open the brewery?"

He shakes his head. "My mom offered to cover for me."

"I really should get going," I say, even though today is a late start day for me because of an event I have tonight.

"Please," Cameron says, his grin developing like a picture.

Dang it. His perfect smile and perfect eyes, pleading for me to join him.

This is a bad idea. The worst.

"Okay," comes out of my mouth.

"Great. I'll drive," he says. We walk down the hall, me following Cameron. He finds his mom and says something to her. Kit smiles at me, and I see where Cameron got his charm.

"Are you going to come for Sunday dinner? I'm making pot roast."

I look at Cameron. Sundays are my only day off, and usually I spend them alone in my house, reading romance novels and organizing. A Sunday dinner would be nice.

My parents rarely check in with me, and an evening with the Finches sounds fun.

"Maybe," I say.

"Please come," Kit says, grabbing me for a hug. "Five thirty."

"Let's go," Cameron says as he pulls me by the hand out of the brewery. "I can't believe my mom asked you to Sunday dinner. Once you get into their home, all bets are off. They get really personal there. Sunday dinners are for interrogations. We will just have to continue pretending, I guess."

My hand is still in his, and he's not letting go.

I can be levelheaded about this. I can resist temptation.

This will be fine.

Still, a small part of me wishes he would kiss me again.

16

CAMERON

Annie looks damn good in the front seat of my truck.

I don't know what she did, but she looks different than usual. Whatever she did makes her eyes pop and her lips look extra plump. She's wearing some tight jeans today that hug her in all the right places.

I've snuck a couple peeks at her ass, and it's looking *real* nice.

We stop at Subtown and I get her sandwich order, and it sounds delicious so I get the same. Turkey on Dutch Crunch bread with bacon, avocado, no mustard or mayonnaise, lettuce, tomato, onion. I'm usually a cured meat with some mustard kind of guy, but everything Annie does, I want to be a part of.

We chat continuously on our drive out to the lake. She tells me about her author friend and how they became close. It sounds like Annie reads constantly. I haven't opened a book since high school.

"Maybe I should pick one up," I say.

"You...want to read a romance novel?" she asks with a laugh.

"I'm secure in my masculinity," I say. "What's a good one to start with?"

Annie covers her eyes with her hands. "There's so many kinds."

"I want a really sexy one," I say. "Sex on page two. No page one."

"I can think of a few."

"Do you think I'll pick up any tips?" Cameron asks.

"You might know them all already."

"We'll see. I'm always open to new ideas." I wiggle my eyebrows at her, and she flushes bright pink. I've thought about sex with Annie more than I'd like to admit, and imagining her reading dirty scenes, touching herself while reading them, makes me shift in my seat.

We pull up to visitor parking at one of the beaches at Tin Lake on the edge of town. It's an extension of the American River, and the pride and joy of Goldheart, since tourists rent cabins, fish, and hang out on jet skis there during the summer. Woody Finch is gearing up and hiring summer help, because our taproom becomes a madhouse after Memorial Day.

For now, though, we'll enjoy the peace and quiet of the lake until all the out-of-towners show up.

I grab a blanket from the back of my truck, and Annie holds the sandwiches and our drinks.

We walk down the bank and pick a dry spot. I spread the blanket down, and Annie helps. There's a quiet ease between us as she unbags our sandwiches and cracks open her Diet Pepsi to take a sip. I've known Annie my entire life, but it's like I'm finally getting to *know* her, the real her.

"This is nice," Annie says, stretching out her legs and

crossing them, cradling her sandwich in her hands. "I forget to come out here. I always assume it's crowded."

"I do, too. Jackson is the only one who comes out here regularly. Every day, even in bad weather. Usually at golden hour."

"Stop it, you're going to make me cry," Annie says. I watch her catch a tear and sniffle. She's thinking about what happened to Jackson, and I can't think about it too long either or I'll get sad, too.

I unwrap my sandwich. "You were great today. With my family. Thank you for doing this. And neither confirming nor denying."

"No, thank you. All the pretending was worth it," she says. "Your family practically lost it when I picked up your eyelash."

I touch my cheek where the eyelash landed. I remember how the brush of her finger felt like a hot poker. I can only laugh to mask how it rocked me. "It was a great improvisation moment."

"What did you wish for?" she asks. I can hear her gulp.

I lean in with a wink. "It's a secret."

Jesus, I can not *not* flirt with her.

I wished for another kiss. Another kiss to figure out if the first time was a fluke. A kiss where I will know for sure if I have something with Annie, or the ruse just made a simple peck of the lips feel like a nuclear explosion.

We both take quiet bites of our sandwiches, staring off at a lonely buoy in the middle of the lake.

"I'm so excited for this event. I've wanted to do something like that at the winery, but I'm stuck to birthday parties, wine dinners, and weddings. Theo doesn't really think outside the box."

Theo Banning, the owner of Banning Cellars and Jason's

father, is a Grade A asshole. Theo and my father have never gotten along, and he even tried to stop my dad from opening Woody Finch. It would make sense he wouldn't want to do a fun event for the community; all he cares about is making money.

"Is Theo okay with you helping us?"

"I don't know. I didn't ask," Annie says. She raises an eyebrow at me as she takes a bite of her sandwich.

"Is Ms. Annie Stewart being rebellious?"

She muffles a laugh through the chipmunk cheeks of sandwich in her mouth. Her forefinger and thumb create an inch or two.

Her eyes sure do sparkle.

"How did Jason take our little stunt the other night?"

"I haven't seen him at work yet to find out, and he hasn't texted me or anything. The look on his face was pretty great, though." Her gaze looks off across the stillness of the lake.

"Do you still love him?" I ask.

She shrugs one shoulder. "I don't know. I thought I did, but I'm not sure if the excitement of dating him was actually anxiety since I didn't know what he was going to do."

"No guy should make you feel like that," I say. "That's why I'm really upfront. 'This is just casual, we'll have fun, and it will be over.' So no one is shocked or surprised."

Annie's gaze studies me, and it makes me uncomfortable. It's like she sees through my bullshit.

"Have you ever been in love?"

I shake my head. "Nope."

"Does love scare you?"

"Yes and no," I say. "I love my life. I love my freedom. It's enough for me right now. I don't like saying never, but it's looking like never."

I take a deep breath. Annie is still looking at me, her

gaze ripping me open. My mouth dries, and I take a sip of my iced tea.

"You make me nervous," I say. "It's math tutoring all over again."

"Me? I make you nervous?"

One sip was not enough to wet my mouth. I take another long sip. "Definitely."

"Is that a compliment?"

"Yes," I say, holding out my palm. "Feel how clammy my hands are."

She presses into my palms with the pads of her fingers, and she nods. "You're definitely up to something."

"Me? Never," I say.

I take a bite of my sandwich, chew, and swallow, the bite scraping down my esophagus. Wisps of golden fire hair brush against Annie's face. I can't stop staring at her.

I have to get it together. Annie's closeness to me jumbles my thoughts, makes me incoherent. I'm surprised I can form full sentences right now.

We chew in silence, and Annie is the first to speak.

"Who's going to be the first lucky lady now that our deal is off?"

I want it to be you.

No, Cameron. Stop it.

"I have no idea," I say with a laugh. *Because I haven't been interested in anyone but you.* "I figured I would continue my celibacy. Out of respect."

"Wow, for me? Thank you for your sacrifice," Annie says.

My mouth drops. "Are you teasing me?"

"A little," she says. "I've gone without sex for almost three months. A few weeks won't hurt you."

I almost suggest we break our dry spell together, but I keep that in.

Old Cameron might've said something like that, but New Cameron has self-control.

"Maybe you're coming to your senses?"

"What?"

"Maybe you're realizing meaningless hookups, one after another, doesn't fill the hole you're trying to fill with it."

That knocks the wind right out of me. Acting like I'm Annie's boyfriend has really made me question some things.

Question everything, really.

Meanwhile, Annie takes the last bite of her sandwich, like she didn't just turn my world upside down.

"I don't know. Maybe I'm finally growing up."

"Oh," Annie says with one eyebrow raised. "Is Cameron Finch finally going to find the right woman? Some lucky gal?"

"The girl would be lucky?" I test.

"Come on, Cam," she says. "You know it. Don't deny it."

"Indulge me," I say. I finish off my sandwich, crumple the paper into a ball, and lounge across our blanket.

"You know you're good-looking, charming, fun to be around."

"A great kisser," I add. *Please give me some confirmation it was good. Give me permission to do it again. Make my wish come true.*

"You are," she agrees.

I pump my fist, and she giggles.

"Are you interested in anyone? Ready to get back out there?" I ask, taking a sip of my iced tea.

She shakes her head, looking over the water again. "It might be time to get cats."

"No! I mean, get a cat if you want to, but you're great. Don't close yourself off because of fucking Jason," I say. I can't think of Annie being all alone. She has so much to offer a partner.

If I was the kind of guy who could do the husband thing, the family thing, I would offer it to her in a heartbeat. But I don't have it in me. How can I take on the responsibility of a wife and family when my own sister has put me on a babysitting freeze?

She came home to a dirty kitchen after a very fun food fight one time.

"I've had a string of bad luck," Annie says. "I pick men who don't want me. Jason and I break up, and he immediately gets engaged to someone else. Same thing happened to my boyfriend in my early twenties. I've never been good enough for someone to commit to."

My neck grows hot with anger. Who do these fuckers think they are?

"You are the best, Annie," I say. "A man would be out of his mind not to be head over heels for you."

"Jason always used to say I needed to relax. Have some fun."

"First off, I love how anal you are," I say. *Why did I say anal?* "I don't think you need to change a thing about yourself, but if you want to have fun, you've come to the right place."

She looks at the ground and back up at me. "I'm not going to sleep with you, Cam."

My dick hardens.

Calm down, we can't fuck Annie, I tell my dick, but blood keeps rushing to it, scrambling my thoughts.

Making me want to do bad things to her.

"Damn," I say in response.

"I know. You're disappointed," she says, dejected.

Does she think I'm being sarcastic?

"You're my friend," I say. "I want to stay friends with

you."

"I like having you as a friend. You come in handy when I need arm candy."

"I will always be your arm candy, Annie. Even when we're old and gray."

She laughs, and my brain explodes once I think it over.

That sounds like I hope we're together. In the very distant future. As old people.

I bet Annie would be a hot silver fox. I've always had a thing for Helen Mirren.

"I will always be fun, too," I say, standing up. I look at the lake. It's March, so it could be cold. We've had a couple warm days lately, but there's a good chance this will be a polar bear dip.

What the hell.

I take off my shirt.

"What are you doing?" Annie asks, shielding her eyes. I unbutton my jeans, pushing them down my legs. Thank God my dick calmed down, or I would have some explaining to do.

"We're going to run into the lake. Start off this whole 'loosen Annie up' thing that I don't think you need anyway. I find your PowerPoints scorching hot."

"I can't go into the lake. I have a meeting later," Annie protests. "It's probably still cold, and I don't do cold."

"Come on," I say, walking toward the waterline. I look back. "Let's do it. Be impulsive. This is the beginning of you taking risks and living a little."

"I live!" she shrieks.

I set my hands on my hip like a disapproving teacher. "Prove it!"

She studies the lake, and I know she's weighing the pros and cons. She stands up with a huff.

"If I get hypothermia, you're nursing me back to health," she threatens.

I smack my hands together. "Done."

"Okay," she says. She pulls her shirt over her head, leaving a tissue-thin tank top on her body. She shimmies out of her jeans, and I can't stop staring at her legs. I got an eyeful at the engagement party with that short dress, but this is so much better.

She walks toward me, and I have to remind myself to keep my tongue in my mouth.

"We run in together," Annie says. I offer my hand, and she takes it.

I can't get enough of her hand in mine.

"Okay, here we go. One, two, three!" We charge the beach, hand-in-hand. Once the water hits me, it feels like tiny knives puncturing my whole body. Annie screams and then laughs as we surge waist deep and then chest deep. I dive underneath, just to get used to the water quickly, and when I burst to the surface, Annie's dry head is above water as she treads, her mouth stretched wide.

"It's unbearably cold. This was a terrible idea, Cameron Finch."

"Oh, come on. This is fun," I say, my teeth chattering.

"I can't feel my arms," Annie says.

"You know what helps?" I ask.

"What?"

I dunk her like we're twelve. Annie comes back up, flailing with her eyes closed.

"That's not funny, Cam!" she yells, water dripping down her face, her hair plastered to her head.

"You look adorable wet," I say, then gulp. Any mention of wet or anything that can be a sexual innuendo is not good around Annie. My blood gets pumping for no reason, even in the freezing cold water.

"We should get out of this lake," I say, pulling her to me.

"I'll never forgive you for talking me into this."

"Come on," I say, wrapping my arm around her back, hooking my hand under her armpit to pull her in. It's a good thing I can't feel my fingers because I think they're close to a boob.

I pull her arm around my shoulders as I swim with one hand and kick, pulling her like I'm a lifeguard, her cold cheek against mine. I know I shouldn't look back. Our lips are too close to each other's.

I might lose my mind and kiss her again if she turns her head.

"Are you okay?" I ask.

"Yes," she says. I'm pretty sure she can swim since I remember her doing decent laps in high school PE, but she lets me swim her in. I get to hold her longer this way.

We reach the shore, and we're back on our feet. The air hits my skin, and I shiver, my skin slick like a fish's.

I catch a glimpse of Annie as she crosses her arms across herself, shivering as she tries to pull her jeans back on, tugging with effort.

I try not to look. I really try. Her tank top sticks to her skin, showing the outline of her breasts as they bounce with her effort to tug on the denim. Her nipples poke out, and I can see the lace of her bra through the tank top.

Annie catches me looking, but I don't turn away.

She must know that I'm attracted to her. That kissing her completely fucked me. That I want to make her moan.

I stand there, in the middle of the beach, so she can see me. Shivering, but hard as a rock in my wet underwear. For her.

Her eyes see it, but she turns around, pulling her polo shirt on, the lake water creating wet spots on the knit.

"I really need to go to work," she says, as she slips into her shoes.

We don't say anything to each other as we drive back to her car at the brewery.

Any moment we had is gone.

I know it'll come back, though. Something about Annie and me feels inevitable.

17

ANNIE

I'm still soaked through when I arrive at work. When Cameron dropped me off and gave me a confusing hug, I wove my hair into a braid over my shoulder. The tail of the braid drips, creating another damp spot on my shirt. Thankfully, I have a backup polo shirt in my office, and I hope to God I still have my backup khakis there.

No matter the clamminess, my skin has been on fire since the lake.

I don't know what possessed me. It's not like me to run into a body of water like that, in my thin tank top with a man I feel confusing feelings for. My sister, Raegan, is the risk-taker, the daredevil. Not me.

It was worth it, though. For Cameron swimming me in like I was drowning, touching his hard torso, taut with muscle and ripples, seeing the length of his cock solid for me in his drenched boxer briefs.

I liked it.

Saying yes to lunch and running into the lake must have hit my boundary, because our lips were inches from one another, and I did nothing. I could've kissed him again, tasted the cool lake water on his lips, let our tongues twist in desire with a blatant disregard for later.

However, the sensible side of my brain halted it. I know he's not husband material. Cameron is a good time who refuses to settle down. I'd be bound for another heartbreak.

Still.

If I went back and kissed him, for real this time, what would it have been like? We would kiss until our breath ran out, I could run my fingers through his floppy hair and wrap my legs around his waist. Or we would've realized that one kiss at the party was a fluke. The excitement of *Operation: Fake Date* was just that.

Cameron is a terrible idea. I've been there once with Jason in an impossible relationship, and I don't care to do it again. However, I can't stop daydreaming about him. More than anything, I wish for a chance to go back and think of the consequences later.

I don't hear Jason knock on the door. My heart skips a beat when I see him there, right in front of me. This is the first time I've seen him since the party, and my first chance to gauge if the plan worked.

He smiles as he walks in my office without an invitation. I sit up straight, clasping my hands in front of me on the desk. He walks around it and rests his ass inches from my computer. Attention like this used to thrill me to my core; now, I'm just feeling slightly annoyed.

"Hi," he says, looking down at me.

"Hi," I mutter, dropping my purse on the floor next to me.

"Why are you all wet?" he asks, looking at me.

I fling my braid over my shoulder. "I went for a swim in the lake."

"In all your clothes?"

"In my underwear," I say. "I'm trying to be more spontaneous."

He laughs. "You, spontaneous? You weren't like that when we were dating."

No, no, I wasn't.

"I assume you had a good time at the engagement party," Jason continues. He breathes out, like the day's stresses are leaving him. I used to think it was sexy, the hum of his voice at the back of his throat.

Now it feels like he's seeking attention.

"I had a great time," I say. "It was lovely."

"Morgan really enjoyed meeting you."

My eyebrows raise involuntarily, and I turn my head. "Really?"

"Really," Jason says, picking up my keys, studying the keychain of the Eiffel Tower my sister got for me when she was in Paris. Why is he touching my stuff? He puts my keys down.

"So. You and Cameron Finch. I did *not* see that coming."

Neither did I. I nod.

"I hope he's changed his ways. I know you didn't ask me, but he's all wrong for you."

My eyes narrow. Cameron has treated me with more respect than Jason ever did. How he held my hand to proclaim I'm with him, how he's been nothing but a gentleman.

We were aiming to make Jason jealous, and I have to say, mission accomplished.

I know Jason well enough to know that this is a cover. It bothers him I'm not wallowing over him. That I'm different.

"Anyway, Morgan wonders if you two want to join us for a double date."

"What? Why?" I ask.

"I know. I know it's weird. Morgan just thinks it will clear the air. Since I dated you while we were broken up."

"Why does Cameron need to be there? Why do you need to be there? We could go get a glass of wine and settle it."

Jason purses his lips, and the twitch of his jaw tells me he wasn't expecting me to question it.

He was expecting I would say yes, because I always told him yes.

Jason looks away and clasps his hands over his head. "I'm getting married soon, and a double date would clear the air. We dated, and I want to be cool with the guy you're dating now. It just kills a flock of birds with one stone."

I cross my arms and lean into my chair. "I wouldn't call what we did dating. It was more sneaking around and having sex."

He lets out a one-note chuckle and looks at the ground. "I don't know how you saw us, but I saw us as important. It helped me shape who I am today."

Funny how men see that as a compliment. *I don't want you, but you made me a better man for the next woman I dated.* Makes me feel *great*.

Two months ago, I would've eaten this up like cookie dough ice cream. Now it sounds fake. And the oddest part? I feel nothing.

He rests his hand on my shoulder, and it makes me cringe. "Think about it. I would love to hang out with you. And Cameron."

Cameron is an afterthought. I see how his jaw clenches when he says his name.

Why would Morgan want to go on a double date? I would rather stab myself in the eye with a nail file than talk to the new lady in any of my exes' lives.

"I'll think about it," I say.

"Great," Jason says, standing up. He walks to the door, and I seriously wonder what I ever saw in him.

An imaginary light source blinks over my head, and I feel calm all the sudden.

I think I'm over him.

I think it finally happened.

A big grin breaks across my face.

Jason turns around at the doorframe. "I'm going to get some iced coffee at Gold Roast. Do you want me to get you anything?"

"No, I'm okay," I say.

"Okay. Ask Cameron about going out, and then we can plan it."

"We'll see," I say. The door closes after him, and an energy surge flows through me.

I'm over him. I don't feel a thing.

I stand up without a plan, but I shimmy my hips in excitement.

"I'm over him. I'm over him," I sing to myself as I point fingers in the air. There's exactly one person I want to tell.

"Hi Annie," Raegan says, picking up on the second ring. She's supposed to be in school, teaching.

"Hi! I didn't expect you to pick up."

"I have a free period, so I'm just translating your friend's book. Thank you so much for throwing her my way. This book is steamy goodness. I had to find Henry last night after reading it."

My sister speaks fluent French and majored in it in college and even spent some time abroad in Paris. My romance author friend Whitney has been trying to get into translated markets, and I suggested my sister for her to get her feet wet and Whitney to get a discounted translation.

In the past, I would've felt some jealousy deep in my gut.

Raegan's relationship with Henry is truly rare. Cameron and I are not together, but our interactions so far make me so giddy that I'm not worried about what my sister is doing or what my ex is doing.

I'm content.

"I wanted to tell you something."

"You're not pregnant, are you?"

I laugh. "I haven't had sex recently."

My cheeks heat. Oh no, do I want to? Does Cameron have venereal diseases? My worrying brain catalogs that for later.

"I have something else to tell you. I think I'm over Jason."

"Finally!" Raegan whoops so hard, it hurts my ear.

"Jason and Morgan want to go on a double date with me."

"That's...weird," Raegan says. "If they invite you home with them, say no. I can't handle the nightmares."

I laugh. "No, I would bring someone."

Not sure why I say that. My sister gasps and starts rapidly word-vomiting how excited she is. I can't tell her it's Cameron. It's not even real. What do I do?

"Tell me who it is. Now," Raegan demands.

"I can't," I say, hoping she doesn't guess. Was our lunch at the lake a date? It felt sexually charged to me, but I could be misreading the situation.

"Is it Reid?" she asks.

"No," I say with a laugh. Our conversation earlier was weird, but he swears he doesn't have feelings for me.

"You need a guy like that," Raegan says. "Like my Henry."

I love Henry for Raegan, but he's not my type at all. Henry is sweet and loves my sister, which is all I could ask for. However, he's specifically dorky and weird with my sister in a way that can't be recreated.

I've always had an affinity for bad boys, men with endless charm that could break my heart into a million pieces. I thought I was over that, moved on.

Now, I want to tame the ultimate Goldheart heart-breaker.

What is wrong with me?

Cameron is so different than those other men. The other men led me on, made me think it's something we're not. Cameron isn't afraid to be straightforward and I can trust him to be honest with me. He makes me want to take risks and try a new way of looking at the world.

He makes me feel...alive.

"I'll tell you who it is eventually. I don't want to jinx it."

"You better," Raegan says. "Whatever. I'm proud of you. For being over the douchecanoe deluxe."

"Thank you. I'm proud of myself, too," I say.

"Just watch your heart," Raegan says. "I want you to be happy, but I also don't want you to be sad again. Seeing you sad makes me sad."

"Thanks, Raegan. I love you," I say.

"I love you, too. Tell your friend to write faster. I need Gustavo's story, like pronto."

"Will do."

We say goodbye and hang up. My fingers hover over my screen. I want to call Cameron so bad. Talk about what happened, tell him I'm finally over Jason.

Laugh with him over going on a double date with Jason and Morgan.

Tempt fate a little bit more.

I find his number on my phone, and without thinking, I click it.

"Hey," he says, picking up quickly.

"Hi," I say. "So, the funniest thing just happened."

"What?"

"Jason came in and invited us on a double date with him and Morgan."

"No way," he says.

"Yep. So weird, right?"

"Right," Cameron says. "While tempting, I don't think we should go."

"I agree one hundred percent," I say. I pause before saying, "I think I'm over Jason. For real."

"For real?" Cameron asks.

The line is quiet, and I wonder if he's still there.

"My mom texted me to insist you come for Sunday dinner. It takes her four minutes to send a text message," Cameron says. "I can tell them that you're busy. Having everyone together is a lot, and we'll have to continue to neither confirm nor deny a relationship until our fake breakup..."

"Yes," I interrupt. "I would love to. Eat dinner and keep pretending."

"We don't need to pretend anything. We can just be Cameron and Annie. No pressure."

Cameron and Annie. I love how that sounds together.

"We can do that," I say.

"Perfect." I can hear the smile through the phone. "You remember where it is?"

"Yep."

"Perfect. Five thirty. Sunday."

"Okay," I say. "I'll tell Jason a big fat no."

"Perfect," he says. He's quiet before he adds, "We really gave a show, huh? They should give us Tonys *and* Oscars for our performance."

My heart sinks. He still thinks it wasn't real. That that kiss didn't change...everything.

The line is quiet again. Then, Cameron says, "I had a really good time with you today."

"Likewise."

"Okay, I better go. Take care, Annie. I'll see you Sunday."

I sit back in my chair, damp from the lake, and think over everything.

A smile crosses my lips. Even, if nothing comes of whatever this thing with Cameron is, even if we remain good friends, I'm relieved to feel nothing for Jason anymore. He no longer tethers me to him with his false promises. I'm finally free.

Now that I feel free, now that I jumped in a lake, I want to put some very real moves on Cameron and see what happens.

I dance in my office as a celebration of my decision. I will be brave. I will be fearless. I will make Cameron kiss me again.

18

CAMERON

"Is she coming?" Emily asks, pouring the dressing over the salad. She takes the tongs and peers over the counter at the front door.

"Who's coming?" Olive asks, walking in with a handful of Goldfish in hand.

"A special lady," I say, kneeling down in front of my niece. "Hit me."

I open my mouth, and she lobs a Goldfish aimed at my chest, but I contort myself to catch it on my tongue. She giggles and attacks me with a hug. I never turn down hugs from my best girl.

"Olive, I told you not to get into Grandma's snacks. We're about to eat," Emily says.

Olive crunches down on a cracker to make a point. I hold up my hand, and she slaps it with a high five. "Rebel. I like it."

"Stop encouraging her," my sister says. "Seriously, where is she?"

The doorbell rings, and I scamper to it. When I open the door, I find Annie standing there, holding a tinfoil-covered pan. Her hair is up in a messy bun, but she's wearing those tight jeans again.

"I made cobbler," she says.

"I can't wait to taste it." *And you.* I keep that last bit to myself.

I take her in a half hug and kiss the top of her head. It might be my imagination, but she leans into me, nuzzling against my cheek.

I could be hallucinating because I am so turned on right now.

"Annie!" Mom says, rounding the corner. "Thank you so much for coming."

"Thank you so much for having me." She hands the dish to my mother. "It's blackberry cobbler. My mom's recipe."

"It's always a pleasure to eat some of Jane's cobbler," Mom says, walking the dish into the kitchen. She comes back and takes Annie in an aggressive hug.

She pulls away to take a look at her. "It's wonderful to have another tall woman around. I'm not sure what happened with Emily. We joke that she was switched at the hospital."

Mom is five-ten, while Emily is a full foot shorter than I am. It must've skipped a generation since Olive is in the top one percentile of her height and she might be taller than her mom one day.

"I love that she's tall. My neck doesn't hurt as much," I say.

"Well, let Cameron entertain you while I get the sides going. Help yourself to anything," my mom says, walking back into the kitchen.

Now, it's Annie and me, alone in the living room.

"How are you?" I ask. We haven't talked since our phone call after the lake, and I've been trying to find ways to run into her. I stop by Gold Roast every morning for a breakfast sandwich and a black coffee, but I never see her there. Tara has given me the stink eye twice. I find myself staring at my phone, waiting for a text, a random call from her, but nothing.

I've almost texted her a hundred times.

What would I say? *Hi, I want to see if you'll go to dinner with me and then let me stick my dick in you?*

Now she's here, her coconut scent surrounding me, her lips glossy and plump, and I want to pull her into my parents' giant linen closet.

"Annie," Reid says, walking from the bathroom. He hugs her one-armed like usual. Totally friendly.

She pressed her pelvis against me.

"Can I get you a beer? Wine?" Reid asks.

Dammit, I should've thought of that.

"Whatever your mom is drinking is great."

Reid nods once and leaves.

Annie lets out a ragged breath.

"Don't be nervous," I say, lowering my head toward her. I'm so close I could kiss her. I whip my head back and yelp. I'm too old to do that type of jerk with my neck.

"Are you okay?" she says with a nervous giggle. She brings her hand to my neck and starts massaging it.

I should've whacked off before I came because I'm as hard as a motherfucking tree trunk.

"Keep doing that, and I'll marry you," I joke. Annie's eyes go wide, and she drops her hand. That was the unfunniest joke I've ever made. When did I lose my game? When do I ever *joke* about marriage?

"Here you go," Reid says, bringing Annie a glass of red wine. "I have to go help Dad before he lights himself on fire."

Reid walks out to my parents' porch, and Annie's lips part in confusion.

"Dad's a big fan of searing," I say. "He lost half an eyebrow last year."

We hear a whoosh from outside and see an orange-yellow fireball explode from the grill.

"Best we get away from the windows," I say, ushering her away from the living room.

Jackson walks by. "Hi, Annie."

"Hi, Jackson," Annie says, as he turns the corner and leaves. "Is he okay? About being back?" she asks me.

"As good as he can be. Goldheart just has a lot of memories for him. Some good, some terrible."

"Absolutely," she agrees. "How's the event going?"

"Great," I say. "We booked the DJ and the catering company. We're getting a photo booth and some other goodies. Thank you for the referrals, by the way. Mom's been raving about you to Dan, our investor."

"No problem," Annie says. "You let me know if you need any help."

"I will," I say. My chest puffs with pride, and I smile, bobbing my head. "I think I have it under control. Watch out, or I'll take *your* job."

"Oh now, don't get too cocky," Annie says. "Wait, that might be impossible."

"Hardy har har," I say, slinging my arm around her shoulders. She matches me with an arm around my waist.

I look down at her, my laughter fading. She doesn't look away from me. Does she want me to kiss her?

Her hand drifts lower, settling on the crest of my ass, and my dick jumps at her finger graze. Did her hand slip? Did she mean to do that?

Olive turns the corner, holding another fistful of Goldfish. She stops mid-arm raise when she sees me with Annie. Annie's hand jerks from the danger zone, and she presses her arms to her sides.

Dang it, kid.

"Who are you? Are you Uncle Cam's girlfriend?"

A croak leaves my lips so Annie skirts the issue like a champ. "I'm Annie."

Annie as my girlfriend—I like the sound of that.

For the first time in my life, I haven't cringed at it.

"You interested?" Olive asks, popping a cracker in her mouth. "He needs one."

"Why?" Annie asks. Her cheeks flush rose.

Olive shrugs one shoulder. "My uncle Cam is the best. He would be a good husband and dad. I know he's not my dad, but I like to *pretend* he is."

My eyes water. I've cried two times in my life, both concerning Olive. Once, I found Emily sobbing in the corner when Olive was a year old. I told my sister to take a break, and I watched a YouTube video on how to change a diaper. It wasn't the prettiest wrap job, but my niece's little butt was covered.

Baby Olive looked up at me with her big eyes, blue at the time, and I promised her that night if she didn't have her dad, I would be her dad. I moved in that day to help. I never went far, building the tiny house eventually to give them and myself space.

Second time was during her ballet recital. I knew that routine by heart, because I'd practiced it with her. Emily caught me doing a tiny version of the arm movements in my seat. When I handed her a bouquet of roses, a few tears left my eyes and I told her how proud I was for how hard she worked.

Now, Olive is telling Annie I would be a good dad, and

that's why that little girl is my ride-or-die. She's the only one in my family who looks at me like I hung the stars. A tear settles at the corner of my eye, and I quickly wipe it away.

"That's so nice of you to say, Olive," Annie says, looking at her and back up at me.

"It's the truth," she says. She leans in and whispers against her hand, "You should give him a chance. You're the first lady he's brought home."

Annie laughs. In that moment, there's nothing fake about how I feel about her. She is the best woman I've ever known. But all my shit is keeping me from reaching out and seizing this.

Being a pretend dad works out fine because Olive is amazing and easy. Getting a kid of my own is scarier than the deranged clowns I saw once in a haunted house that benefited the blood bank in town.

It feels like it would be less scary if it was with Annie.

I think I need a minute.

"Come on," Mom says, ushering us into the dining room. "Dinner's ready."

We enter the dining room as my mom is rearranging the place settings.

"Annie, you sit here," Mom says, pointing to a chair under the infamous dog as a nobleman picture. For Christmas one year, Reid sent in Woody's picture to a company that puts pets in Renaissance nobleman outfits and prints it like it's an oil painting. We all laughed so hard we were gasping for air, and the real Woody had no idea what was going on.

Sometimes I catch my dad staring at it when no one is watching.

"Cameron, you can sit here," she says. I slide in next to

Annie, and her hand immediately goes to my thigh. And squeezes.

"What are you doing?" I whisper. She smiles, leaving her hand there, curving inside my thigh.

"Living a little," she says.

Oh, she's into me. Annie Stewart, possibly the smartest fucking woman I've ever met, is into me.

I shift so my hardening dick has room, but it bucks against my zipper and threatens to bust it.

After my mom and Emily bring all the food to the table, we begin passing hamburgers and side dishes. After dropping a cheeseburger on her plate, Annie winks. I'm a gentleman so I wink back.

Mom studies us. "Have you stayed in touch since high school?"

"Kind of?" Annie says. "A couple weeks ago, I had had a really bad day. I always get a banana split from Ice Dream when that happens, and then I walked it next door to the Swift..."

"I was there at the Swift," I interject.

"We figured," my mom says.

Annie squeezes my thigh again. I wish she was squeezing my dick.

"So, I'm crying into my banana split and bourbon, and Cam really lifted my mood," Annie says, turning to me with a smile.

If we were actually together, a kiss right here would be appropriate.

However, I don't want to give her a nice little peck.

I want to push her against a wall and give her a kiss she deserves. I want to push my fingers into her hair, feel her skin under my fingertips, sweep my tongue in her mouth.

We catch each other's gaze, and we both smirk.

She's into me. *Me.*

"You two are adorable," Emily says, lifting her wine glass to her lips.

"Uncle Cameron, do you have sex with Annie?" Olive asks.

The drink of water I just took ends up all over Reid, who sits directly across from me. A little bit gets on Jackson.

"Olive Jean, *where* did you hear that?" Emily asks, her tone mortified and trying not to laugh.

"From my friend Kenzie," Olive says. She looks around the table and slumps, confused at what she's just asked.

I did not hear that kind of stuff when I was eight. I now have a deeper appreciation for the nineties.

"I'm so sorry, Reid. Did I get you, Jackson?" I ask, covering my mouth.

"It's fine, Cam. I would've done the same thing," Reid says, wiping his face and smothering a laugh into his napkin.

I look at Jackson, who sits there stoically.

He moved home four months ago, but the eggshells we walk around him are made of glass. Anything could set him off, even getting a little bit of water all over him.

Jackson lifts his napkin to his face and towels off. We all hold our breath, waiting for a reaction from him, but he says nothing, just wipes his face. He stands up and grabs his water glass.

"I'm going to the bathroom," he says, walking off.

The table lets out a collective sigh. Annie smiles at me once I look at her, and it warms me to the pit of my stomach.

Not in a million years did I think this would ever happen to me.

I think I'm falling for her.

19

ANNIE

Olive's question throws me for a loop.

Where did she learn that?

Second, bless her so I could see Cameron's reaction. I think it was good?

Me being me, I catch glimpses of a future that's not possible. A future where I get to come here for every Sunday dinner, where Cameron's hand is always on my shoulder, rubbing his thumb against my skin, creating shivers down my limbs. Where he wears my ring and gets me pregnant and we're blissfully happy.

It's all a fantasy. One I cannot think about.

Because the urge to have sex with him is so strong, I'm crossing my legs tightly under this table.

I want him to take me back to his tiny house and have sex all over it. There might not be many spots, but I want it all. I've never felt this carnal before, this ready to be taken, however it is. My usual process of being scared or nervous about a first time with a guy is not even a thought in my mind.

I squeeze his thigh under the table, and my pinky flirts

with the seam of his jeans, inching closer to his bulge. He flinches, coughing on his bite of potato salad, and takes a sip of water. The corner of my lips curl up, like a cartoon evil cat.

At one point, Cameron looks at me after Jackson leaves the table, after he spit out water on his two brothers because Olive asked if he had sex with me.

I hope he will. I try to communicate it with my eyes.

"Annie, may I have a word?" Cameron asks.

"Sure," I say, standing up. Terror seizes me. Why does he want to talk? What's going on?

Cameron opens the front door for me so I can go through first.

The air is chilly, and I pull my cardigan tighter across my front. Dusk has fallen so the sky already has an indigo hue.

"What are you doing?" Cameron asks, his arms folded in front of him.

"Nothing," I say. But I can't help it; I smirk.

"That's more than letting people think what they want to think," he says, pushing his hand through his hair. "I mean, you were basically going for my dick. I'm not complaining, but...was it a hand slip? Did you mean to?"

I shrug a shoulder.

"So, this is confusing for me. It's almost as if..." he says.

"It's almost as if what?" I ask. *Say it. Say what we've been dancing around for weeks.*

"It's almost as if you want me. No pretend, no bullshitting, no letting people think what they want to think. Full-on, let's do this shit."

I bite my lip. The old Annie would deny it, push the feelings down deep where she can't access them. However, the old Annie wouldn't jump in a lake. The old Annie wouldn't be so bold. Old Annie would deny something so right because it wasn't safe.

The old me is not here anymore. Ever since I decided to fake date Cameron, she is nowhere to be found.

"What if I do?" I ask.

"Then I'm going to kiss you for real. I'm going to kiss all the breath out of you until our knees are weak and we're holding each other up. And there *will* be tongue."

I take one step toward him, looking down, wetting my lips. I grab the back of his neck, crashing my lips into his and it is all over.

He pulls me close against his hard chest, and our mouths mingle together. I'm not sure where I end and he begins. His tongue wastes no time dipping into my mouth, searching and hot, and I meet his with mine. Our collision is hard and bruising, the opposite of polite and considerate. My lips move across his as a frenzy.

This is a kiss of destruction.

His hand is on my ass, his dick is hard against my pelvis as I grip his neck, trying to pull him closer so we can consume each other. My nerves are a wildfire through dense, dead brush, igniting me, setting me ablaze at an uncontrollable spread.

He pulls away and looks at me, pressing my face between his hands. His gaze brands me, burning what resolve I have to ash.

"I need to get you alone. Now," he says.

"We're not done with dinner yet," I say, reaching my lips to his for another taste. He steps away from me, his hand going through his hair again. He's walking in circles on his family's lawn as I giggle behind my hands.

"The prior kiss was great, but *that*? That was the best

fucking kiss I have ever had," he says with a finger point, his eyes not looking at me. "You've been here, *the entire time.*"

"I have," I say, giggling harder.

"I've known you for twenty-five years, and *that* was there, *this entire time.*"

"Yep," I say, doubling over in laughter. I feel drunk from Cameron's unraveling, pride erasing all my doubts.

"And I *like* you," he says. "I *really* like you. You're smoking hot, but I also like hanging out with you. This is blowing my mind right now."

"Are you going to kiss me again?" I ask, setting my hands on my hips.

"I can't because if I kiss you again, I'm going to fuck you on my parents' front lawn, and the neighbors will definitely call the cops."

"We can't have that."

"No. Especially since that one time I got caught with my bare ass out at the mines. I got off with a warning, so I don't think they'll be too kind a second time," he says.

I turn toward the front of the house and catch the curtains shaking violently, as I notice a flash of a brown ponytail whip the glass.

"I think we had an audience."

"Fuck," he says, stepping onto the brick path to the front door. He steps closer to me, and I can see the debate in his eyes. If he touches me again, I can't promise what I'll do.

"This is no longer pretend for me," he whispers.

I swallow, a hard lump in my throat impossible to ignore. "Me either. I want you, too, Cameron. I don't want anyone else. I want you. Only you."

"Oh my God," he says, brushing his lips against mine again. It sends a whip of nerves firing through my body. His lips stamp imprints down my neck, and I gasp.

"We need to finish dinner with your parents."

He kisses me again, stealing my breath, my thoughts, my feelings.

"Do we?" he asks through gasps for air.

"Yes," I say, tearing myself from his arms, jogging inside before he catches me in another kiss. We make it inside, our shirts askew from our hands and embrace.

I walk into the dining room first, to a bevy of eyes staring at me. They definitely saw us making out on their front lawn.

"Everything okay?" Kit asks, with a bright, fake smile.

"Fine," I say, walking to my seat. Cameron pulls his chair out and I sit down. His fingertips brush against the fabric of my cardigan, and it creates lines of fire.

The dinner started with my hand on his thigh. It's ending with his hand in mine.

Emily and I lock eyes, and I know she knows. She smiles as she takes a bite of green beans.

"We are really excited about the event," Randy, Cameron's dad, says to me. "I told Dan about it, and he's excited too."

"Have I met Dan?" I ask.

Reid lets out a laugh. "You would definitely know it if you met him."

"Dan is our investor," Randy says. "He says he is going to try to make it for the prom, so you'll meet him there."

"We'll have to make the final arrangements this week," Cameron says.

"Cameron has been working so hard. I don't know what kind of sorcery you worked on him, Annie, but..."

"It is all Cameron," I say, rubbing his back. His hand squeezes my thigh. "It'll be great."

Cameron leans in, lowering his voice to a whisper. "I was serious about you being my prom date."

"Of course," I whisper back. I wish I could go back in time and tell seventeen-year-old me that she only has to wait seventeen more years to have a daydream come true.

Everyone finishes eating, and Kit stands up. "Annie, can you help me get everyone's dishes?"

"Sure." I collect mine and Cameron's. His hand brushes my forearm as I pick up his plate, and I smile to him. Reid hands me his, and I pick up Jackson's, still three-fourths full of food. He didn't reappear after he stormed off.

Kit stands over the sink as I cover Jackson's plate with foil I find in a drawer and stick in the fridge for later.

"I'm really glad Cameron found you," Kit says, not turning around to face me. "Cameron has always needed to find his own way with things. You're too modest to admit you've had an effect on him. He's the same boy, but it's like his light turned on."

Any doubt I have that Cameron and I are not the right thing floats away with his mother's words. She knows him better than anyone and confirming that he has changed, that he's not the typical Cameron anymore, calms me.

It's why there's nothing wrong about heading into this face first, hoping I don't fall.

It's time to take a risk.

Kit wipes her hands with a towel and takes me in for an embrace. "Thank God for you."

I swallow the emotion down into my throat as I hold this sweet woman. A woman I've known over the years marginally, and now she feels like a friend.

We wash the plates and get most of the kitchen cleaned up. Cameron walks into the kitchen, looking at his mother first and then at me. His hand finds the small of my back, and I ache to touch him, to kiss him, to let him undress me.

"Everything going okay in here?" Cameron asks, moving his hand up and down my back. My eyes flutter closed with his touch, but I try to keep it together.

"Everything is great," Kit says. "I'm sure you want some time to yourself tonight. We can let you go. As long as you promise to bring this wonderful woman back around."

"Deal," he says. We look at each other, and I notice his stare.

He is hungry for me.

"Mom, I think we're going to get dessert on our own," Cameron says. He winks at me, and my cheeks warm.

"What about Annie's cobbler?"

I flip my hand down and lie. "I have another pan at home. Please enjoy it."

"Okay," Kit says. She looks between us, and I blush, knowing that she knows we're leaving early to devour each other.

"Thank you so much for having me," I say, squeezing Kit in a hug. She kisses my cheek and lets me go.

I hug the rest of the family before I leave, except for Jackson, who's still MIA. Randy gives me rapid pats on the back with our pelvises so far from one another. Emily squeezes me like her mother did, and Reid takes me in a friendly side hug.

We wave as the door closes and my hand is in Cameron's.

He walks me to my car parked on the gravel shoulder in front of the neighbor's house and their mailbox. Trees shield us from prying Finch eyes, so I don't see the harm in a little flirting.

I lean against the car, and Cameron leans in, his hand planted on the roof.

"So."

"So," I say, hooking my finger in one of his belt loops.

"Your house or mine?" he asks.

I think about how many female visitors he has had over the years, and I'm not quite ready to compete with all the memories. Jason never liked to go to my place; I always went to his. So, the choice is obvious.

"Mine," I say, closing my eyes. "But I won't have sex with you."

"Really," he says, leaning in to kiss my neck. He finds the spot again, and my mouth creeps open.

"I want you to get tested first." It's easier to say this now, while we're fully clothed. I add, "I got tested when I broke up with Jason, and I'm free and clear. I haven't been with anyone since."

I wait for him to protest, but he lays a small kiss on my nose instead. "I'll get tested tomorrow."

"Perfect," I say. I may be taking risks, but I'm still me. They need to be calculated risks.

"What about other things?"

Swallowing is really hard right now. "Like what?" I squeak.

"Can I touch you?" he whispers. "These beautiful breasts…" His fingers trace the side of them and my body responds… "Or in between your legs on your clit…" His hand drifts down my hip, his thumb creeping closer to apex of my legs.

I gasp out a breath and swallow. "I'll allow that."

"Good," he says, kissing me on my neck. "Because I want to make you feel good."

I feel a whoosh of air as I close my eyes. Once I open them again, I see Cameron walking to his car. My body still hums like a live wire from his words, and I can't think straight.

"See you back at your place," Cameron says.

20

ANNIE

I arrive first at my place, parking in my usual spot. Even though I've parked here a thousand times, this time feels different.

As I drive on the highway and turn onto my road, I can't stop thinking about what will happen. All those years of being curious, of wondering what Cameron was like in bed, and now I get to find out.

Intellectually, I know it's smart to require a negative STD test from him. Emotionally, I'm angry at myself that I will not have his legendary dick inside of me tonight.

You will not let him stick his penis inside of you, you will not let him stick his penis inside of you, I repeat to myself over and over.

I *will* let him touch me. I will probably give him a hand job. But nothing more than that.

I'm still repeating my mantras and my game plan for tonight while I pace in my living room when I hear Cameron's truck pull into the driveway. I grin when I hear two knocks.

Dang it, I should've put on some lingerie.

No, that's too tempting. I think.

I pull the hair tie out of my hair, shaking my waves loose. It's five-day hair, and I curse myself for not washing it today. It's caked with tropical dry shampoo. He's going to taste pina colada in the back of his throat.

When I open the door, I act casual, like I do this kind of thing all the time.

The sight of Cameron, that tall drink of water, here to do bad things to me, reminds me I'm a total amateur.

I can't remember the last time I've given a hand job. I'm not even sure I'm any good.

I don't have long to think because Cameron's lips are on mine as he backs me into my house, slamming the door behind us. He spins me and pushes me against the door, taking my lips in his, plunging his tongue in my mouth. Desire swirls within me, my skin buzzing with his hands and his kisses.

"Put your hands on me," I say, and his one hand immediately palms my breast and his other cups my ass, pulling me closer. I feel his cock, hard and long against my pelvis, and I know it aches for release.

Cameron is taking his time.

His hands stall at the edge of my shirt. He pulls away and murmurs, "May I?"

I nod, trying to breathe as he pulls my shirt over my head. I'm wearing a simple bralette since I don't have much, but he looks at me like he's starving and it's Thanksgiving.

He kneels before me, and I gasp as he takes my jeans off slowly, like he has all the time in the world.

He runs his hands down my skin as he applies kisses to my thighs. He helps me step out of my jeans as I rest a hand on his shoulder to balance.

Without warning, he scoops me up like a fairy tale

princess and sits us down in my favorite purple chair, me in his lap. I'm in only my underwear, my panties damp in anticipation.

His smooth hands press against my thighs. I lose my mind when he pushes my legs apart, his fingers teasing the lace of my underwear. His fingers stop.

"Is it okay?" he asks. "To touch you?"

"I'm a little nervous," I admit.

"We'll go slow," he says, kissing my neck. His right hand dips in my panties, and I buck against him as he flirts and teases me. When his fingers touch my clit, my back arches and I moan.

He cups my breast through my bralette, his thumb rubbing my nipple. "I'll wait to use my tongue on these until I can taste all of you."

"Okay," I say, as his hand moves in my underwear. I pull them off and fling them on my bed, spreading my legs wider so his fingers can dip into me and feel my wet heat, how turned on I am.

"Are you doing okay?" he asks.

I nod. "Wonderful."

"You tell me what you like," he says into my neck.

"Move the pad of your finger, up and down," I instruct.

His finger does as it's told, and a whoosh of breath escapes my lips. I'm so close already. He squeezes my breast gently, pushing the fabric away so I'm exposed. His fingers dip in and out of me, as his thumb stays on my clit, and suddenly I'm soaring. His breath on my skin, his fingers on me, his hand on my breast sends rolling waves of pleasure through my core, and it's building like a tidal wave. I moan loudly.

"Are you enjoying this?" he asks, his breath hot against my ear.

I say nothing as I turn my head to kiss him, fill my mouth with his tongue as his hands continue to work.

It's building and building until he says, "Just...let...go."

"Oh God," I say before I cry out, my walls pulsing violently, so strongly that my body jerks on top of him. Cameron knows the perfect moment to pull his hand away as soon as everything gets sensitive.

I lie there, on top of Cameron, dumbstruck. He rubs his palm against my thigh, and I sit there, eyes closed, totally numb.

Holy shit, if he's that good with his hands, what is he like with his tongue? With his cock?

He chuckles again. "Are you okay?"

"I'm fine. Give me a minute." I shake a hand at him, keeping my eyes closed, overcome with bliss from that transcendent orgasm.

He nuzzles against my neck, leaving a whisper of kisses. "I assume you enjoyed that."

I turn my head and give him a long kiss. He takes his hand from my breast to cradle my chin, kissing me slowly, letting our tongues meet each other.

"Now, it's your turn," I say, sliding off of his lap. "To be honest, it's been a long time since I've given one."

He grabs my hand and looks up at me as I stand before him.

"I'm sure it'll be over quick since you're the one doing it."

21

CAMERON

I knew I was good with my hands, but damn. Her body reacted like poetry, convulsing with her orgasm, violent and dangerous. Afterward, she lay there in a state of bliss that made me swell with pride. I did that.

She turns her head to me. "Your turn."

You don't have to tell me twice.

We switch places, and now this woman I'm obsessed with is kneeling in front of me. I know what's coming, me, regardless of what she does. She could just *look* at my cock, and I might come on my own.

Her hands on me, fisting my cock, will be epic.

She shimmies my boxer briefs off of me, and my dick springs free, completely hard and completely ready for whatever she has for me.

I'm going to last fifteen seconds, tops.

I open my eyes to see her sitting on her heels, just staring at it. A chuckle leaves my lips because she looks shell-shocked.

"What?"

"It's...big," she says.

"Thank you," I reply.

Annie says nothing as she spits on her hand and grips me, taking her fist in a long, slow drag down my shaft.

"Yes," I gasp as she pumps me slowly in her fist. Closing my eyes, I let the sensations take over me. Her hand is slick against my cock as it goes up and down. I try to imagine it's her mouth on me and her grip is replaced by those pink, plump lips. Imaging her riding me, her eyes closed with pleasure, is enough to get me close.

My mind races with the possibilities. There's a different sensation, soft like a pillow against me.

When I open my eyes, I see her bare breasts, teasing my crown. Her bra is on the ground, discarded with a mission.

That's enough to get me there.

When her eyes catch mine, I come undone, spilling cum all over her tits with a moan.

I'm proud of myself since I managed to make it at least thirty seconds.

She gently places my cock on my thigh, and I settle in the chair, spent and satisfied.

I'm going to need a serious pep talk with myself once she lets me have actual sex with her, or it's going to be two thrusts and I'm done.

Annie stands up calmly, covered in my cum, and walks naked to her bathroom. The water runs, and she emerges with a wet towel so I can clean myself up. I pull my underwear and my pants back on, while Annie dresses, covering her perfect body with a baggy T-shirt and leggings. My shirt hangs from a lamp shade, and I grab it.

"So, I guess you're leaving," Annie says, looking at my keys on the kitchen table.

"Who said a thing about leaving?" I say, wrapping one

arm around her waist. I check my watch. "It's only eight o'clock."

"Are you looking for seconds?"

I bat my eyelashes at her. "Maybe. But I just want to hang out with you."

"I usually veg out after eight o'clock and go to sleep around nine-thirty."

"Perfect."

"Do you want to stay over?"

I usually say no to women's invitations, but I want to spend every free moment I have with Annie. I want to feel her in my arms as I fall asleep.

"Only if you want me to," I say.

"I want you to," she whispers. I kiss her sweetly, and her hands tangle in my hair.

"Let's watch some TV then," I say, dragging her to the loveseat and plopping down. She giggles as she slides onto the cushion next to me. "What are we watching?"

"Ever since it was suggested we do a nineties-themed prom, I started my rewatch of *My So-Called Life* for the billionth time."

"Wasn't that on for less than a season?"

Annie nods. "It's one of the biggest missteps of American TV programming. It deserved at least three seasons."

"I don't think I've seen it."

"I don't think you will like it," she says.

"Try me," I say, kissing her on the head.

She smiles at me while she presses a button on the remote to power up Hulu. *My So-Called Life* is the first in a long line of Continue Watching on the app. Annie hesitates clicking on it.

"Something up?" I ask, tucking some hair behind her ear.

"I'm really confused."

I lean on my elbow. "What are you confused about?"

"I didn't think you would hang around. You know, after hooking up. You don't usually, right?"

"I don't usually," I say, kissing her head again. "Maybe I'm turning over a new leaf. Trying something new."

"And what is that?"

I take a deep breath. *Boyfriend.* It was a weird concept for me until we faked it. Then I realized I liked the way it felt with Annie. Holding her hand, coming home to only her, it feels right.

"Seeing where something goes instead of ending it before it has a chance."

I'm still not convinced I'm the best for her. That I can give her everything she needs. Annie is the kind of woman you wife up fast before she comes to her senses and realizes you're a piece of trash and unworthy.

Annie's phone rings, cutting the tension in half. She looks at the screen and shows it to me.

Jason. That absolute tool.

"Answer it," I say, suppressing the swirl of heated jealousy I feel in my veins. I can be cool with her talking to her ex. Totally cool.

She picks it up and doesn't move off the couch, needing privacy.

The transparency is healthy, mature.

"Hello?" she asks.

I hear Jason's voice barely from the phone. She nods in reaction before she looks at me.

"I'll check," Annie says, pressing the mute button. "Jason's asking about the double date again. What do I say?"

While I want to go on a date with Annie, I don't want the other jokers around.

"Tell that fucker no," I say.

"Okay," she says, pressing the mute button. "Jason, we're going to pass."

I think I hear Jason whining over the phone. It takes five minutes for her to say goodbye.

When she ends the call, she throws her phone onto the couch cushion and drapes her legs over my lap and flops back on the pillows.

"He would not shut up," she says. "It's weird he asked, right? I mean, why?"

I know why. Jason still wants to keep tabs on Annie, or it could be Morgan wanting to feel Annie out, both for Jason and for me. I slept with Morgan over a year ago, so I hope she's over it and it's not something where I end up tied to a chair in a basement.

I should tell her about Morgan.

Nah, I should keep it to myself. Everything is going so well; it'll just create drama if I tell her. It's one of those "it's best if I keep this to myself" things. This is too delicate to risk ruining right now.

My heart beats like a jackhammer in my chest, and I release a deep breath.

"How about we go on a date? Just the two of us."

Her face softens, and I wonder if she's going to cry. Oh no.

"Really?" she asks.

"Really," I say, pushing hair out of her face. "Maybe I'll be tested by then and we can have sex all night long afterward."

Her skin flushes against her freckles. She's so beautiful, I can't stop looking at her.

"Is that a yes?" I ask.

She nods once. "A real date. Just you and me."

"Just you and me."

Annie kisses me in response, and I take a fist of her red hair in my hand. She tastes like paradise.

I need to get that STD test done as soon as humanely possible.

22

ANNIE

Wednesday rolls around and I'm so nervous, I drop a makeup brush three separate times.

"You'll be fine. You're fine," I tell myself as I sweep my tried-and-true blush on my cheeks. Compared to Jason's engagement party and the armor I piled on for it, I feel like myself right now, wearing my favorite swing dress and sandals.

We've had a couple warm days for April, but I grab a light sweater, just in case it's chilly when the sun goes down.

A smile has permanently planted itself on my face since my dinner with his family. Cameron texts me constantly and FaceTimes just to say hello, and he's slept over a couple times. He doesn't complain about only hand jobs until he gets his STD results back. He drove to Roseville first thing Monday for his test.

For our date tonight, I shave my whole body, just in case.

A soft knock comes at my door at six sharp, and I shake the nervousness from my hands as I walk to the door.

I open it to my arm candy wearing a suit jacket over a crisp white shirt, his jaw clean-shaven, his hair combed back, looking sexy as hell. He takes an eyeful, his gaze raking over my dress and my exposed legs.

"Wow," he says, pulling me closer by the waist. "I should've come earlier."

He kisses my neck, and I almost suggest we stay in instead.

"I'm shorter than you this time," I say, kicking up one of my feet.

"You are short," he says, something I hear never. It's nice being around someone as tall as Cameron. I rarely get to feel petite.

He takes my hand as we walk to his truck. Opening the door like a gentleman, he smacks my ass like a scoundrel when I get in.

"I made us a nineties playlist so we can start deciding on songs," Cameron says, syncing his phone to his Bluetooth in his car, the first song blasting through the speakers.

"Whatta Man" by Salt-N-Pepa begins through the speakers.

"You planned this one," I say.

"I think this song is my nineties anthem," he says. He takes my hand and kisses my knuckles. "You can't honestly listen to this song and not think of me."

"That's presumptuous of you, Cam."

"Excuse me, I made you come last night within three minutes. That's a record."

"Yes, yes, you did." My thighs squeeze together at the memory of his fingers on me, in me, resulting in an orgasm so quick and fast, it shocked me enough to fall off the bed.

Cameron only laughed at me a little bit.

"I guess I need to work harder so you don't think of any other man when this song plays."

"I only have eyes for you."

"I hope the fuck so," he says, turning onto the highway. I squeeze his thigh playfully. "You better stop, or I'm going to find a pull-off and rip that dress off of you."

My hand travels closer to his bulge, and he squirms in his seat, taking turns on the road, careening around curves and bends.

"Are you trying to make me crash, woman?"

"You're right," I say, removing my hand. "It would be a shame to die before we actually have full penis-in-vagina sex."

"I agree," he says, taking another turn in the road. We drive for thirty minutes, chatting about our days and skirting around the issue. He would've mentioned if he got his results, if we could have sex tonight by now, right? I guess we're still waiting.

Cameron pulls off the road into the shopping center surrounded by tall redwoods. We're in Auburn, thirty or so miles from Goldheart. He pulls into a parking space and cuts the engine. He lifts my chin with his fingers and lays a sweet kiss on me.

"You look really cute tonight."

"Really?" I ask, cooing.

"Really," Cameron says, leaning in again, this kiss more sensual than a quick peck. "Oh, I have something to show you."

He opens his phone, tapping on some buttons, and turns it around. It shows test results of his STD screening. He got the works done, and it all shows no traces or negative.

"How did you get the results so fast?"

"I found a place that did rapid testing, and I may have greased the wheels a little bit. Magic happens when you're nice to people and flash money and donuts at them."

I smack him on the shoulder. "Why didn't you tell me before we left?"

"Because I wanted to take you on a date first. Change my ways." He leans in and kisses me sweetly. "I'll make love to you..." He croons. Badly. "It's on the playlist."

Cameron leaves the truck first, walking around to my side to open my door. He offers a hand so I can step out. He pulls me close as we walk to the restaurant. It's a small unit, between a dry cleaner and a dark bar, like the Swift.

La Scarola Family Italian.

"Wait, isn't this Emily's favorite?"

"Yes, she comes once a month. Says she doesn't run into anyone she knows. Well, she ran into Dan that one time..."

"Your investor?"

Cameron nods. "It was when he was secretly dating his now-wife. Emily accidentally caused drama."

He opens the door and leads me to a table in the middle of the restaurant since it's self-seating. A server appears and takes our drink orders. It's nice I don't see Banning Cellars on the wine list. It's like they have taste here.

"Wow, I haven't been on an actual date in months," I say, resting my forearms on the table.

"Jason never took you on a date?"

I shake my head. "The only time he asked me on one was the weird double date with Morgan. Which I'm so glad we said no to."

"I don't want to share you," Cameron says, holding out his hands. I tuck my hands in his, and his thumbs massage my knuckles. "This is a date. A real date."

My stomach flutters with butterflies.

We discuss the merits of each dish, but I go with my tried-and-true chicken parmesan while Cameron orders pasta primavera. The server drops off a breadbasket, and we dive in, slathering creamy butter on thick slices of home-made sourdough. The first bite makes my eyes roll back in a mouth orgasm.

"The way you're eating that bread is turning me on," Cameron says.

"It's just so good," I respond.

"I hope I can get you to make that face later," he says. My chewing slows so I don't choke. A flash of Cameron's head between my legs makes me squeeze my knees together.

"I hope so, too," I reply, running my foot up his pants leg. He adjusts in his seat, grumbling as he takes a sip of water.

I wonder if he's as turned on as I am.

"You better stop, or we're getting the food to go."

"I'll stop," I say, smirking at him. I take the napkin from my lap and drop it on the table. "I need to wash my hands."

"Go for it," Cameron says, taking a sip of his beer.

As I lather soap in my hands, I look up, alarmed at my appearance. I look like a feral version of myself—baby hairs creating a halo over my head, my cheeks so red you can't make out my freckles, my skin full of goosebumps, even though I barely touched his leg.

My stomach twists at what's going to happen tonight.

I will have sex with Cameron Finch, and it will be incredible.

I could orgasm from the fantasies alone, right here in the bathroom.

When I leave, someone grabs my hand and pulls me down the hall. I'm pushed against a wall, and there Cameron is, with lust in his eyes so strong, it might burn me.

"I wanted to do this," he says, taking me in a scorching kiss that consumes my breath. He kisses me like he might undress me right here. A moan hums at his throat as he turns his head to taste me deeper. His hands presses against my ass, and I feel his hardness against my pelvis, making me break with desire.

"We can't do anything here," I say as he kisses my neck. My eyes scan for an employee or another patron, seeing us make out in the back of this restaurant.

"Should we get our food to go?" he asks.

"I think so," I say. He pulls away, peers into my eyes, then kisses me one last time. He takes my hand, and we walk back into the restaurant. He finds our server, a guy in his early twenties, and we tell him we want our meals boxed up to go.

At least, we *tried* to go on a date. I'm ready to lick marinara sauce off of his body.

23

ANNIE

My stomach still twists as I step into Cameron's tiny home, and I take it all in. It's clean and organized, with zero clutter. There's a ladder leading to one loft and a slender stairwell leading to another loft. There's a small couch under one of the lofts and a galley-style kitchen with a counter facing a window overlooking some trees I can barely make out in the dark. I glance at a notebook filled with his handwriting, with brainstormed ideas and to-do lists for the event.

I don't care what anyone else says. He's changed.

After Cameron puts our food in the fridge, he stands in front of his door as I explore. The car ride back forced us to calm down, and now it feels like some of the urgency of the night has died along with it. I'm not sure how to get it back. I've always felt awkward about seducing a man.

"I've never been in one of these before," I say, looking in the bathroom. I point to the shower. "Is this big enough for you?"

Cameron nods, his hands in his pockets. "I had this custom designed so I can fit in the shower. We *will* not be having shower sex in here because I barely fit. We'll save that for vacations."

My cheeks warm since he's thought of a future for us that includes going away together. I run my fingers along the countertop and sit down on the couch. It's comfy and so plush that I disappear into the cushions.

"You don't have a TV," I say.

"I don't need it," Cameron says. "I watch stuff on my laptop. Cuts down on the stuff in here."

"I don't know where you keep everything."

"I don't need a lot. I really don't believe in having a lot of stuff."

"So, you're a minimalist?"

Cameron shrugs a shoulder. "Not really. I just don't see the point in taking up more space than I need."

I think I'm falling in love with you rattles in my brain, but I keep it inside. Who knows what he's feeling or thinking.

All I know is he wants me.

Cameron sinks into the couch next to me. He takes my hair and drops it over my left shoulder. He kisses my neck like a feather and my head rolls to the side. My skin singes with his kisses as his hands grip my waist, his arm pulling me closer.

I appreciate that he wants to take his time, but I want his cock inside of me immediately.

"We should close the windows," I say breathlessly.

"Sure," he replies, standing up and drawing the shades. I unstrap my sandals, stepping on the coolness of the hard-wood floor. I grip the banister and step onto the stairs, climbing to the loft. A mattress is visible from the ground floor so I assume that's where the bedroom is.

"Where are you going?" he asks, turning around from drawing the last shade.

"Going to your bedroom. Giving you a hint."

He climbs the stairs with three steps, the railing shaking with his charge. He spins me around, taking my mouth with a hunger left over from our kiss at the restaurant. Cameron takes over my mouth as he grabs my ass. The passion swirls around us as he lowers me to a stair, my back leaning comfortably against the last one leading to the loft.

He crouches over me, his all-consuming, wet, firm, powerful mouth against mine. A gasp leaves my lips as his hand disappears under my skirt, rubbing me through the fabric of my underwear, making me see stars.

Cameron squats down on a step three below, pushing the skirt of my dress up.

"I'm excited I can finally do this," he says, pulling my underwear down, spreading my legs as wide as the banister allows. He dives into me, and the pleasure is instant.

He laps at my clit lazily, and I arch against him as I brace myself against the black railing, bucking into his mouth. He focuses solely on it, sucking, licking, flicking his tongue. One finger goes into my wet heat, then two, finding the spot within me that makes me dizzy.

"You taste so good," Cameron moans, as he continues his work, his expert mouth against me. His hand finds the strap of my dress, pulling it down to expose one of my breasts. His fingers tease my nipple, and the ecstasy makes me squirm. I'm so close to coming undone.

I pull his face to see me eye-to-eye, his lips slick from me.

"I want you inside of me when I come," I say. "If you don't get inside me right now, I will die."

"Okay," he says, scooping me up, and taking me the last few stairs to his loft. He drops me on a soft mattress, while he leans over to grab a condom.

"Let's get you undressed," he says, finding the zipper on the back of my dress. He pulls it down slowly, peeling the straps from my shoulders. He takes my breasts in his hands, massaging them as I press my back into his chest. My body is on alert as he flings the dress away from us. I lie down, and his eyes drag from my head to my toes. His look makes me writhe with anticipation.

His head travels down my body, taking my nipple in his mouth, licking my clit again. Just once, and I'm delirious.

He removes his own clothes quickly, his cock thick and long for me. I've seen it many times over the last few days, but it still makes me gasp. We're finally going to be together, connected. After Cameron rolls the condom on, he lies back, pulling me on top of him.

"I want you on top. I want to see your face," he says.

I line up his cock so that he can slide into me, and we let out a release of air together.

His hands settle on my ass as I lean down to kiss him. He wipes my sweaty hair from my face and locks our eyes.

"Fuck, Annie, you feel so fucking good." I can't respond since the ecstasy steals my words. His cock stretches me deliciously, filling me, and I can't think as the desire builds within my core. I roll into him, my clit hitting his flesh. I'm back to my build, reaching higher than before. His thumb finds my sensitive nub, rubbing it as I ride him.

He sits up to kiss my neck, taking one nipple in his mouth and then the other one, his hand still between us. I reach the point of no return and fall off the cliff, my mouth stretching wide as I let out a cry as the orgasm takes me over.

"That's right, baby," he says into my neck. "Just fall."

He still moves within me, and I want him now. All of him.

"Now you on top," I say.

He grabs me by the ass and flips me over, his strong body now over mine. He interlaces my fingers with his and leans down to kiss me until we both need breath again. His slow pulses are driving me to madness as he takes his time, retracting and railing into me, his velvety cock sliding against my walls in powerful strokes.

Seeing Cameron's face so close to mine, knowing that I am giving him all these sensations, makes me bold.

"Fuck me harder," I command. His thrusts speed up, the smack of flesh echoing throughout the tiny house, and I spiral out of control. His thumb massages my sensitive clit as he slaps into me and my nails dig into his ass. This is raw and primal.

This is perfect.

"Oh yes," I say between moans, and I scream as another orgasm builds within me, growing, getting away from me. I cry out when my walls pulse around his cock again. He grunts into my neck as he spills into me, filling me up, kissing my cheek, my neck, my hair. Our bodies are slick with sweat as he punctuates our time together with a long kiss.

"Annie," he murmurs.

I love the way he says my name, drunk off of his desire for me.

"Cameron," I say, kissing the tip of his nose. He gazes into my eyes, his breath on my face as we look at each other with no words. "What?" I ask when it lasts a little too long.

"Just thinking about how lucky I am," he says, kissing my nose in return.

He pulls out of me and steps over me. I lay there, in bliss, in utter disbelief of how hot that was. Him inside of me, as I climaxed twice. How I'll spend the night in his arms again.

Cameron finds me a clean towel and lets me shower first.

He's absolutely right that two people our size could not fit comfortably in this shower.

After a few tries, I figure out the shower knob and enjoy a delightful flow of water as I wash myself. I can't help but smile as I wash the soapy suds off of my body. When I step out with the towel around me, he is waiting there with a bottle of wine and a T-shirt folded in his hand.

He holds it up, and I nod. "I have this for you to sleep in. That is, if you want to sleep over."

"Of course," I say. "I would love to."

"Good," Cameron says. "I have to warn you that my bed is small, and since we're two tall people, it's going to get even smaller."

"We'll test it," I say.

"I might accidentally push you off the mattress."

"I'll risk it," I reply.

"I might wake you in the middle of the night to fuck you."

"I would be disappointed if you didn't. Can you put the shirt on me?" I ask. I raise my arms, letting my towel fall. His eyes fix to my bare skin, my peaked nipples, the goose-bumps. Cam gathers the shirt and pulls it over my head, picking up each arm to thread through the arm holes. His hands drag the shirt down my stomach. He does the same with my underwear, delicately touching each ankle as he places my foot in each hole, slowly pulling them up.

"Now that you've put those on slowly, you should take them off quickly."

"Oh, really?" His head drops to kiss me.

We make love on the couch again, and it's as explosive as the first time. When our stomachs rumble, we eat our dinner, heated by the microwave. After one more sex session, Cameron and I climb to the loft, exhausted, and pass out on top of each other. It's a little uncomfortable, but we make it work.

We wake up to a rumbling. It's dark outside, except for a spotlight directly shining into the tiny home.

"What the hell?" Cameron asks. He lifts the shades and squints. "What the fuck?"

"Cameron Finch, I love you!" a distinct voice says, amplified by some microphone or other device.

"Oh no," Cameron says, exploding from the bed like there's a fire.

"What's going on?" I ask, alarmed.

"Let me handle this," he says, opening the door.

"There you are, you fucker!" the female voice yells, and I stand up cautiously, creeping down the stairs. I peek behind the shades of one of the windows to see a car with its headlights on and the outline of a body, holding something in front of them.

"What are you doing here, Morgan?" Cameron asks.

"Cameron, how does it feel to be a piece of shit?"

What? I wrack my brain.

24

CAMERON

Why is this happening to me?

Morgan stands in the middle of my sister's property, spotlighted by her car's headlights. All I can see is her outline, hair big, body language unhinged, a bullhorn in her hands.

It was one hookup, one weekend. She should have moved on by now.

Apparently she hasn't.

The headlights are bright on my eyes so I shield them with my hand.

"You're going to wake up my sister and niece," I whisper-yell, pressing the air down with my hands, encouraging her to quiet.

"Let them know you're such a piece of shit!" she says again into the bullhorn, louder and more obnoxious. "You're some coward for not going on a double date with us."

"Going on a double date is weird, Morgan," I shout back.

Calling the cops seems extreme, and they might laugh at me. Lance, one of the night officers, is a good friend of mine, and he will make fun of me until the end of time if I call this in. I bring my hand down my face. I need to figure out what to do.

As I stand here, unsure on how to diffuse the situation, another set of headlights drives onto my sister's property, and I turn back to my house. What now?

Once the truck stops, Jason Banning climbs out.

This is a nightmare. An actual nightmare.

Looking back, I see Annie standing there, her brown eyes large and confused.

"Who is it?"

"It's Morgan. And now Jason has showed up," I say. I maneuver her so she's not visible to Morgan. Who knows how she'll react if she sees Annie, looking good and fucked in my house?

"Morgan, you came here? Here?" Jason asks, pointing to my house.

"Yes, I did."

"Why?" Jason and I ask in unison.

"Because Cameron needs to know what he did. We lost a year and a half of being together because of *him*."

I cannot believe this. We flirted once at a party, I didn't know they were together, and I found out after the fact when Jason cornered me and threatened to fight me. The owner of the pool hall, Marty, threw him out by the scruff of his neck.

"I'm really sorry about that," I say, although I have nothing to apologize for. Morgan lied to me, and I got embroiled in a hot mess, one I've been trying to separate myself from.

"Is it happening again, Morgan? Because I thought we agreed that when I put that ring on your finger that it would be different this time."

Morgan raises the bullhorn to her mouth, although Jason is mere feet from her. "It is different. I need closure."

"Well, I'm closed so..." I say walking back inside.

"Hey, who is that?" Jason asks, pointing behind me.

"Hi, Jason," Annie says and I close my eyes slowly. Here we go.

"You're *living* with him?" Jason asks, eyes wide.

"Not yet," I blurt out. That really makes Jason swell with rage.

"Not yet, Annie? Not yet? Him?" Jason asks, his voice going up two octaves. "This stupid piece of shit?"

My fists clench by my sides. I'm not the type of guy who starts fights, but Jason is asking for a swift punch to the face.

"The only stupid piece of shit here is you, Jason," Annie says. "Cameron might be the smartest man in Goldheart because he wants me. And takes me out in public."

Jason scoffs, and Morgan looks at him. "You told me you were over her."

"I am," Jason insists. I don't believe it for a second.

"Did you cheat on her with me?"

"No!" he shouts at her. I wonder if I can retreat into my house, close the door, and they can fight among themselves and eventually disappear. I really don't want a text from my sister.

I step back before I hear a scream that could be heard in the next county.

"What is that?" Morgan asks, dropping the bullhorn and screaming again. In the outline of the headlights, I can see her lifting her feet, avoiding something on the ground. "Get away from me, you fuckers! Why are they coming for my feet? Why?"

I hear the melodious squeak of our raccoon friends, Thelma and Louise. They must be scared or maybe Jason and Morgan smell like trash. They swarm Morgan and Jason's feet, hissing. Jason tries to kick one, but it lunges at him, attaching itself to his pant leg.

"Shake it off like Taylor Swift," I yell with a laugh, and Annie cackles behind me. The raccoon is still hugging his leg, and Jason is doing a terrible job at disengaging with the raccoon.

God bless Thelma and Louise.

"Get it off of me!" Jason shrieks, his voice hitting an octave only dogs can hear. Annie wheezes with laughter behind me. Her butt hits the ground with a thud, and I'm cackling as I watch Morgan scramble into her car. Jason jumps in his own car, finally rid of the raccoon on his leg.

Morgan left the bullhorn as a present.

The wheels of their cars peel out, and I double-check Thelma and Louise aren't harmed. They run away, chittering as they go toward the road. I'm surprised they didn't take the bullhorn as a trophy.

I look back to find Annie sitting on the step, laughing so hard she's crying and hyperventilating.

In that moment, my heart balloons. The realization hits.

She's perfect for me.

Annie is organized where I am a mess. She's smart when I am not. While we're different, we find the same things funny. The sex is incredible. I respect her, I like her, and I fucking love her.

My phone buzzes on my kitchen counter, and I pick it up after I see my sister's name.

"Don't worry, Emily, they're gone now," I say immediately.

"What the hell is going on?"

I start laughing again. "Jason and Morgan came, and Thelma and Louise attacked them."

My sister knows about my one-night stand with Morgan and how Jason hates me. Hearing Emily laugh from the depth of her gut was worth the awkward moment. She rarely laughs anymore like that, and all it took was a raccoon attack on literal human garbage.

"Is Annie there?" Emily asks.

"Yes," I admit.

"How do you feel about her?" Emily asks.

Annie's still on the step, taking deep breaths since her laughing turned into hiccups. I'm looking at this woman, in my T-shirt, laughing because our former lovers showed up with a bullhorn. I feel a tightness in my chest.

I love her.

I really love her.

"She's it," I say.

25

ANNIE

I realize today that I can hyperventilate from laughing too hard.

But once I stop laughing, all the pieces of the puzzle come together in a perfect picture.

Morgan and Cameron were involved at some point. Jason wouldn't have suggested a double date without an outside influence. At first, I thought that she was curious about me because Jason dated me when they were broken up, or that Jason was jealous that I was with Cameron now.

How wrong I was.

The late-night visit, amplified by a bullhorn, made it clear that she is jealous that I'm with *Cam*, not that I was with Jason.

I've always hated raccoons, ever since they tipped over our trash cans constantly as a child, but now I have to say—God bless raccoons.

I laugh through his phone call with his sister, asking what's going on.

He checks outside to make sure they're gone and closes

the door. Now that my laughter has died down and I got rid of the hiccups, all that's left is anger.

"That was so funny," Cameron says, walking back inside to find me cross-legged on the floor. He notices my demeanor and tilts his head. "Are you okay?"

"Did something happen? With Morgan?"

He rubs the scruff of his chin. "Yes. About a year and a half ago."

"What happened?"

"We hooked up *once*. She broke up with Jason to be with me because she took flirting at a party as something more. I didn't know she was even with him until after the fact." I stay quiet as he sits down in front of me, taking my hands. "For the record, since we started together, fake or not, I haven't gone out with anyone else, looked at anyone else, flirted with anyone else. I'm all yours."

I know he's telling the truth, but jealousy blooms in my chest. Cameron slept with Morgan before me. Me, a woman he's known his entire life, who he only started seeing because he wanted to help me. Because he felt sorry for me.

"It all makes sense. Why he hates you."

"We've hated each other long before all this. I thought it would create drama to tell you about Morgan, and I don't kiss and tell. No matter what people think."

Tears well in my eyes. We had a beautiful night together, and now it's ruined.

"I'm with *you* now." His hand comes to my cheek, but I can't look at him. "It doesn't matter what happened in the past. I want to be with you. You only."

He lied by omission. Maybe he didn't think anything of it, but he has to know this will not fly. I'm done letting men get away with things, and Cameron needs to know that if we move forward, I refuse to tolerate this. I've stayed silent before, but *this* is too important to stay quiet.

It's time to stick up for myself, no matter how much I'm falling for Cameron.

"I wish you would've told me. You lied to me," I say. My head hurts, and I want to burrow in my own bed. I know I won't be able to sleep next to him after this, and I need a really good night of sleep to sort through everything.

"I didn't lie to you," he says. "I would never lie to you."

"You did," I say, swallowing back tears. "You didn't tell me when you had multiple opportunities. That's a lie by omission."

I pull his shirt off my body and find my dress crumpled in a pile under his counter.

"What are you doing?" Cameron asks.

"I want to go home," I say.

"Why? I thought you were going to stay here tonight."

"Can you take me home, please?" I pull the dress down my body and slip my feet into my shoes. His forehead crinkles and his lip part.

"You can't leave," Cameron says. "We can fix this."

"We can talk about it tomorrow," I say. "I promise. I'm really tired and want to go home."

He swipes his keys off the counter and follows me to his truck. His body language is tense and hunched, and I almost give in. I almost tell him to forget it and let's go back to his house. Fall asleep in each other's arms.

If he apologized, I would've.

We drive in silence back to my house, and when he pulls into my driveway, he can barely look at me.

"Good night," I say, opening the door.

"Good night," he says. He tries to smile, but sadness floods his face.

Hold your ground. Be strong, I tell myself.

Cameron doesn't make a move to kiss me, and I don't either.

Once I'm inside and my door is locked, I crumple to the ground and begin sobbing.

It takes a few sobs for me to fall asleep on the floor of my house.

I wake to a buzzing and sunlight piercing my eyeballs.

Why is Whitney calling? I don't have a book of hers, and she doesn't have a release coming for a couple months. She's so busy, she rarely calls me just to chat.

"Hi? Whitney?"

"Hi," Whitney says, her voice clogged with tears.

My heart drops. Oh no.

"What's going on?"

"Now's not a bad time, is it?"

"No," I say as I rub my eyes. I cross my legs and lean against my door. "What's up? Are you okay?"

"Brad and I are getting a divorce, and I've been keeping it a secret. I don't know how to tell people...I..." She hiccups through tears over the phone. I'm so confused. Her social media is full of pictures of them together, childfree and blissfully happy, on adventures around the world. Her posts about him are so true and full of love.

"What happened?"

She lets out a sob. "He decided he wanted to be a father."

"What?" I ask. I thought he was completely on board with being childfree-by-choice.

"We talked about it before we got married and agreed we would be childfree. Then, eight months ago, he takes me out to dinner and brought up having a baby. Supposedly, he had a dream. I thought he would give it up, but he didn't."

"I'm so sorry," I say. "Are you okay?"

"No," she says. "A part of me thinks I should give in, but I don't want to be a mother. It's not in me to do that. You know?"

Last night comes flooding back. Whitney stayed true to who she was, and I will stay true to my new sense of self. It's tough, though, when you're in love with someone. To create boundaries.

Am I in love with Cameron?

"You have to do what's best for you," I say. "What do you need? Do you want to come to Goldheart?"

We've talked about Goldheart in the past, that it could be perfect inspiration for a small-town series. Whitney has expressed interest in seeing it, since I love it so much and talk about it often. I would love her to visit.

"That's a sweet offer, but I shouldn't," she says.

"You can show up in Goldheart at any time, you know. You don't even have to call. Just show up."

The line goes quiet and I ask, "Are you still there?"

"I'm thinking," she says. "I've been wanting to come."

"Seriously, come," I say. "I have a light day today and no events so we can go out to dinner. Go to the Swift. I have a great couch."

"You're too sweet," she says, and then she's quiet again. "What if I did come today?"

"Please," I say. "I can tell you the best coffee shop to write while I finish up work."

"What the hell," Whitney says. "I'll come. If that's not too much of a burden."

"Absolutely not," I say. "Come."

"Crazy, huh?" she asks. "We've met twice, and you know more than eighty percent of my in-real-life friends."

"It's not. Romance books bring people together."

Whitney's voice brightens. "I'll pack some stuff, and I'll be down the hill in the next few hours. Hit me with your best coffee shop. A change of scenery might help me get the words down. The words *have not* been flowing."

I send her Gold Roast's information since they have cozy tables and free refills on coffee. Even if Tara talked about me in the bathroom, her shop is still the best shop in town, and I want to support women in business.

Whitney tells me she will text me when she gets into town and I promise to get all my work done so we can hang out as soon as possible.

My excitement about Whitney coming almost makes me forget about my fight with Cameron. Makes me stop obsessing on how he rationalized telling a lie by omission. By making me question why he agreed to help me in the first place.

Almost.

Whitney texts me at two, and I burn through the rest of my work, even drinking my emergency energy drink in the fridge. Jason passes me in the hallway as I go to grab something off the printer, and he barely acknowledges me.

It doesn't matter that I see Jason, or Cameron and I are in a disagreement—I get to hang out with my friend.

Before I go into the coffee shop, I call Cameron. It goes straight to voicemail.

Hey it's Cameron. You know what to do.

I ache at the sound of his voice. Why did I take such a hard line?

"Hey it's me. I want to talk. Call me or text me. Whatever. Bye."

I feel defeated as I open the door to Gold Roast, seeing Whitney sitting at a table covered in open notebooks, chunky earphones on, typing away furiously. Her dark hair is tied back in a colonial-man ponytail, and her glasses, used only for writing, slide down her nose. When I tap on her shoulder, she jumps five feet.

She stands up and wraps me in a bear hug.

"Oh my God, I was writing a torture scene and you scared the crap out of me," she says, hugging me again. She must be writing one of the soldiers' books in her mafia romance series. Whitney's smiling like she just got a check for ten thousand dollars and a puppy, not a divorce.

"How are you holding up?" I ask.

She points at her laptop. "I'm great. I just wrote six thousand words nonstop since I got here, and I have so much energy. I can't tell you the last time I got that. This shop is freaking amazing."

I turn around and see Tara standing behind the register. The last time we saw each other was in the bathroom at Banning Cellars during Jason's engagement party.

She looks just as thrilled to see me. I think Tara is a good person. Women gossip sometimes, especially if they're feeling insecure. I know I've done it. Still, I don't quite trust her yet.

"Hi, Annie," she says. "Is this your friend?"

"Yes," I say, pointing to Whitney. "This is Whitney. She writes books for a living."

"What kind?" Tara asks.

"Romance," she says confidently.

"Cool," Tara says. "Hey, Annie, can I talk to you?"

"Excuse me, Whitney," I say.

"Go for it. I think I have another thousand or two in me," she says, pushing her glasses up her nose and putting her earphones back on.

Tara walks out from behind the counter and motions for me to sit at a table.

"Look, I'm really sorry with what happened at the Banning engagement party," Tara says sincerely.

"It's fine," I say.

"I think I'm just really jealous. Of you. When I get jealous, I'm not my best self. I tend to turn into...well... a total bitch."

I wonder if she would be jealous to know that Cameron and I slept together and I left, just like she did, but he wanted me to stay.

"It happens," I say. "No worries."

"Your friend's been typing like a madwoman," Tara says. We look back at Whitney, hunched over her laptop, focused on her work.

"She's a really good writer," I say. "People give romance novels such hassle, but the women who write them are special. Really special."

"They must be," she says. "Anyway, I would love to grab a drink or something with you. Sometime."

"Whitney will be here a couple of days, but we can plan something in the future."

"Sounds good," Tara says. "I'm really sorry for gossiping. You seem like a cool woman, and I just let my jealousy get the better of me."

"We'll do something soon. Give me your number," I say, handing her my phone.

She types in her number and then I text her so she has mine.

"We'll go out soon," I say.

"Sure. That sounds like fun," she replies.

We stand up and I walk back over to Whitney's table. She's typing so fast I cannot believe this woman is in the middle of a divorce. It's like nothing else matters when she's writing. The same thing happens to me when I read her books.

She sees me in front of her, and she looks up.

"I got another eight hundred words in," she says, stretching her arms above her head. Her smile is so wide, I see gums.

"You do not look like someone going through...well... you know."

"I'm crushed inside, don't get me wrong," she says, cracking her knuckles. "It's just been a long time since the words flowed like this. This shop is magic."

"Do you want to work some more or..."

She closes her laptop. "I should probably stop for the day. I don't want to jinx it by overworking today. This was great, though. Thank you for inviting me. I think I need a drink, though. An alcoholic one."

"I can find you a drink," I say. "What about our local watering hole, the Swift?"

"Sounds perfect," she says. "I want to get freshened up. I finally feel like taking a shower."

My eyebrows scrunch. "When was the last time you took a shower?"

Her mouth twists. "You don't want to know."

I text her my address and offer to let her follow me.

We take turns in the bathroom and grab burgers at Moe's before we head to the Swift. It's still early, and I breathe out a sigh of relief that Cameron and his best buddy Thumper aren't here. I don't think I could take it seeing him flirt with anyone but me.

"This is great," Whitney says. Her dark hair is down and straight, over a simple back dress that gives her some of the best cleavage I've ever seen. Her blue eyes pop against her porcelain skin, and she looks like one of the heroines she writes about. She doesn't need a fairy godmother; she just needed a shower.

"The usual?" Carl calls from behind the bar to me. "Keep your friend away from Pete. He's in the bathroom right now."

I lean into Whitney. "Pete tries to hit on every new woman who comes into the bar."

Whitney nods once. "I can handle him."

"What are you drinking?" Carl asks.

I look at Whitney. "I'm boring. Jack and Coke."

"Two Jacks and Coke," I order. Carl bobs his head from side to side and fills two slender glasses with ice. We find an open tall table by the dart boards.

"This is fun," Whitney say, clasping her hands. "This is exactly what I envisioned for Goldheart's hometown bar."

"Too bad you don't write small-town romance."

"Yeah, too bad. Maybe I should," she says, looking around. "Hey, what's going on with that guy? The one you pretended to date?"

"Oh," I say. "It's...complicated."

Whitney leans on her hand. "Feel free to tell me anything. Just know, it might end up in a book."

I laugh. "I figured."

My heart drops as I think about Cameron. We're at the table next to the one he found me crying into my banana split. It's been less than twenty-four hours since I left Cameron's place, and I miss him. I should've stayed and worked it out. Now, he won't call me back.

Carl sets down my drink on our high top, and I hand him my card to open a tab.

I take a sip of my drink and shiver. It's sugary with a bite, and I want to gulp it down and forget about my sadness.

"I'm ready for the full complicated story," Whitney says.

I shrug. "I thought we were going somewhere. We had a romantic date that we cut short, I went back to his place, we...you know...."

"Fucked," Whitney says. My mouth must've dropped, and she says, "I'm sorry. I'm a romance author."

"Fair enough," I say. "Well, his ex and my ex came over in the middle of the night with a bullhorn."

Whitney sprays her sip, sending sticky liquid all over my face.

"I'm so sorry," she says, grabbing a napkin. "What?"

"Jason's fiancée Morgan was involved with Cameron," I say.

"Is that a problem?" Whitney asks. "Sorry, I've been out of the game for so long."

"I didn't know they had been involved until she was shouting it through a bullhorn. We're just starting out, and he lied by omission."

"Are you his first real girlfriend?"

"I think so," I say, although I'm not sure I'm his girlfriend. The booze is loosening my tongue. There's no one I really can talk to about this with and Whitney might be the best person, although it might end up in a romance novel that thousands of people will read.

"Cam hasn't called me back or texted me. I'm worried I messed it up by not staying to work it out like he wanted." I drop my forehead into my hands. "I don't know what to do."

"How old is he?"

"Thirty-four."

Whitney grimaces.

"What should I do?"

"You did the right thing by leaving. He'll know that you will not tolerate it. Don't call him again. For now," Whitney says. "Between your relationship trouble and my divorce, you and I deserve more booze." Her drink is already gone, only clinking ice cubes remaining. "Should I meet a man tonight? What do divorcing people do?"

We scan the room. Every man is at least twenty years older than us, and I know too much about all of them.

"Slim pickings," I say.

"We'll just get drunk, then," Whitney says, standing up to go to the bar. Pete and his buddy Winston do flirt with her, but Whitney smiles and keeps her body out of arm's length.

We order another round and another. The Swift fills up more and more, and we laugh harder with one another about romance novels and authors. She gives me some good gossip on who's shelling out serious advertising money to get to the Top 100, and we talk about other stuff, like *The Bachelorette* and the remaining four men on the current season. We pull up the promo photos from the website and discuss, reading their bios and making fun of them.

An actual man interrupts us. He's around our age, not terrible-looking, and genuinely friendly. We entertain him, although I'm thinking about Cameron the entire time. While Whitney hasn't cried, I've seen waves of sadness cross her face, and I know she's hurting.

The longer Cameron doesn't contact me, the deeper I sink. However, I don't have it as bad as Whitney. At least we can be miserable together.

I see nothing wrong with talking to this man, especially after he buys us another round. Carl makes sure to deposit them directly in front of us, in case this guy is a creep.

"Tucker," the man says, holding out a hand to me first. I shake his hand and feel the callouses on his fingers.

I don't notice Cameron's death stare from across the Swift.

26

CAMERON

"You're acting like someone told you your penis no longer works," my buddy Thumper says as he opens the door to the Swift. "What happened to you?"

It's the fight with Annie that's making me moody and unfun.

It's a busier-than-usual night, with most of the high tables filled with Goldheart residents and the usual suspects at the bar. The gang is all here—Pete with his green trucker hat and his buddy Winston, who hang out here six days out of the week. Pete isn't crying, which is uplifting. His girlfriend gave him an ultimatum, and when he said he didn't want to marry her, she left with his best friend and his plants on the back of the best friend's Harley.

He's a Goldheart cautionary tale.

Waving, I find a spot near the stack of kegs and saddle up while Thumper knocks on the table.

"You need a good stiff drink," Thumper says. "I'll get you something."

"No absinthe or Everclear, Thumper. I mean it."

He looks back with a finger point, but I know he's going to come back with a concoction that will fuck me up.

I didn't want to come, but Thumper called me several times in a row. And when I didn't pick up, he drove out to my house and beat on my door. My phone has been dead since eleven, with all of my checking and when I got home, I plugged it in and passed out in a nap. I didn't sleep at all last night. When I stumbled down the stairs, I bumped into the wall and then the railing. I stopped and looked at the exact place I ate out Annie like a gourmet meal.

Thinking about Annie creates a gaping hole in my heart.

What can I do to fix everything? I don't know.

Tonight, I fully intended to hang out in my bed, napping on and off, with a Netflix show on my laptop and fall asleep early, but I ended up in Thumper's truck, and somehow, we're at the Swift. Thumper refused to let me take my phone. So, I didn't check it.

I rest my head on the table like I did during math class in high school. Math now means Annie to me. I'm going to lose her if I don't figure it out soon.

A knuckle nudges my bicep, and I sit up. Thumper slides a suspicious-looking pink drink in front of me. "Drink."

"How much alcohol is in this?" I ask, holding it up. It's way too clear.

"Don't worry about it. Down the hatch."

I take one sip, and there's no bitter aftertaste. Knowing Thumper, if I drink three of these, I'm ending up in the ER.

Oh well. I drain half the glass.

"I've never seen you like this. Is this about Annie Stewart?"

I nod. "We had a fight last night. I don't know if I'm cut out for this boyfriend shit."

Thumper shakes his head. "I can't believe you're dating

her. I bet she's wild in bed. I know you won't tell me, though."

"Nope."

"What happened?"

I shake my head again.

"Well, let's find you another lady. Let's see," Thumper says, looking around. I don't have the heart to tell him that I have no interest in any women tonight. At all. Plus, I really don't want to fuck it up with Annie, because I can't be certain I one hundred percent fucked it up.

I should've told Thumper to fuck off and grabbed my phone.

My eyes zone in on the fluorescent sign over the bar when I hear Thumper mutter, "Oh shit."

"What?" I ask.

"Annie is here. With a total smoke show."

My head shoots up like a telescope from a submarine. I look across the room and catch the flash of red hair and dark hair of a woman I've never seen before. Yes, she was good-looking, but next to Annie, she might as well be a raccoon. Annie is wearing a slinky black top over those form-fitting jeans I love, and my breath catches from seeing her.

They're talking to an even bigger douchebag than me.

Tucker Redmond. That absolute tool.

He worked on a crew with me once, and he was super proud of himself he left his wife and two kids in North Carolina to move out here. That guy is a bigger asshole than Jason.

"She moves on quickly," Thumper says.

"There's no way she can be into Tucker," I say. She might've dated Jason, but she's smarter than that.

Tucker laughs and touches Annie on the shoulder. That's *my* shoulder to touch. *Motherfucker.*

"Are you going to say something?"

"No, I..." I can't stop staring at Annie, how her body shakes with laughter, the way the freckles on her back dust her skin.

"What happened last night? Did she ask you to be exclusive or something?"

I shake my head.

"Then, what was it?"

"I didn't tell her I slept with Morgan. And then Morgan showed up at the tiny house."

Thumper slams his beer bottle down on the table. "Are you fucking serious?"

I nod. "With a bullhorn."

"What the fuck?" Thumper asks. "Do you have a magic dick or something?"

"You know it," I say as we bump our fists together.

"So, what's wrong?"

I tilt my head with a shoulder shrug. "Annie got mad and asked me to take her home."

"Did she say you all broke up?"

Did she? "I don't think so."

"Dude," he says, dropping his head back. "That wasn't a breakup. You got in a fight. I bet you haven't even texted her yet to apologize."

"You wouldn't let me bring my phone!" I yell. "I was charging it since it went dead. That's why I didn't get your calls."

Out of nowhere, a slap comes upside my temple and my eyes cross for a moment. I cover the impact spot with my hand.

"What was that for?"

"Make sure your phone is charged, like a man."

Thumper points a finger at me. "This is your fault. If Tucker marries her, you should give the best-man toast."

"Thumper, I already feel like shit."

"Is she worth it?" Thumper asks, looking back. "I've known Annie since birth, just like you. She's a good woman. Not sure what she sees in you, but she sees something. You should lock it down before she wises up."

I've never thought about marriage seriously. Not until Annie. With her, I can picture us drinking coffee on my deck, me kissing her neck while she works on her laptop, pulling her close to snuggle before drifting off to sleep. Having a couple tykes and going out on my family's boat.

Thumper is right. It was just a fight, and I'm doing my usual shit of bailing before anything else can happen. Well, not anymore.

How do you apologize? Going up and saying "I'm sorry" doesn't feel like enough for Annie. Plus, it makes my skin crawl to realize I'm wrong. This is my fault, like Thumper says.

I need to make it right.

"I'm going over there," I say.

"Attaboy," he says. I stand up and walk over, coughing into my hand. Tucker sees me and stands up from his leaning on the table.

"Hey Cameron," he says, shaking my hand.

"Can I borrow Annie for a moment?" I ask. Annie freezes in her seat, and her head turns slowly. There's no joy in her eyes when she looks at me, which is alarming. She stands up and walks past me, outside.

"In case it rains," Thumper says, throwing his keys at me.

We walk outside, onto the sidewalk. I hope the gray clouds don't foreshadow how this conversation is going to go.

"What's up?" Annie asks, crossing her arms in front of her.

"I want to talk."

"Did you get my message? I was hoping to hear from you all day." Her arms cross tighter, like a cage around her.

"I know."

"Did you follow me here?"

I shake my head and push my hair out of my face. "No. Thumper and I ended up here tonight."

Her eyes glow hotter with anger, and I'm not sure why she's mad. I thought women liked not being stalked.

"You aren't here to pick up women, are you?" she asks.

"No!" I shove my hands in my pockets. "Are we over?"

Her mouth gapes, and she stares at me.

"Are we?" I ask.

"I didn't think so, but now that you're asking, I..." She looks like she's going to cry. I'm messing this up royally.

I take a step toward her, and she doesn't step back. This is a good sign. "I haven't been a boyfriend in a really long time. Ever, really. I know I screwed this up, but I want to fight. For you."

"You lied by omission," she says. A tear falls down her cheek. Great, I'm already making her cry, something I didn't want to do. "All I wanted was an apology."

"I'm sorry," I say with a wince. Then the heavens open up, and it begins pouring like we're in a Nicholas Sparks movie.

"It was tough for you to say that, wasn't it?" Annie asks. She stays put, as the rain comes down around us, dripping off our noses.

I nod. "Admitting I lied is rough. I don't lie. And I lied to the most important person in my life and that kills me."

Annie relaxes her arms to her sides as we stare at each

other, a few feet apart.

"Are we having a moment?" I ask, shouting over the thunder that booms in the clouds.

"I think we are," Annie says.

The cold rain pelts me like thumb tacks. "I should've told you about Morgan the second we talked about going to the engagement party."

"Keep going," Annie says, pointing to the ground. "Grovel."

"Oh shit, I wasn't planning on this," I say, getting to my knees on the wet ground and looking up. "Is this good?"

"Perfect," Annie says. "Now tell me how wrong you were."

"I was so wrong. You're always right. You make me a better man, Annie. I would do whatever you ask me to make it up to you. Do you want foot massages? Flowers? I can do continual cunnilingus..."

"Keep your voice down," she says, resting her hand on my cheek.

"All I know is I'm falling for you," I say. Her face softens as she looks down at me. Her hair is completely wet, and her mascara runs down her cheeks. I pull her to me, hugging her legs, pressing my cheek against her knees. "Please accept my apology and this grovel."

"Okay, you're forgiven. Now, get up," she says, pulling me up by my armpits. She's in my arms again, and my body relaxes. Her hands play with the hair at the nape of my neck. "Okay, kiss me in the rain, and then we'll go inside because this is not as romantic as I thought it would be."

I kiss her, her lips warm although this rain is liquid ice on my skin. When we pull apart, I hold up Thumper's keys and motion to Thumper's old Chevy parked across the street from the Swift. "We're getting soaked. Do you want to go to Thumper's truck?"

"Yeah," she says, stepping into a puddle on the street. It splashes me, and I yelp, making Annie double over in laughter. We get into the covered bed of Thumper's truck. He converted it a few months ago so he could sleep in it when he goes camping with his black lab, Bambi.

"My friend is staying at my house tonight so we can't do anything," she says.

"Well, we have this truck. Thumper will understand."

"I've never had sex in the bed of a truck before."

After I rack my brain, I say, "I don't think I have either."

Her face lights up.

"Are you thinking what I'm thinking?"

"Hell yeah," I say.

"Do you have a condom?"

"Always," I say, covering her mouth with mine.

Clothes start flying, and we're naked in less than a minute. The windows steam with the moisture on our skin and the heat. I kiss her cold skin, and she licks some rain from my cheek. I lick between her legs until she pulls me up her body, grabbing for me. I pull out an emergency condom from my wallet, and she rolls it down my shaft, stroking me, making me groan. When I bury myself into her, we sigh at the same time, laughing at the sounds we make. Like our first time, I fuck her hard as her cries get louder, and she screams my name out loud when I rub her clit with my thumb.

Makeup sex feels so fucking good.

I let go as I hover over her, banging my head on the top of the camper shell. Flopping on top of her, she runs her nails up and down my spine.

"How's your head?" Annie asks, touching the tender spot where I banged it.

"Fine," I say, wincing.

"Maybe we don't do this again."

"I think Thumper will allow this one time only." She giggles as I kiss her breasts. It's only been a day, but I missed them.

Annie shivers, and I grab a folded blanket tucked in the corner and pull it around her. "Romance in the rain is really overrated."

"Oh absolutely. It's miserable," I say. "Even that ninety-seven-percent-alcohol drink Thumper got me did nothing to warm me up."

"We'll just have to find other ways," she says, kissing me on the neck.

"Yes," I say, kissing her again. I pull my wet shirt over my head, and I hear her voice, small, but clear.

"Cameron, I'm falling for you too."

"Mom, you know Cameron Finch," I say, gripping his hand tight, standing on the stoop of my parents' house. My mom smiles wide and opens the door, letting us walk through.

Whitney stayed with me for three days, going to Gold Roast every day to write. After she left to go back home, Cameron didn't leave my house for forty-eight hours. We made up for lost time and took full advantage of our privacy.

I just started walking normally again.

"You're going to break my hand," Cameron whispers in my ear, deliberately close enough to tickle me.

"Just don't leave my side," I say, walking through the foyer and into the living room. My younger sister Raegan is home for the weekend, and it's the first time I'm telling her about Cameron. She doesn't trust him because of his reputation, so I hope she can see the man I see.

My sister's mouth falls open when she sees Cameron holding my hand, in our parents' living room. She doesn't usually make a scene, but there's a first time for everything.

"Hi," Raegan says, her voice higher than usual. Her fiancé Henry stands up and extends a hand.

"Good to see you again," he says, shaking Cameron's hand.

"Likewise buddy," he says.

Henry takes me in for a hug, squeezing a sound out of me. Raegan always says that the hugs were what made her fall in love with him. I can see why.

"Raegan," Cameron says, offering his arms. I hold my breath as Raegan stands up, looks Cameron dead in the eye, and walks past him to hug me.

"Cameron," Raegan says flatly and then turns to me. "Do you want my mojito?"

I nod, and she hands the drink to me. "I wish Mom would learn how to make something else. I just can't handle drinks that has stuff floating in it."

"I'm definitely more of a beer or bourbon guy myself," Cameron interjects. That comment hangs in the air.

Mom turns the corner, breaking the tension. "Who wants charcuterie?"

"Me," Raegan says, holding up her hand.

"Honey, how did you get a drink?" she asks me. I point to my sister who holds her hands up like Mom is a cop. Mom shakes her head.

"Where's Dad?" I ask.

"Tinkering in the garage. I'll go get him."

Once she leaves, it's awkward again.

"Thank you again for helping with our engagement. It went awesome," Henry says.

"You're welcome. It was my pleasure."

Henry is a good man for trying to break the tension. He wraps his arm around my sister who lets out a huff. He keeps trying, God bless him.

"I got your newsletter, and you're doing a nineties-themed adult prom? I want to go. I'm a nineties kid myself," Henry says.

"It's the same day as Landon and Erin's wedding." I'm not sure how Raegan knows the date.

"Oh that's right," he says, snapping his fingers. "Sounds great, though."

Cameron nods, his shoulder relaxing. "Annie has been so helpful on how to plan it. I would be lost without her."

"Is that how you two got together?" Henry asks.

"Something like that." Cameron kisses my hair, and Raegan scoffs again.

"Can I get a recommendation for a cherry-red hair dye, Raegan?" I ask. Her eyes glimmer with my question. My sister frequently dyes her hair fun colors. It's currently a bright blue with purple tips. She's been wanting to dye my hair for years. It's one of my tactics to butter her up.

"Why?" she asks.

Cameron pulls me tighter. "We talked about going as Jordan and Angela from *My So-Called Life.*"

My heart flutters at the comment. Cameron and I have been watching it in between orgasms, and he knows how much I love it. He was the one to suggest it for the prom. I've already picked out the perfect flannel and found black bike shorts and a lacy halter crop top. I just need the hair.

"You already have red hair, but we can punch it up," Raegan says, with no smile. "Angela and Jordan—that makes sense. Especially since you've had a crush on Cameron since high school."

"Really?" Cameron asks, hooking his arm around my shoulders. "Since high school, huh?"

"'Crush' is a loose term," I say, my cheeks flushing with embarrassment.

"Please, you wrote 'Annie Finch' a couple times. I *caught* you," Raegan says. I could kill her.

Cameron grins harder. His grip on me grows tighter, and it makes my stomach churn. Old Cameron would run away. This Cameron seems excited to hear I had a crush back then.

"So, I heard the wedding is coming soon?" Cameron asks.

Henry nods. "July. We're doing it at City Hall in San Francisco. It doesn't sound fancy, but the interior is spectacular."

"I'm so excited," Raegan says. She bursts with happiness. That could be Cameron and me one day. Many, many months in the future. My sister got engaged after three months, which is way too quick for me, but I already feel so comfortable with Cameron. Ever since our makeup sex in the back of Thumper's truck, everything's been going well.

Talking about the wedding has loosened Raegan up and she no longer looks like she's plotting Cam's murder, so I'm cautiously optimistic.

My dad Neil walks in from the garage, wiping his hands on a cloth. Neil adopted me when I was five, after my bio dad terminated his parental rights. I was the maid of honor in my mother's wedding and I love my dad, but he can be... overbearing. He had a three-hour conversation with Henry when he showed up to sweep Raegan back to San Francisco.

"Hi, I'm Cameron," he says, dropping his arm from around my shoulders to greet my dad.

"I know who you are," Dad says, looking Cameron up and down. Cameron's shoulders rise with tension.

"Sir, I would like to talk to you privately," Cameron says. They walk outside, and I wish I could listen in.

"He's so brave," Henry whispers, his arm around Raegan.

I cross my arms. "You don't think Dad will yell at him, do you?"

"Dad doesn't yell. That's the scariest thing about him. How quiet he gets," Raegan says. Her face is expressionless, which is alarming.

"Are you mad?" I ask her.

"I need to observe more," Raegan says.

"I'll go see if Jane needs any help in the kitchen. I can wash vegetables like a champion," Henry says and makes a quick escape.

That man is great.

Raegan leans in. "I just want you to be careful. Jason destroyed you. Decimated you. I don't want your heart to be broken again."

"Cameron and Jason treat me totally differently," I say. "The difference is shocking, actually."

"Cameron's slept his way all over this town. How do you know you're different?"

I pause. That's the thing that's nagged at me. What makes me special? I'm just an incredibly tall woman, with a string of bad relationships, in a dead-end job, who still lives in her hometown.

I just know the way Cameron acts with me. The way he grabbed my hand when we walked into the room. How he's proud to be with me, how it feels like it's getting stronger with each day we're together.

For once in my life, I need to have hope. Cameron and I can make it. That a happily ever after is possible for us, and I can be as happy as a heroine in one of Whitney's novels.

"I appreciate your concern," I say. "But if this is a mistake, you have to let me make it. I'm your big sister, after all."

"Just take it slow."

"That's interesting, coming from you."

"Do as I say, not as I do," Raegan says. "You need more time. Just don't rush into anything. Cameron's never been in a relationship before, ever."

"I know that, Raegan," I say. She hugs me and sniffles against my ear.

"I just want you to be happy," she says, wiping away a tear. "I want more than anything for you to meet the one and settle down and have kids if you want that."

I don't tell her I've already envisioned a full future with Cameron. How I've thought out the trajectory of our life and that I can't see my future without him in it.

It's new, but it feels real. Even if it started as a lie.

"Just be careful," Raegan says. "I love you. So much."

"I love you, too. Just give him a chance. Please."

"Okay, fine. I'll give him a chance," she says.

I hear the door to the garage open and manly laughter waft in. My dad is slapping Cameron on the shoulder, and they're laughing.

Cameron broke down my dad's defenses in twenty minutes. Impressive.

"We were just discussing the Broncos," Dad says, smiling wider than I've ever seen him. "You didn't tell me that you would bring home a fellow fan."

"I saw the flag in the garage," Cameron says.

I didn't know he was a Broncos fan, but I smile because that's one of the few ways to get my dad talking.

"Yes, Cameron, you can date my daughter," Dad says. "Although she's a grown woman and can make her own decisions."

"Noted," he says, serving me with a wink.

"Dinner's ready!" Mom announces.

We sit down, and I just love watching how giddy my dad

is to talk about sports with another man, when he spent his life surrounded by women. Even the dogs were female.

The dinner goes perfectly. We pass the dishes, and Raegan and Henry do their usual schtick, full of inside jokes back and forth, making each other laugh about innocuous things. Cameron's hand rests on my thigh as he smiles and laughs, fitting in with my family like he's been coming here for years.

"Are you having a good time?" I ask after everyone disperses and I've cleared the table.

"A blast. You have a great family," he says, kissing me on the cheek. "We'll have to talk about your crush on me in high school, though."

I don't know why I feel like I could explode with mortification at that when his head was between my thighs two hours ago.

"I have another secret I didn't tell you," he says. "I had a crush on you, too."

My mouth falls open. Me, braces-wearing, gangly, flat-chested teenage me?

"It's true," Cameron says. "I was so turned on, all the time, when you tutored me. I almost kissed you once."

I say nothing, in shock, and Cameron grabs me in a hug. "Did I just blow your mind?"

"A little," I say.

"It was when I told you I passed my test. I'm not sure if you noticed."

I play-slap him on the chest. "I thought that was all in my head. Really?"

He nods. "You believed in me when not a lot of people thought I could. People believed in me with sports and girls and stuff, but school wasn't ever for me. My mom kissed the paper when I showed her I got a C."

It was so long ago, but the look of pride on Cameron's face is scarred in my memories, how happy and relieved it made him that he could pass a test by such a high margin. Math didn't come easily to him. It wasn't his fault it didn't make sense.

"I just never forgot that. I kick myself all the time I didn't stay in touch more when we were seniors. Especially lately," he says, wrapping his arm around my shoulders. "I always wondered who the lucky guy was who would end up with you. It's kind of miraculous it might be me."

That turns me into a pile of feelings.

After we say goodbye to my family, Cameron grabs my hand as we walk to his truck. "I think that went well. Your parents like me."

"You charmed my dad, for sure," I say. He opens my door for me, and I climb in. His hand finds mine after he starts the car and pulls off of the gravel shoulder.

"He's an easy guy to like. Once he knew I was in it for the long haul with you, he relaxed."

These words create some tingles within me, enough to break a smile and make me want to scream with release. I've spent my dating life searching for what I have with Cameron.

He takes me back to the tiny home. We make love, and he falls asleep while my eyes remain wide open.

Everything feels good. Everything feels right.

Too right.

I, Annie Stewart, am not lucky. There's no way I can charm Goldheart's resident fuckboy into a committed relationship. Before I drift off into sleep, I examine it from every angle. Something is bound to go wrong. There's no way I can get everything I've ever wanted with the most unlikeliness of unlikely choices.

28

ANNIE

My uterus hates me.

I'm popping some ibuprofen when I hear a knock at the door.

Opening the door, I have a heating pad clamped to my pelvis, wearing my rattiest but most comfortable sweatpants.

"I asked my sister," he says, presenting me with a pizza from Booker's Pizza and patting a huge tote over his arm. "I also have chocolate, ice cream, and more wine."

The hormones make me want to cry.

The pizza smells phenomenal. Cheese, grease, pepperoni definitely. I crack the lid, and my mouth waters.

"You might break up with me since you're about to see me eat an amount of pizza that's unladylike," I say.

"I might propose on the spot if I'm impressed," he jokes. That makes me freeze.

"It's a joke," Cameron says, kissing me as he heads to my kitchen to get plates out.

"I know," I say, smiling. I'm not sure what I'm feeling besides a dull ache in my lower back.

Cameron grabs two wine glasses from my cupboard. "Let me pour this wine, and you can start mainlining pizza."

"Perfect," I say. I take the box over to my coffee table and flip it open. When you're on your period, anything goes.

"This is so sweet," I say, a sob leaving my throat. "You are the sweetest."

"What is happening?" Cameron asks, alarmed, walking toward me with an outstretched glass of red.

"Hormones," I say. I pull it together to take my first bite of pizza, and I'm ready to cry again.

"Tell me about it. My sister yells at me every month."

"Just wait until Olive is old enough. They'll sync."

"What?" Cameron asks. "You all sync?"

"Like witches under a blood moon," I say. "Thank you for this. You are so thoughtful."

"I didn't used to be this way," Cameron says. "I'm growing up. Changing."

"At thirty-four."

"At thirty-four," he repeats. He looks at the half of slice in my hand. "You're slow to start."

"I'm savoring it," I say. After I set down the wine glass, I readjust on the heating pad, resting my socked feet on the coffee table. "I think my uterus hates me for not giving it an embryo."

Cameron pauses, with the pizza inches from his mouth, resting the wine glass on his knee. "When would you want to have kids?"

The thought of having kids with Cameron, marrying Cameron. Wow, it's quick. We've only been dating for a few weeks. I didn't start talking about marriage or kids with my boyfriends until we were almost a year in, and it was always casual.

This feels serious.

This question seems like it should come far in the future. Although I want to be a mom with my full being, sooner rather than later, this all seems too quick. I need to plan, to strategize.

We need to figure out so many things. I just don't think we're ready yet, for marriage or for kids.

"Kids are a big step," I say. "When I turn thirty-five, I will be considered a geriatric pregnancy, so ideally in the next couple years."

He nods once. "We can have fun practicing then."

"Definitely." I finish my piece of pizza, and I lay my head on his shoulder. He takes his non-pizza-holding hand and brushes my hair away from my face.

"This feels nice," I say.

"I agree," he replies, kissing me on the head. It's one of my favorite things he does.

"This is perfect for now," I say.

"I love you," he says quickly.

I lift my head. "What?"

"I know, I know," he says. "It's quick. I just needed you to know. I love you."

"Wow," I say, taking a sip of wine. My throat constricts, and I cough. "I did not expect that."

"So..." he says, scooting closer.

Only two men besides my dad have told me they loved me. My college boyfriend Christian and Jason. Both times felt like over-the-top glitter and rainbows, a Broadway musical in my stomach and my heart.

Those other guys didn't show me they loved me. Cameron does.

The mint chocolate chip ice cream is proof.

I know I love him. I also know we have a ways to go before I can confidently say I will love him forever. Too many things have happened to me that I have to be cautious and guard my heart. Only time will tell if Cameron and I are meant for forever.

However, I can't help it. I've fallen in love with Cameron Finch. He deserves to know. I lean forward so our noses touch.

"I love you, too."

He kisses me so hard, I fall back with my piece of pizza hoisted in the air. Thank God I wasn't holding my wine.

"Pizza saved!" Cameron says, kissing my greasy lips. He pulls me up by the elbow, and I take a bite as I sit up.

He points to the pizza box. "Show me what you're made of."

29

CAMERON

I'm hunched over my sister's coffee table when she rounds the corner. She jumps back, startled, and I lift my head with a smile.

I've been up for two hours, and I've lost count of the cups of coffee I've had.

"Hi," Emily says, walking around me carefully like I'm a rabid raccoon.

"The coffee is fresh," I say. "I just brewed another pot."

"How much coffee have you had? How long have you been up?"

"Since five." I point to the laptop and then at the binder. "The event is this week."

"I know that, but..." Emily is still unsure as she looks down at the coffee mug I set down. I pulled her favorite *Friends* mug and already prepped her two sugars with a little creamer.

"I've almost gotten through my to-do list today. I've prepped the reminder email to the attendees, I'm going through some last-minute projections, and I just finalized the playlist. There are some jams!" I say. I hold my phone up. "Listen!"

"Gangsta's Paradise" by Coolio begins playing. Olive turns the corner, and Emily motions for me to turn it off.

I hold it higher in the air and sway my arms.

"Uncle Cam, what is that?"

"Only a classic," I say. I rap along with the song from memory. Olive giggles while Emily rolls her eyes, just giving in.

Emily takes her first sip of coffee and looks down.

"It's a special oat milk vanilla creamer Annie turned me on to," I say. "It's delicious, right?"

"You've been seeing a lot of Annie recently, huh?" Emily asks.

"Yep," I say. I can't help it; I smile, and Olive gets in my face.

"Are you in love, Uncle Cam?"

I swear Emily leans in to hear. "What if I was?" I ask, switching off the song.

"Then you would have hearts in your eyes."

"What else, Martini?"

"And ask her to marry you."

"Let's not get ahead of ourselves, sweetie," Emily says. "Uncle Cam just got his first girlfriend."

"It's time for you to get married. You're getting old," Olive says.

Emily and I crack up, while Olive looks back and forth, unsure why we're laughing.

"You may have a point, Martini," I say, shaking my phone at her. "This song is older than you are."

"Olive, go get dressed for school. We're leaving in twenty minutes. I'll let you have a running-late muffin if you hurry."

Olive says nothing as she clomps off to her room.

"A running-late muffin, huh?" I say. A running-late muffin are these chocolate-chocolate chip muffins my sister saves for when we're late. Olive found them once when she was five and ate three before we found her, covered head to toe in chocolate. Now they're hidden above the fridge.

"It's so I could get rid of her," Emily says, looking down at her coffee. "What has gotten into you? You're up early to work, you're making the coffee, you're actually dressed and ready to go."

"What, you don't like that I'm finally taking the job seriously?"

"It's great, it's just...surprising is all," Emily says. "It's like you've changed."

"I have," I say. I've been proud of myself the last few weeks. Ever since Annie and I got involved, I now give a shit about things. I never was interested in the success of the brewery—I just wanted to serve beer. Now, I want this event to be great, and for my family and Annie to be proud of me.

"Are you getting serious with her?" Emily asks.

I nod, breathing in and out. "I think I want to marry her."

Emily sits down, her eyes large. "Wow."

"I was thinking about asking her," I say.

The flash of inspiration happened last weekend. Annie and I had breakfast together at Moe's and made love before she left for her Saturday event. When I let her go and went to the brewery for my shift, it hit me like a wrecking ball.

I wanted to marry her. I wanted to have babies with her. I never wanted her to leave me. I wanted forever to start as soon as possible.

On my lunch break, I went into a jewelry store five minutes before it closed and put a deposit down on a ring. I'm going to drop down on one knee at the prom.

I've always trusted my gut. My gut says this woman is it for me.

"You just started dating, Cam," Emily says, resting her hand on my forearm. "Ease into it. Get used to being each other."

"Didn't you say that you were going to marry Olive's father after a week?"

"Well, look how well that turned out," Emily says.

Olive's father spent a week at the lake with his family and met Emily by chance at the snack bar. I met him once, and he seemed to be really into her.

Until he left her pregnant and alone and disappeared off the face of the earth.

"Annie and I are perfect for each other," I say. "It's none of your business when we decide to make it official."

"I know that," Emily says, wrapping her arm around my shoulders. "I just know you like to rush into things without thinking them through."

"I've thought it through," I insist. "I'm a grown man. I can make my own decisions."

"If you're there, just make sure she's right there with you," Emily says, rubbing my hair, making it spring up higher than usual.

"Thanks, Em," I say. She stands up, sipping her coffee. "Do you have any songs you want added?"

"Just make sure you have 'Wonderwall' on there."

I scroll through. "Done."

A FEW DAYS LATER, I arrive home with a bag holding a very important piece of jewelry. Emily took Olive to dance tonight, and Annie is working late so she can go to the prom with me tomorrow.

After grabbing a beer from my sister's fridge, I sit down at the patio table and prop my feet up. I pull out the black velvet box in my pocket, just to stare at the ring. I picked out a gold band with a ruby in the middle, with two diamonds flanking the main stone. I spend a few minutes staring at it, picturing it on Annie's finger. A symbol that she will be mine forever.

Picking up the ring makes this real, so real it's making heart thunder in my chest. This proposal signals how far we've come, how far I've come. I'm ready to take the next step in my life. With Annie.

My sister's words haunt me as I rub the metal between my fingers.

Yes, we just started dating, but we love each other. That's enough for me to know we can weather anything when we're together.

I'm lost in my thoughts until I hear a squeak next to me, and I look down to see a raccoon eating the cat food again with its tiny, creepy, black hands.

While I'm grateful to the raccoons for attacking Jason and Morgan, I kind of wished they would move on already.

Oh well, if they're going to eat the cat food, they can be my therapist, too.

"Thelma...or Louise, I'm not sure which one you are," I say. The animal looks up at me and continues to stuff its face like I do when I find a good buffet.

"Do you think I'm rushing into this?" I ask. "I mean, I'm in love with her."

The animal doesn't answer me. Disney lied to me.

"She's it for me. I don't want her to leave me, you know," I say. Another swig of beer, and then I keep going, although the raccoon is probably thinking about the leftover Wendy's it found when it tipped over in our garbage three days prior.

You have to drive to the next town over to get Wendy's so it's a delicacy.

The raccoon looks up at me like it's listening. "What do you think?"

It lets out its racoon sound. I'm not sure what it means.

"Thanks, little critter," I say. I almost extend my hand to offer a high five but decide against it. These raccoons might be family now, but I'm not trying to catch rabies.

I finish the last of my beer, and the raccoon runs away. Halfway across my sister's lawn, the raccoon looks back, like it's saying, "You got this."

That's all the sign I need to move forward and execute the plan.

"Wow," Annie says, walking into the space.

"I wanted to show you before everyone shows up," I say, squeezing her hand. After studying the few episodes of *My So-Called Life*, I think I nailed my Jordan Catalano costume. I found the perfect blue flannel at Goodwill and paired it with a white shirt and baggy jeans I kept from high school. I'm wearing a choker. My hair, usually combed back, is parted down the middle.

I may look good, but Annie is dazzling.

I attacked her when she showed up at my house, her hair a vibrant candy apple red, stark against her black outfit, accentuated by a red flannel tied around her waist. All of this ends up on my floor as I make love to her quickly, her ass on my kitchen counter as we get a quickie in before the event.

Her brick-colored lipstick stays through the whole thing, and I'm flabbergasted at the sorcery of makeup products.

Watching Annie see my work for the first time, how happy she is, makes me happy.

I plan to up the ante on how happy we can be tonight. The ring is in my pocket.

We've decorated the brewery like it's a prom from the late nineties teen movies, like *She's All That* or *10 Things I Hate About You.* Lots of balloons, sparkly glitter, a banner stating "Class of 1999" strewn over a makeshift stage where a nineties cover band will play the latter half the night. The first half will be DJ'ed by Thumper, who has strict instructions to stick to my playlist.

Annie looks around and leans into me, and I kiss the top of her head. "This is wonderful."

"We sold out," I say. "I couldn't have done this without you."

"You did it all yourself. I just gave you some direction," she says. She walks around, looking at the food spread, which includes the classics, like Bagel Bites, Dunkaroos, and the catering's version of Lunchables. She laughs at the sign I thought up, "When I Dip, You Dip, We Dip" next to the improvised Handi-Snacks spread.

I spent an embarrassing amount of time on Pinterest.

"Did I do a good job?" I ask.

"You did a great job. I know your investor will be pleased."

"He'll be here later. You'll get to meet him and his wife, Makenna."

"I look forward to it," she says. She kisses me and hugs me. "I'm so proud of you, baby."

When she pulls away, I sneak another kiss.

"I kind of like this hair," I say, smoothing it down.

"Don't get too used to it. Raegan assured me it'll come out after a few washes."

"I dig it," I say. Staring at her, I look for a sign not to drop to one knee tonight, not to ask them to play "Crash into Me," not to ask the love of my life to marry me.

My stare makes her laugh nervously.

"What?" she asks.

"Nothing," I say, kissing her forehead.

I hope she says yes.

30

ANNIE

Cameron is acting strangely, and I don't know why.

He's been staring at me off and on. There are jitters in his voice when he speaks.

It has to be nervousness about the event going well.

The room looks great with all the perfect nineties touches. I loved all the teen movies with big proms like this, even though I was in middle school at the time. Now I'm in the middle of one, having my redo on the high school prom I never went to. It looks glittery and over-the-top and perfect.

And I have the cutest date I could ask for, even if he's acting weird.

Cameron holds my hand in a death grip as we walk around the room, welcoming people to the prom. The costumes are the best part of this event, including Thumper and his buddy Dallas dressed up in the powder blue and orange *Dumb and Dumber* suits. We walk up to a couple dressed as Richard Gere and Julia Roberts from *Pretty Woman*. The man is dressed in a double-breasted suit with a gray tie, while the woman wears Vivian's signature white and blue dress with cut-outs on the sides. Tattoos snake up her torso, and her makeup is perfect. She's one of the most stunning women I've ever seen.

She's rocking the boots, making her tower over her date. I appreciate a shorter man confident enough to be with a woman taller than him.

"Annie, I want you to meet our business partner, Dan Price, and his wife, Makenna."

"Oh my God, Angela Chase," he says, taking me in a hug. The way they described him, I expected a scary, stern tyrant.

I am so confused.

I shake Makenna's hand. It's always awesome to interact with a woman taller than me, even if it's because of her boots. Doesn't happen often.

"This party gets an A plus," Dan says, looking around. "Such a good idea. There's some strong nostalgia for the nineties, and I love that you capitalized on it."

"We sold out," Cameron says. "My family is already talking about doing one next year for Y2K."

"That would be great. I could bleach my hair again. I miss the frosted tips," Dan says.

"Baby, that didn't even look good on Justin Timberlake," Makenna says.

He pulls her to him by the waist. "You would love it," Dan says. The way he looks at her is what every little girl dreams of.

"I'm very pleased with this," Dan says, looking at Cameron. "You did a great job. Your sister sent me all the clippings of the press coverage you're getting."

"This is just the beginning," Cameron says. Dan offers a hand, and Cameron shakes it, a handshake of respect and mutual admiration.

Getting praise from Dan has always been huge for his family. It's all because of Cameron.

I'm so proud of him.

He's acting like a whole new man to the one I've known all these years. There's drive behind his eyes, and he's dedicated to something other than having fun. He has a path to follow.

Dare I say, Cameron Finch has finally grown up.

"I heard that you had something to do with this lovely event," Dan says, looking at me. "The Finches can't stop raving about your contributions."

"Cameron did all the work. I just gave him a little bit of guidance."

"I want you to come work for me," Dan says. He looks me dead in the eye. "I'm serious. Are you looking?"

"No, I..."

"Here's my card. Everyone who works for me tells me I'm the best boss they have ever had. I've been known to give out Chanel purses when I feel like it."

His wife leans forward. "It's true. He'll do Dior or Louis Vuitton, if that's more your speed."

The card feels heavy in my hands. His name is written in plain black font, but it feels elegant against the cardstock. I've worked at Banning Cellars for so long that I don't know anything else. It's gotten tenser since Jason and I broke it off and even more awkward since the night of the raccoon attack. I've done job searches in the last few weeks after a couple glasses of wine, but nothing serious.

It's like the universe is smacking me in the face.

"Thank you," I say.

"You're welcome. Think about it," Dan says. He wraps his arm around Makenna's midsection again. He points at Cameron. "I'm going to bid an ungodly amount of money to win Homecoming King. Also, Cam, please play some old school *NSync."

We decided to make Homecoming King and Queen a silent auction item, and Cam deliberately picked out a fur-substitute robe because Dan was guaranteed to bid a lot of money to get it.

"'Tearin' Up My Heart' coming right up," Cameron says.

"I see someone I know. Check you later." Dan walks away with his arm still around his wife's torso.

My mouth gapes at the interaction. Once they're out of earshot, I say, "Wow."

"I know. Dan can be a little much," Cameron says. We watch Dan dip Makenna to kiss her and almost drop her on the way back up.

I hold up the business card. "I was not expecting this."

"Dan goes off of instincts. He's a brilliant businessman. We're eternally grateful to him for everything he has done. You should call him," Cameron says. "I would work for him in a heartbeat."

As we start another perimeter lap, I tuck the card in the waistband of my bicycle shorts. We say hello to Emily and Olive, dressed as Thelma and Louise. Olive's wearing a black cutoff shirt with a skull on it and jeans while Emily is dressed in a simple white tank top tucked into jeans. I say hello to Kit and Randy Finch, Cameron's parents, who are dressed as Al and Peg Bundy from *Married...with Children.* Reid is dressed as Wayne, wearing a long brown wig, a black hat with a black T-shirt. I have to assume Jackson is Garth, but he's nowhere to be found.

"Hey, Reid," I say. I feel bad I've been slow to text him back since I started dating Cameron. I see him at Sunday dinner, but our interactions haven't been as carefree as they've been in the past.

"Hey," he says, taking me in for a hug.

"How's it going?" I heard he broke up with Callie, but he hasn't told me yet. They're so off and on that I'm not sure if it's permanent.

"I'm fine," he says with no smile or his typical happy-go-lucky nature. I can tell he's hurting.

"Something's not fine," I say. Cameron is busy talking to a guy dressed up like Zack Morris from *Saved by the Bell* so I pull Reid down the hall.

Reid looks anywhere but at me.

"I heard about Callie," I say.

He nods. "To be honest, it was over a long time ago."

"Are you okay?"

"I'll be fine." Reid's jaw clenches and he looks up. "Can I ask you a question?"

"Sure."

"Why him?" We can see Cameron from where we're standing and he raises a hand, a wave.

"Why are you asking me this?" I ask. Reid has always felt like the little brother I never had, the soft place to fall. I've never had an iota of romantic interest in him, but I always wondered if he did for me.

Reid looks down like he's thinking, a gesture he's done since we were kids. I wonder what is going through his brain.

"Never mind," he says with a smile.

My skin crawls with discomfort; I need to do something to get out of this situation.

Like another sign from the universe, my phone buzzes in my hand.

Whitney: I'm here!

I hold up my phone. "My author friend Whitney is here. You should meet her."

Reid always talks about writing a novel. While he wouldn't write romance, it might lift his spirits to speak with an author making a living from her writing. Like a coward, I walk away from the conversation to find Whitney, wearing a short brown wig, a jean jumper, and a red turtleneck, holding a mallet.

"I'm Annie Bates from *Misery*!" Whitney says. She hugs me and says, "I'm not saying you're obsessive like my character, but I felt like this costume would be hilarious."

It is. Whitney's told me about a couple of stalker readers, one who messages her every day at five a.m., reminding her to write.

"Whitney, this is my friend, Reid Finch," I say. They stare at each other without saying anything.

"Whitney Ferguson?" he asks.

"Reid 'Wannabe' Finch," Whitney says, crossing her arms.

"Do you two know each other?"

"'Know' is a strong term," Reid says. "'Blocked out mentally' is a better one."

"We were in the same creative writing class at Byron University," Whitney explains. "He called my short story 'trite' and 'predictable.'"

"And she said my short story was a Salinger-Faulkner-Steinbeck circle jerk."

"I didn't say it *out loud*," Whitney says. She pauses. "I wrote him five pages of feedback."

"Okay, calm down," I say, holding my arms out, like I'm a hockey referee. "It's been, what, how many years?"

"A person never forgets their first nasty review," Whitney says.

"Well, I've forgotten all about you." Reid crosses his arms.

"Maybe you should avoid each other," I say. Like another sign, Emily taps on Reid's shoulder.

"Reid, we need to change a keg and I have no upper body strength so..."

"Excuse me," Reid says, smiling at me and scowling at Whitney. Whitney sticks her tongue out at Reid's back as he leaves.

"I didn't realize your friend Reid was the Reid I hate," she says. "Really, he was such an asshole in college. High and mighty about literature and the classics. I mean, who reads *Ulysses* for fun? If you're reading *Ulysses*, it's because you want people to think you're smart."

Between Reid's somber attitude, then the utter flip of a switch to hatred for Whitney, and then Whitney flustered and fired up when she's usually chill, my head is spinning.

"I need a nice walk outside," Whitney says. She holds up her mallet. "Don't worry about me. I have a weapon."

"Okay. I'm sorry about Reid, I didn't know," I say.

"It's okay. I don't waste my breath on my enemies."

Whitney walks outside, dragging her mallet.

My head spins as I walk to Cameron, now talking to a couple dressed up like *Baywatch* lifeguards. My baby is so good at this, lighting up as he welcomes residents to the brewery, inviting them to try the limited-edition beer called As If, a New England IPA brewed specifically for the event. I'm so proud to be his date, and he's hotter than Jared Leto as Jordan Catalano, which I thought was impossible.

Nirvana wafts from the speakers and the mirrorball spins, projecting shattered light onto the dance floor. Attendees swarm the dance floor, jumping around like they're in a mosh pit. I'm concerned about the half full beer in Thumper's hand as he jumps around in an orange suit.

My shoulders are still tense.

"Do you feel the nostalgia yet?" Cameron shouts to me.

"Definitely. It feels like a middle school dance in here."

"I hope you hold me closer than we did in middle school."

"Missed opportunity," I shout.

"That was baby Cameron being a fool. I only want to dance with you from now on."

"Good answer," I say. His arms circle my waist, and he pulls me closer.

I feel something hard and round in his pocket, and I look down.

"What's in your pocket?" I ask.

"Nothing!" he blurts out. He looks over my head at someone and waves. "Excuse me."

He plants a kiss on my lips and walks past me.

I'm so confused. Again.

A tap on my shoulder makes me turn around. It's Tara, dressed in a baby doll dress with a choker and chunky platforms.

"Hey girl," I say, hugging her. We had a coffee date and realized we have lots of things in common. Tara is a great person. She apologized again, and I forgave her. I look past Tara, but no man is sticking close to her. "Did you bring a date?"

Tara shakes her head. "I'm perfectly happy being single right now. I need to get my head right."

"Thumper is still single."

Tara grimaces. "No thank you. Thumper is a man-baby."

Thumper walks toward us like he's been summoned. "Hello, ladies."

"Hey, Eugene," Tara says, using Thumper's real name.

He stops and cast his eyes down at her like a disapproving middle school teacher. "Excuse me?"

"You heard me," she says, laughing behind her fingers.

"I'll pretend like you didn't call me that," he says, throwing up his palm. "Talk to the hand."

We both laugh at the nineties phrase we haven't heard in forever.

"So, *Dumb and Dumber,* huh?" I ask.

"I've been waiting for this moment my whole life," he says, straightening his jacket.

"I love it," I say while Tara grumbles.

"I see your man is shaking hands and kissing babies," Thumper says. We turn to see Cameron scooping up Olive and dancing with her around the dance floor to "Hold On" by Wilson Phillips. The little girl giggles a high pitch as he swings her around, her long legs flopping one direction and another.

"This is so cute," Tara comments.

Sure is. I have visions of having children with Cameron. Marrying Cameron. Every day that passes, the vision gets stronger, more possible as our lives mix together. Seeing him with Olive always warms my heart, but today it's practically exploding my ovaries.

We have a long way to go before that. Cameron and I still need to learn how to communicate, which became clear to me the night of the raccoon attack. While my sister fell into an easy relationship with Henry and got engaged three months later, I don't see the same trajectory for us.

Cameron may have said "I love you," but he hasn't even called me his girlfriend yet.

We're on our own timeline, and I'm perfectly fine with that.

"Free Your Mind" by En Vogue begins, and Tara jumps up and down.

"Please dance with me," she says, pulling me onto the

dance floor. I begrudgingly go, shaking my hips and throwing my arms up in the air. Tara spins, slapping her fanny pack, making me double over in laughter.

Turning, I see Cameron, holding up one of his family's beers, a deep smile across his face. He raises his beer in a cheers, and I wave.

Everything is perfect, just the way it is.

When we leave the dance floor three songs later, sweat is dripping off my chin. Every song that came on brought me back to nights in my room, taping songs off of the radio on my pink boombox. I remember all the CDs and tapes I had and how easy it was back then, before I had to grow up and date and have an adult job.

"You looked like you were having fun out there," Cameron comments as he hands me a glass of water.

I take a gulp. "Yes. This playlist is all that and a bag of chips."

"Wow," Cameron says.

"I'm going back to the nineties and never coming back. I don't like the twenties. It is not the roarin' twenties, like the first time."

"No shit," Cameron says. "Come with me."

He takes my hand, and we walk to the middle of the dance floor, dodging flannel and platform heels. As the previous song ends, he nods to Thumper who's in charge of the music until the band gets here, and he nods back.

What is going on?

"Crash into Me" by Dave Matthews Band begins. I slap my heart with my hand and purse out my bottom lip. Cameron takes me in his arms, and we begin swaying. "Oh," I coo as he pulls me tighter.

"I think I knew that night," he whispers in my ear.

"What?"

"That you were meant for me," he says. "I love you."

My chest still swells when he says the L word.

"I love you, too," I say.

He squeezes me, and when he pulls back, he leans in and kisses me. This time it's real, not our fake staged kiss at Jason's engagement party. Now, I get to kiss him whenever I want, and it feels like the first time, every time.

The dance floor clears, as we stay in one spot, barely turning, barely swaying.

I love this man. I cannot wait for our future of getting to know each other, growing with each other, and Cameron one day dropping to his knee to propose to me.

I didn't expect he would do it fifteen seconds later.

31

CAMERON

I should've grabbed the ring box *before* I dropped to one knee.

My hands shakes as I wrestle it out of my pocket, all while holding Annie's hand and every guest watching me.

I should've practiced.

After awkwardly retrieving it from my pocket, I open it in front of Annie, who jumps back and covers her mouth with both hands.

The party quiets, with a lady directly behind me gasping so loud, it makes me flinch.

"Anne Jane Stewart, please make me the happiest man and agree to be my wife," I say, holding up the ring.

I hope she likes it.

She looks down at me in shock. Something is wrong.

My knee aches against the concrete of the floor as I look up at her.

Please say yes. Even if the answer is no, say yes and we can discuss it later.

"Cameron, I..." Annie says, looking down at me and at the box in my hand. Does she not like the ring?

"I thought this was a good ring, but if you want something else..."

"Cameron, can I talk to you? Privately?" she asks. Annie pulls me up from my kneel, and her arm wraps around my waist.

This is not good. Not good at all.

I look around, holding up hands. "I do this all the time. Joke like this. Don't mind us," I say to the crowd with a smile. I see pity in their eyes as we walk hand-in-hand toward the exit, past my brothers shaking their heads and Olive whispering something in Emily's ear.

The cold air hits me, and I untie the flannel from my waist to put on, crossing my arms to keep myself warm. Annie sits down at a picnic bench in our outdoor area, a couple smokers at the edge of the space.

"Annie, I..." I say, pacing, too uncomfortable to sit down.

She looks down at her hands set on the picnic table. Her shoulders shake and I want to take her in my arms.

When she looks up at me, I see the regret in her eyes and I know I can't.

Fucking shit to hell.

"Cameron, I love you..." she starts. My eyes close as I wait for the gut punch of words. Her voice is small as she says, "We're not ready. There's so many things we need to talk about."

"Like what?" I say. The words tumble out faster than I can prepare for them. "We can figure everything out when we get married. I'm in this forever with you. We can take on whatever happens. I'm sure of it. I've never been surer of anything in my life."

She lets out a shaky breath. "This has been a really weird night. I'm not saying no, but…"

I don't hear the rest of her words. Stabbing me in the heart with a dull blade would've hurt less than this. I sit down opposite her, even if my nervous energy supercharges my veins.

"What do you need to say yes?" I ask.

"Time," she says. Her lips part as she looks at me. Tears stick to her bottom lashes. This is really not good.

She tries to grab my hands, but I rip mine away. The wind whips through my flannel. Turning around, I look at her, with a hand on my heart.

"I'll give you that," I say coolly.

I walk away before I say something I regret. Something childish, from a place of anger, something Old Cameron would say.

The ring box feels like a boulder in my pants pocket as I walk away, leaving the love of my life on a picnic bench. My heart breaks with the distance growing between us.

If time and space are what she needs, I'll give it to her. It was definitely not the right time to propose to her, that's for sure.

Cameron Finch, failing again.

I'm a different man to the guy who found her crying into ice cream that day at the Swift, but I'm still me. A good time, but not someone serious, or someone that a woman like Annie Stewart can be serious about.

Since my failed proposal, the party is picking up as "This is How We Do It" by Montell Jordan plays. The band sets up behind Thumper as he sways his arms with the crowd. Thumper has been watching the playlist off and on the whole night, and he's standing behind the phone dock. When he sees me, he mouths, *Did she say yes?*

I shake my head.

Thumper's eyes widen as he presses a button, and Toni Braxton's "Un-break My Heart" begins playing.

I flip him off, and Thumper doubles over in laughter. Then, he lifts his hands and scampers off the stage, like the coward he is. It looks like that's his last song before the band starts.

I feel a tug on my flannel.

"Uncle Cam, I've been looking for you everywhere," Olive says. "I want to dance."

"To this song?" I ask.

"Yes," she says, tucking her tiny hand into mine.

I wonder who put her up to this.

She pulls me out into the dance floor. Dozens of pairs of eyes stare at me, wondering what happened when we went outside. I've spent the majority of my life being talked about, so the attention is nothing new. Let them watch. Everyone already knows I failed anyway.

My niece asked me to dance, so I'll dance.

I pick her up although she's getting big. She holds my hand out like *Sleeping Beauty,* and I make it dramatic, doing large sweeps back and forth.

"Uncle Cam, are you sad?"

"Me? Why would I be sad?"

"Annie's not here anymore," she says. She looks at the exit.

"Yes," I say.

"What happened?" she asks, her brows knitted in confusion.

I consider not telling her. She is a kid, after all. However, her big green eyes look at me, the same ones as her momma. I could never lie to Emily, so I could never lie to her daughter.

Olive is the love of my life, too.

It's important for her to know that dreams don't work out exactly the way you want.

"Well, I asked Annie to marry me, and she didn't say yes."

"Just ask again," Olive says. "I'm sure she'll say yes if you ask again."

"I don't know about that."

"Well, I love you, Uncle Cam," she says as she wraps her arms around my neck and pulls me close. A hug from my niece is the actual best.

"I love you, too, Martini. This is helping."

"Did she tell you to leave her alone?"

"Kinda."

"Uncle Cam?" she asks, her voice tiny.

"Yes?"

"I think you should keep trying. Like you tell me with ballet. Never give up because I love it. If you love Annie, you shouldn't give up."

Fuck, I did say that. Nothing like kids throwing your advice back in your face.

I lean in so our noses are inches apart.

"Did your mother tell you tell me that?"

Olive shakes her head with a goofy smile.

She's my dance partner for the rest of the evening, but I keep checking the entrance to see if Annie will walk back through the door.

She doesn't.

32

ANNIE

My eyelids are sore this morning.

I tried my best to mask the redness and puffiness, but I look like I've been crying all night.

Because I have.

Images of Cameron on one knee, everything I ever dreamed of, and I couldn't say yes.

In my heart, I'm in love with him. I see a future with him.

Still, I couldn't say yes.

The look in his eyes kept me up all night. I crushed him. I broke his heart.

I found Whitney and her mallet in the parking lot. We drove back to my house, stopping first at the gas station for cheap whiskey and candy. We both cried as we drank whiskey and ate Sour Patch Kids (not a great combo) and fell asleep to Dorinda yelling on *The Real Housewives*.

After a brunch with more crying and mimosas, I hugged Whitney, who planned to write at Gold Roast before heading home to Reno.

As I went through my usual Sunday chores, I went over every part of my relationship with Cameron. I just wish he would've talked to me about this before it happened. He would know my thoughts on our relationship, that an engagement was possible one day, but not right now. And I wish he hadn't done it in front of the entire prom, their eyes boring into us, their collective held breath that turned to pity and shared mortification.

It made me cringe for Cameron. The overall night was odd and cursed, even though the event itself was a smashing success.

I have a meeting with a potential client at eight-thirty this morning, so I need to pull myself together. My hair is still cherry red; a shower only made the dye patchy and fade. I try to make my drive to the winery as normal as possible, finishing a true crime podcast about a double homicide in Florida that was insane. A wife killed her husband and his lover, removing the husband's heart and kept it in the freezer because he had been cheating on her.

Lost in my own thoughts, I barely register Jason as I walk to my office.

I jump and grab my chest when I see him standing in my office door frame.

"Hi, Jason," I say, dropping my purse down on the desk.

"Good morning," he says. He meanders in and fiddles with the framed photo of my sister with Henry and me when I visited her in San Francisco.

"What do you want, Jason?" I ask. It's funny how I used to melt when he visited me.

Now he's just annoying.

"I heard Cameron proposed to you and you said no."

I am not in the mood for this. I sit down, taking a long

drag of my coffee from Gold Roast, as I turn on my computer.

Looking up, I said, "From now on, I think we should be professional and only discuss business."

"Come on, Annie, I thought we were friends."

Closing my eyes, I exhale a deep breath. I rub my temples.

"We were never friends," I whisper, leaning forward, logging into the system.

"We weren't?" His voice raises. I'm a nanosecond from kicking him out.

"No, we weren't."

Jason slaps the back of one of my visitor chairs. "Oh, I'm sorry for caring about you and wanting to be a good friend. I always tried to be a good friend to you."

That's it.

I've bitten my tongue. I've sobbed and agonized over this man. He doesn't get it.

It's about time he gets it.

I stand up and look him square in the eye. "Jason, we weren't friends because I was in love with you. You fucked me over when you hid me for over a year because you said you were afraid. A friend wouldn't do that. If that's your defi-nition of being a friend, you're a really shitty one."

"Wow," Jason says. "I've never heard you curse." He immediately looks to the floor and shoves his hands in his pockets. When he looks up, I see some moisture in the corner of his eye. Alligator tears. This man doesn't care. He just wants to have control over me. The second I started being happy without him, he became interested again.

"I broke up with Morgan. For good this time. I don't know what I was thinking. I should've picked you."

I'm not sure if he knows what happened at the prom, but his timing is suspicious.

He rounds the corner and reaches for my hand, but I back away. I hold up a finger.

"Watch yourself," I say.

Jason freezes in place. He knows his family needs me. Our events account for thirty-two percent of our revenue, and I'm the reason. This winery would not be popular without the word-of-mouth referrals, the beautiful events that create more business because a guest sees what I can do.

"Annie, please don't be like this," he says, his hands up in a "don't shoot" pose.

I place my hand on my chest. "I have no idea what I saw in you."

"Really?" Jason says. "You pick Cameron Finch? A guy suckling off of his family's business? A guy who lives with his sister? A guy who doesn't even consult with you before proposing to you?"

"Cameron Finch is twice the man you are," I say. "You dangled commitment over my head for a year, and I *fell* for it! Also, who do you work for? Who pays the mortgage on your house?" Every little thing I've ever noticed about him spits out of me like poison. He has ridden on the coattails of Banning Cellars for years, doing the same goddamn thing as Cameron, only hiding it, keeping up appearances, lying up and down about his contributions. Lying about me.

I see Jason for who he is now. He's an arrogant, self-entitled prick who I let rule me for far too long. I was blind to it because I was so in love with him. Now, I'm repulsed by the sight of him.

Jason has not moved from behind my desk, and he has about three seconds before I slap him.

"Get out of my fucking office. Now," I tell him, the tears behind my eyes threatening to break free. Jason walks to the door and turns around, his hand flat on the wall.

"I think you should be respectful of who you're talking to. You work for us."

Between Cameron and the party and now Jason openly threatening me, my thoughts are jumbled and I can't think straight.

I look in the mirror attached to my monitor, tighten my ponytail, and walk myself into Jason's father's office. My boss.

The door is ajar so I see him at his desk. Theo Banning ushers me in with the crook of his fingers. My boss is an older version of Jason, with thinning hair and a protruding belly, but a way better personality. I respect Theo greatly since he gave me my first job out of college and we've grown close over the years. At one point, I hoped to have him as a father-in-law and feel less like an outsider here at Banning Cellars. Now, his son is making my employment at his winery a living nightmare.

Over the year and a half Jason and I were seeing each other, I'd dreamt of telling Theo. I wondered whether he would be happy or disappointed that his son was dating me. Now, I need to get him involved. For my sanity. For my self-worth.

"Theo, can I talk to you for a second?"

"Of course, Annie. I see we have the eight-thirty for the fiftieth wedding anniversary."

"Yes, I've pulled some ideas for them, and I think they'll be pretty excited."

"What did you want to talk about?" he asks.

He motions for me to sit down. I sit down across from him and he focuses on me, lacing his fingers together like a baseball mitt.

"Theo, I wanted you know that Jason and I were seeing each other for a little bit, but we're not seeing each other anymore," I say.

"Oh," he says. His gaze focuses on his desk. "Why didn't you tell me?"

Your son didn't want to.

"Jason wanted to see if it developed into something serious."

"I assume it wasn't if you are not together anymore."

"I thought it was."

Maybe I was never in love with him. Maybe the thrill of the relationship was just instability and anxiety from the secrecy and the manipulation.

My relationship with Jason was fake. What I had with Cameron was real.

"Did Morgan break you two up?" Theo asks.

I shake my head. Whether or not we overlap is a mystery I don't necessarily want answered. "I wanted you to know so there's full transparency between us."

"I appreciate you coming to me," Theo says as he takes his glasses off to rub the bridge of his nose.

I relax in my chair. *This is going well.*

"The real reason I'm here is it's getting increasingly difficult to work here because of Jason," I say.

Theo closes his eyes, like my truth is too bright. He touches his pressed-together pointer fingers to his lips. I remind myself to breathe while the silence hangs uncomfortably in the air. "I really value your work here, Annie. You're a great event planner for us. But..."

I close my eyes and wait for the blow.

"If there's a conflict between you two about breaking up, it puts me in a precarious spot. I hope you know that."

I nod, knowing where this is going.

"Jason is my son. I know he made some promises he might not have kept or was honest about, but my number one priority is this business. I worked hard to build this, and I can't let it crumble because of drama between my son and a disgruntled ex-girlfriend."

I want to cry, but I swallow the hard lump down. At the end of the day, this is a family business, and I'm an outsider.

I've always been one.

Twelve years of my life dedicating myself to a business, a vision I believed in, and at the first criticism, they insinuate they can't handle my feelings and real concerns about working for Banning Cellars.

I should've seen this coming from a mile away.

"I want this to be a peaceful workplace," he says. "If you don't think you can work with Jason, I suggest you seek other employment. I will keep you on as long as there's no drama."

"I understand, sir," I say, standing up to leave.

"You should get going. Your first appointment of the day is soon."

I stand on shaky legs, turning to the door. I stop before I turn back.

Dan's business card sits on my bureau, and I've looked at it constantly since Saturday. I didn't know why, but I know now.

I've reached a breaking point with Banning Cellars. Maybe I reached it the second Jason broke up with me.

"Mr. Banning, I'm done."

"What?" he asks, his eyes barely leaving his computer screen.

"Sir, I'm done working here. I appreciate the twelve years. However, I can't work with your son another second," I say. "My resignation is effective now."

"What about the Brewers?" he asks, referencing the couple coming in for their consultation.

"You will have to attend that meeting. I'm sorry," I say.

I leave before he can object.

A giant metal bar lifts from my shoulders as I walk back to my office, put my purse on my shoulder, and leave. The sun looks different in the sky, brighter, bursting with hope.

Holy cow, I just quit my job. I quit my job.

There's only one person I want to tell.

Cameron.

I texted him this morning to say good morning with no return text. It shows it was delivered, but that means nothing.

It's time to go over there and tell him we need to talk about this. I asked for time in the relationship, not space.

He can't run away from me just because I said not now.

Woody Finch Brewery is dark, and I see the chairs upside down on the tables. Usually, someone is there by nine, so I cup my hands to look through the tinted doors.

The taproom has returned to its usual purpose, not a prom. Still. I zero in on the spot Cameron proposed to me, and my heart hurts.

I should've explained myself better.

I didn't, though, and now Cameron is not returning my calls.

A figure buzzes through the taproom, and I bang and holler before the person opens the door.

"Annie," Emily says, her mouth stretched in surprise.

"Hey," I say. "Is Cameron here?"

Emily shakes her head. "He went out of town. With Thumper."

"Oh," I say, hands on my hips. "How is he?"

"Sad," Emily says.

My heart drops. I did that. I tighten my ponytail.

"It's none of my business, but if he would've told me what he was seriously planning, I would've tried to talk him out of it," Emily says. "He wouldn't have listened to me, though. He loves you."

"I should've said more. I should've explained myself..."

"Stop it, it's my brother's fault," Emily says. "Come here. You need a hug."

Emily envelops me, and I smell citrus, crisp and fresh.

"I quit my job," I say in her ear.

She pushes me away. "Holy shit. Was it planned?"

"No," I say. "I was seeing Jason Banning."

She nods once. "I had my suspicions."

"You knew?"

"Oh yeah. The whole town knew," Emily says. "Miriam Oliver saw you once."

"Of course Miriam did," I say.

Emily touches my arm. "Hey, if my brother doesn't call you when he gets back, you let me know, and I'll drag his ass over to your house so you can talk." She pauses for a moment. "I didn't think Cameron would ever get married. Until he met you."

A tear drops from my eye. "Thank you."

I hope Cameron talks to me soon. Before I make a pact with the raccoons to deliver him to me.

33

CAMERON

My vision is blurry when Thumper shoves another tumbler of tequila into my hand.

"Thumper, I don't know," I slur as I wobble on my feet, standing at a high top at the Swift.

"Trust me, you need it. I can't believe you cried in my car," he says, shaking his head. "I can forgive the fucking in my car. But crying. Nope."

"I'm sad, okay?" I say, taking a sip of my new drink. It tastes like water, which is a bad, bad sign.

"You don't have a right to be sad. We had a great camping trip, and now we're home at our favorite place."

I sniff back any emotion I have. *I will not cry like Pete in this bar.*

Pete isn't here tonight, and I can't become the Swift's resident crier.

It has been five days since I dropped to one knee and Annie rejected me. Even though she's texted me and called me and Emily said she stopped by the brewery, I can't face her.

I'm not a good man. Annie turning me down reminded

me of that. For a second, I thought I was the man I always wanted to be—committed, loved by a good woman.

It was all a lie.

Now I'm getting shit-faced with my best friend, and it just feels lonely.

"Well, hello," Thumper croons as two leggy brunettes approach us, both holding a bright pink drink.

"Hello, yourself," the one wearing bright lipstick says. "I'm Carrie. This is my friend, Stacey."

"Hi." Stacey flutters her fingers at us.

"My name is Eugene, and this is my friend, Cameron," Thumper says, using his given name. He got his nickname after a drunken night in high school and it stuck.

Through my half-closed eyes, I can admire the women. They are beautiful, and with the way they approached us, they might be in the mood for a good time. I know I will be asleep before my belt is unbuckled.

My heart is also twisting itself into knots every day over Annie, so there's that, too.

"Cameron just got his heart smashed," Thumper says, pointing to me. "But I'm *not* brokenhearted, ladies."

"It was not a breakup!" I yell. "She needs time!"

One of the brunettes, stuck in a half-snuggle with Thumper, looks at me with pity. My head pounds. I want to crawl under this pub table and fall asleep.

"Is he okay?" I hear as I float off and everything goes black.

I WAKE up in my tiny home, tucked in with a puke bucket next to me.

"Oh my God," I say, sitting up, nearly missing the ceiling in my loft. How the fuck did I get up the stairs to the loft last night? The last I remember is two women approaching us and I think I put my head down for a nap.

I hear snoring. Rubbing my eyes, I descend my stairs to see Thumper, sprawled out across my couch. His mouth stretches as he makes sounds from the back of his throat that sound like a freight train.

He didn't even take his shoes off. I nudge his boot.

"Wake up," I say. Thumper shakes his head as his eyes open. When he looks at me, he smacks his lips.

"Good morning," he says, stretching his long arms over his head.

"What happened last night?"

"You passed out at the Swift is what happened," he says, sitting up.

"How did I get home?"

"Carl and I dragged your tall ass out of the bar. Carl got the legs, and I got the armpits. You slept in the bed of my truck. When I got here, you were curled on your side and crying. I figured I'd be a good friend and make sure you didn't choke on your own vomit. My neighbor still has my dog."

I rub my face with my hands. I do not remember that.

"Your sister stopped by. I've never seen her so mad," Thumper says. "I mean, I deserved it since I gave you the tequila..."

"Can you stop talking?" I ask, since my head pounds and his voice is like a dagger in my skull.

"You asked," Thumper says. "You look like you need food. You're buying."

I look down, and I'm wearing the same thing from last night. After sniffing my armpits, I say, "I need a shower."

"I agree. You look like Pete. No one wants to look like Pete."

"I know."

"I'll go chase the raccoons outside while you do that."

Showering and shaving makes me feel marginally better. My chest still feels like a heart surgeon cracked open my ribs.

When I come outside, Thumper has shrunk three inches because my sister is standing next to him.

She's fuming.

"Hey, Emily," I say.

"You. Inside," she says, pointing to my tiny home. I turn back and she follows, yelling back, "Thumper, you stay there!"

"Yes, ma'am." Thumper may have a death wish, but he knows not to mess with my sister when she's pissed off.

"Where were you?"

"I went camping with Thumper," I say.

"You left your *girlfriend* and me worried about you."

"I'm sorry," I say. My head pounds so I rub my forehead and my hair. I sit down on my couch so I can rest my forehead in my hands. "I'm a total piece of shit."

"You're not a piece of shit, you just did a piece-of-shit thing," Emily says. Her tightly crossed arms loosen. "You took two steps forward and three back."

She sits down next to me on my couch and wraps her arm around me. "How are you holding up?"

"It hurts so bad, Em," I say. I sniffle and swallow the emotion down deep, where no one can find it.

"Are you two over?"

"We might as well be."

Emily lets out a deep sigh.

"What?" I ask. I brace myself since Emily is about to tell me something true I don't want to hear.

"Cameron, did you know if she wanted to marry you or not?"

"I figured... I love her, Em. She said she loved me. It's not enough."

Emily breathes in and out again, louder this time.

"What?

"She doesn't seem like the type who would know in three months or a week. I just think she needs more time." Emily slaps me hard on the thigh to make her point. It stings but it doesn't hurt as badly as my heart or head. Emily may be the youngest, but she's the wisest out of all of us. Maybe it was being a single parent at twenty or having a successful jewelry business and buying the property we live on. I've always been the fuckup sibling, the problem child. No matter how I try to change, my identity in this town is unchanging.

That's why Emily's words feel like a painful jolt to my stomach.

"I say this with love, Cameron, but you have a pattern. Things get hard, and you quit."

"Nothing has been easy for me, Emily. I wasn't the perfect student, and I sure as hell didn't go to USC."

Emily pauses. I know that was a low blow. Emily dropped out her senior year because she got pregnant with Olive.

She keeps talking about going back, but it's too hard now with Olive and the brewery.

"You don't need to be a dick, Cameron," she says. She's never called me a name. Ever.

"I deserved that," I say. The dull ache in my temple is now screaming. "God, it was so embarrassing. I used to pity the bastards at baseball games who proposed on the jumbotron, and now I'm one of them."

"Maybe don't propose in public next time."

"I don't know if there will be a next time," I say, rubbing my chest. "Man, I didn't expect this to feel like my ribcage is splitting open."

"What?" Emily asks.

"My heart. Being broken."

Emily nods, and she looks down at her hands. It's been over eight years since Olive's dad, and it's still raw for her.

I hope I can survive Annie. I'm not sure if I can.

"Come here," I say, standing up.

She stands up, and I pull her into me.

"Do you and Olive want to come to breakfast with us? I'm buying."

"We already ate, but thank you," Emily says. She walks to the door and looks back. "You deserve love, Cam. And love can be hard. But you need to fight for her. Even if you're embarrassed. Be the guy I know you can be."

Her words linger like smoke.

Thumper and I end up at Moe's Diner and we choose a booth two over from where Annie presented her PowerPoint for our fake dating ruse. This town is painted with memories of her, and then I remember how no matter how much I changed, how much I wanted things to be different, it was more of the same.

Delilah says nothing and drops a pot of coffee off at our table. Thumper winks at her, then pours me a cup and pushes it in front of me.

"I've never seen you like this before in my life," he says. "You're pathetic."

"I know," I say. "I realized last night why I don't drink tequila anymore."

"It's probably for the best." Thumper tilts his head as he looks at me. "When are you going to talk to Annie?"

I shrug. "I don't know what to say. I know I fucked up."

"I mean, yeah. You proposed to the most anal woman on earth. Of course she needs more time than to process marrying *you*," Thumper says. He taps the edge of the coffee cup. "Drink some. It'll help."

I chuckle. "My sister said the same thing."

"I know your sister hates me, and that's how I know she's smart. Besides agreeing with me."

The first sip of coffee scalds my throat, but I don't care. I drink again.

Tara walks by with her mother and stops when she sees me. I press myself into the booth, hoping I disappear. Her eyes narrow in on me like I murdered her entire family.

"I need to talk to him," Tara says to Thumper, but she stares at me.

"I'm not arguing with you," Thumper says, scooting across the booth.

"Come on," she says, grabbing my arm. I stumble as she pulls me outside.

I try to plan a tactical strategy in case she beats my ass, but she crosses her arms when she looks at me. Her stares are scarier than her fists.

"What the fuck are you doing?" she yells at me.

"Me? I'm getting breakfast with Thumper."

"You know what I mean," Tara says. "You're ignoring Annie."

I look down at my shoes as I kick gravel. "It's none of your business."

"It *is* my business. Annie is my friend, and I assume you love her, right?"

I say nothing, but I'm sure she can tell from my face. I love her. I love her in spite of myself.

Tara smacks me upside the head.

I cover the impact spot. "Ow, that fucking hurt."

"You deserve it," Tara says, crossing her arms again. "Who proposes to a woman when he's not absolutely sure she will say yes? And in a public place, too? You're one of those knuckleheads who orders a band to surprise a woman at a crowded restaurant."

"I saw a guy get turned down like that once. I may not be the brightest guy, but I would never do that," I say.

She smacks me again in the same place. My head pulses now.

"What was that for?"

"Because you're being an asshole. Figure out your shit and beg her to forgive you, asshole."

I rub my head. "Why are you calling me an asshole?"

"Because you were! To me!" Tara steps back toward the entrance to the restaurant.

I was.

Holy shit, I was.

She's smacked me upside the head for a third time., this time with her words.

The third time does it.

I remember all the women I've been with. How callous I was, how cruel I was in honesty. How if a guy treated Olive like that, the police wouldn't even be able to find his body.

"I'm sorry, Tara," I say. "I truly am. For not being clear on what we were. For being rude, asking you to leave the way I did. If you were led on in anyway, that's my bad. Not yours."

"Apology accepted," Tara says. She lightly punches my arm. "That wasn't so hard, was it?"

"No, ma'am," I say.

"Step up. Be the man Annie Stewart deserves. Go after her. Do whatever it takes. Don't give up," she says. She walks back inside, not looking back, leaving me questioning my whole existence.

Instead of walking back into the restaurant, I walk around the parking lot, my boots scrapping against the gravel and the cool air seeping through my thin sweater.

My mind races with all the ways I need to get her back. My instincts tell me to find her and convince her. But she deserves more than that. I want to fight for her. I want to work on this to make something extraordinary with her.

When I sit down across from Thumper, he's cutting a monster bite of pancakes dripping with syrup. He shoves it in his mouth.

It takes Thumper a solid minute of chewing and holding up his finger. When he finally swallows, he pours half a cup of water down his throat.

"I saw you talking to Tara. She's a feisty one, smacking you upside the head. Did you deserve it?"

"I did," I say, rubbing the spot.

"What did you talk about?" he asks, shoving another bite in his mouth.

"Annie."

He nods, taking a sip of his coffee. Once he swallows his pancakes, he asks, "What are you going to do?"

"I'm going to be a better man. So I gotta suck up my battered pride and try like hell to get her back."

Thumper nods once. "I'm finally proud to be your friend. Fucker."

ANNIE

Sweat drips in my eyes as I round the bend to my street. My heart pumps, and my legs feel heavy as my shoes slip against the gravel and dirt. I went hard on my run today, pushing it to six miles. My usual four wasn't enough to burn off the ache in my heart.

I miss Cameron. I miss his smirk, his hands on my body, our talks.

How I felt like the most beautiful woman in the world around him.

I've tried to deconstruct my reaction to his proposal. I love Cameron. He loves me. It feels natural and right.

I just couldn't say yes.

Wine helped for a little bit, but the second night of crying after a few glasses made me drain my currently drinking bottle. Now, it's my fifth day in a row of not drinking when my bungalow grows quiet, as the night fades to dark. My stomach clenches and twists, and sometimes I cannot stay away from the Woody Finch website, needing to look at his face and touch the screen with my fingers.

When I run, I feel nothing, just the wind on my face and the burn of acid in my calves.

I've made peace with it. Men have broken up with me before, and I've survived. I can survive this. Even if I don't want to, I can live without him.

But it still hurts.

I jump when I see a truck pull up beside me. When I see who it is, I fume.

"Thumper, don't sneak up on women like that! That's how women get kidnapped."

"Well, I'm kind of kidnapping you," he says, leaning over his passenger seat. He flings the door open. "Get in."

Is Thumper going to kill me?

"Annie, I've been scared of your dad ever since that field trip in third grade. Would I really kidnap you?"

He does have a point.

"I have this pepper spray," I say, showing him the small canister I run with on my key.

"Understood," Thumper says. "It's because of my Neanderthal of a friend I'm doing this. Get in."

I do as he asks and he peels away down the road before I get my seatbelt fastened.

Within four miles, we're in front of Quartz High School. He pulls into the bus drop-off in front of the library. The fence is open.

"What's going on?" I ask.

"It's Cameron's idea. I have no idea what he planned."

I get out gingerly and turn back. "Are you coming in?"

"I'm waiting out here to make sure you get in okay."

"Is this how I die, Thumper?"

"I don't know. No one knows. Go in. He's waiting for you in the library," Thumper says, exasperation in his voice.

I walk up the stairs, remembering all my years going

here. The library was my favorite place. I spent most of my lunches there, reading or helping students study.

It's where I first got to know Cameron when I tutored him in math. It's where my crush raged like crazy.

The door sticks like I remember as I walk into the familiar scents of old books and wood. I scan the main area to find Cameron sitting at the table where I tutored him.

He stands up in his old letterman jacket, now short in the sleeves. His smile makes me want to run to him.

There's too much hesitation in my heart to do that, though.

"Hi," I say.

"Hi," Cameron responds.

"How did you get access to this?"

"The current principal loves our beer so I promised him some four-packs. And maybe first crack at any new concoctions my brother comes up with." He pulls the chair out next to him and motions to it. "Can you sit with me?"

I walk slowly to the table and sit down. He doesn't touch me, but folds his hands together as he sits down next to me.

"I need you to tutor me," he says.

"On what?"

"How to be in a relationship," Cameron says. He takes a deep breath and continues. "I've never done this before and I obviously suck at it. You got me to graduate high school math so I know you can tutor me in this."

"Cameron, you've pulled away from me twice. That hurt me."

"I know," Cameron says. "You deserve everything. And I want to be better. For you. So I've already started."

"Started what?"

"Trying to be better," he says. "I went and apologized to

every woman I've hurt. You're the last one because I hope you'll be the last. Please tell me you're the last."

"You apologized?" I'm so confused. "For what?"

"I was always straightforward with women that it was only going to be sex, and I thought that was enough. If I was upfront, I wasn't responsible. But I dated lots of women who wanted more, and I knew that. It was wrong of me."

"How did that go?" I ask.

"Some good. Some not so good. Morgan took it as invitation and asked me out on a date. I said no because I can't go out with someone who treats my girls Thelma and Louise like that."

We both laugh since that raccoon story never stops being funny.

"I quit my job," I say.

"I heard. I'm proud of you," he says.

"It was time. I already called Dan."

"Smart. He seems like a great boss." Cameron pauses and then looks at me. Really looks at me. All the hurt falls away as we lock gazes. He takes my hands in his.

"I don't deserve a second chance, but if you give me one, I will spend the rest of my life showing you I can be a better man for you. Because I love you, Annie. I love you so much."

I should make him work for it. Show him how he hurt me for pulling away.

Instead, I wrap him in my arms and pepper his face with my kisses.

He pulls my face away gently to look at me. Really look at me.

"I love you so much," he says, a huge grin across his face.

"I love you, too," I say. "And I'm sorry about what happened."

"Don't be sorry. I rushed into asking you to marry me,

and I know that now. Your reaction was normal, and I understand."

I squeeze him tighter and close my eyes with a deep exhale of relief.

He's here. He's mine. I melt into his arms.

"Why didn't you take my calls? Why did you hide from me?"

"We went camping, and there was no cell service," he says, pulling me by the hand to a bench. "I should've stuck around, though, so we could figure it out. I'm sorry. I was embarrassed, and my usual MO is to give up when things are hard or when things get real. I'm done doing that. You're what I need, and you're worth fighting for."

I say nothing; I just kiss him.

"I called your sister. She was not happy to hear from me at first," Cameron says.

"You called Raegan?" I did call her right after I rejected Cameron, so she knows that he didn't call me back right away.

"She left me a rather disturbing voicemail." Cameron shudders. "I want to plan a weekend to San Francisco so we can get to know each other besides reputations. Well, *my* reputation. I've already done some research since it's been a long time since I've been there."

"You want to go to San Francisco? To visit my sister?"

He nods. "I already got a hotel recommendation. The Octavo. I was told not to use the elevator, though."

My heart melts. I climb onto his lap, straddling him, our lips still touching. We fit together. Feeling him against me, him hardening against the apex of my legs, makes me sink into him. Our kisses are saturated with need.

I have to do it. It's every book nerd's dream.

"Can we get busy in the high school library?"

He nods. "The principal gave us an hour."

He nips at my neck, making me giggle. I feel his lips all over my chest and when his lips travel over my sports bra where my nipple is, I shiver.

"God, I've missed you."

"I've missed you, too."

"I promise not to leave again if it gets hard," he says. "I'll give you as much time as you need."

"Cameron," I say, pulling away from him. His eyes are half-mast as I take his face between my hands. "I love you."

"I love you," he repeats and kisses me, standing up with my legs hooked around his waist. He walks and kisses, dropping me onto the low bookshelf where the dusty, outdated reference books are kept. He pulls my shorts with built-in underwear off of me and immediately dives in, kissing my thighs, dragging a tongue along my seam to my throbbing clit. The first swipe of his tongue causes shudders within my body, as my legs drop over his shoulders.

I can't believe Cameron is going down on me in our high school library.

My breath quickens as his tongue becomes aggressive, making my mind swirl, but my focus zeroes in on him down there.

I pull his face to mine, tasting my arousal on his lips. Our breath is the only sound between us as he pulls his shirt over his head, unbuckling his belt, and pulling his pants down. He finds a condom in his pocket.

"I brought this, just in case," he says, pinching the wrapper between his fingers.

"Smart," I say as he smirks and rolls it on.

Kissing him, I line him up to my entrance, my pussy slick and wet for him.

When he sinks into me, I moan and push his hair off of his forehead.

"Teenage Cameron would've loved this," he says, as his head rolls back. "Fuck, you feel so good."

"Teenage Annie would've, too." I hook my arm around his neck as I come, a cry escaping my lips as I let myself go. Cameron comes a second later, the walls of my pussy pulsing around him.

We're sweaty and spent. I love hearing his breath on my ear.

"Let's do that again at least seven more times tonight," I say. "At my house."

"Are you trying to kill me, woman?"

"Maybe," I say, kissing his nose.

"That's fine with me," he says, pushing my hair out of my face. He presses a kiss to my sticky forehead and pulls me into him, him still inside of me.

"You were always enough," I say, kissing his cheek.

"I was?" he asks.

I nod and kiss him. I cannot believe the love of my life is Cameron Finch, the silly guy who never liked school and never settled down until he saw me crying into a banana split at the Swift.

Until we pretended to be something when that something was always there.

I'm so glad I made that PowerPoint.

CAMERON

nnie's sister Raegan marries her fiancé Henry two months later at the San Francisco City Hall. It's ornate and grand, with white etchings in tall columns, perfect for two San Francisco lovers to tie the knot.

I can't take my eyes off of my beautiful girlfriend as she walks down the aisle, holding white lilies and wearing a sky-blue dress as maid of honor.

I can't wait to take it off later.

Henry's face scrunches with joy as he watches his bride float down the aisle.

Her hair is not her usual blue or pink—it's a soft, natural brown pulled back in a traditional updo with tiny white flowers tucked into twists.

Miley Cyrus's "When I Look at You" plays as Raegan walks down the aisle, flanked by her parents.

People I hope will be my in-laws one day.

"This is a weird song to walk down the aisle to," I whisper to the young-but-graying guy on my right. He's a good-looking dude. If I ever go gray, I want to do it like him.

"Miley Cyrus is a thing for them. Don't question it," he whispers.

Raegan finally warmed up to me right before the wedding, pulling me aside at the rehearsal dinner, telling me she was finally okay with me dating her sister.

She even gave me a hug, but still threatened dismemberment if I pulled any of the shit I pulled earlier again.

Fair.

As Raegan gets closer, I watch Henry. Tears filled his eyes, and while I don't think I'll cry when I marry Annie, I can't guarantee it.

Who am I kidding, I'm gonna sob.

We told our families shortly after our reunion in the library that our relationship started as a ploy to make Annie's ex jealous.

Surprisingly, no one was that mad.

"Maybe it was a way for you to test it. See if it could be real," Mom said after the crowd died down. "It obviously was."

Mom was absolutely right.

Raegan liked me more when she found out.

I catch Annie's gaze during the ceremony, and she winks. The blonde bridesmaid—I think her name is Cassie—blows kisses to the guy sitting next to me. He blows one back, and she smirks, looking back toward Raegan and Henry as they exchange their vows.

When the ceremony is finished and Henry kisses Raegan, they walk down the aisle to "We Can't Stop."

Going to a Miley Cyrus-themed wedding is a first.

Since it appears our women will be preoccupied with photos, I turn to the guy sitting next to me and extend my hand.

"I'm Cameron, Raegan's sister's boyfriend."

"Smith. My fiancée Cassie is the blonde bridesmaid." He shakes my hand, and damn, he has a strong grip.

"Congratulations, man."

"Thanks," he says.

"I'm sure the women will be taking a thousand pictures," I say. "Share an Uber?"

"Sure," he said.

I find Annie talking to the other members of the bridal party and kiss her neck. "I'm going to head over with Cassie's Smith to the reception," I say.

"I'm glad you met," Cassie says. "Just don't get stuck in an elevator with him. He's mine."

"Oh, so *they're* the reason we took the stairs at the Octavo." I drop a tiny kiss on Annie's lips, careful not to smudge her lipstick. "I'll see you over there."

Smith and I have a great conversation on the way to the reception at a Mediterranean restaurant with a rooftop entertainment space, overlooking the streets of San Francisco. It's the perfect breezy night, with warm air flowing through the billows of white tulle hung as decoration. We're a couple drinks in when the DJ announces the bridal party.

More Miley blares from the speakers.

"Really?" I ask Smith.

Smith swallows his gin and tonic. "They really love Miley."

Annie and the best man, Landon, dance their way into the reception to "Can't Be Tamed," wearing big sunglasses and holding blow-up microphones. Cassie enters with Henry's fourteen-year-old adopted brother from China, Charles, and they do a choreographed Hannah Montana dance to "Best of Both Worlds."

Once the wedding party is released from their entrance

duties, Annie runs towards me and jumps in my arms. Cassie, Smith's fiancé, tucks herself under his armpit.

"So, this is your boyfriend?" Cassie asks, nodding her chin toward us.

"Yes, it is," Annie says, kissing me on the cheek.

"Who knows, maybe you'll catch the bouquet," Cassie says.

I laugh as I kiss the top of Annie's head. I'm not sure if Cassie knows about the failed marriage proposal two months earlier. How I'm not asking again until I'm completely sure she will say yes.

"She might have to propose to me," I say.

Annie looks at me with a smirk, and I kiss her head again.

Dan, as well as my dad, offered Annie a job after I told them about her resignation at Banning Cellars.

"Any woman who tells that jackwagon Theo Banning off has the kind of tenacity I like," my dad said. She accepted the offer from both, working out a hybrid plan so she splits her time between Dan's business and my parents' brewery.

It's been fun to sneak off to different storage areas in the brewery and get frisky in lulls of the day.

Last week, I threw out the idea of us moving in together after we had sweaty sex on my couch. I couldn't see her face since she was resting on my chest, but my current game plan is to keep mentioning it until all of her stuff is accidentally there.

Then, get a solid yes before I drop to one knee again.

Every day I see a new item of hers there, a hairbrush, one of her pieces of art. I caught her measuring a few days ago.

After dinner, and the first dance to "Party in the USA", I stand on the perimeter of the dance floor as the bouquet toss happens. Of course, my competitive girlfriend catches it and holds it up in the air, jumping up and down, causing petals to fall.

Raegan points to me and mouths, "You're next." She then makes a signal to the DJ. The DJ nods, presses some buttons, and "Crash into Me" starts playing.

Annie looks at me and then her sister, pointing. Raegan throws up her hands, and they embrace.

I extend my hand to Annie and tuck my other arm behind my back.

"Madam," I say. She takes my hand, and I lead her into my arms.

"It seems like my sister finally likes you."

"She says I'm all right," I say, moving side by side. "She knows our song."

"She does," Annie says.

"You look really beautiful tonight."

"Thank you. You look rather handsome yourself."

"This has been a really good wedding," I say.

"Entirely too much Miley Cyrus."

"Absolutely."

"We will not have any Miley Cyrus at our wedding," she says.

A smirk crosses my lips. "Oh?"

"Absolutely not," she says. "One Miley Cyrus wedding is enough for one family."

I let her go so she can spin under my arm and once she's back in my arms, I look down at her. "Are you asking me to marry you?"

She shakes her head. "I'm not. I'll say yes, though. When you ask me again."

"This is a trick," I say, looking away from my love so I don't burst into laughter. "I'm not doing it now. I've learned my lesson doing it to this song, in public. Besides, proposing to someone at someone's wedding is kind of douchy."

"Eventually. Someday."

"Who says I'll ask you again?" I tease. "You won't even move in with me."

She leans in and whispers in my ear. "I won't live with you until we're engaged."

"Oh, really," I say. "I guess this will be a battle of the wills."

"I guess so," she responds.

"Let the best person win," I say.

"Exactly," she replies, looking up at me with pursed lips. "I love you."

"I love you, too." I kiss her and then rip my lips away. "You're going down, though. I don't care how romantic this song is or how many times you suck me off, I will not give in."

"Noted," she says. She moves her arms to around my neck as we continue to dance to our song. The rest of the world falls away and I look down at the woman I would do anything for.

I became a better man. For her.

I can't thank her enough.

But I will try later tonight when I peel this dress off her in our hotel room.

Then, I'll spend every day trying to get her to propose to me.

EPILOGUE

ANNIE

Five Months Later

"Oh, I can't look," I say, looking at the piece of plastic on the bathroom counter.

"It's been three minutes, right?" Cameron asks. He checks his phone. "We should have the verdict now."

I cover my eyes. "You look."

"No, you look," he says.

We stare at it. This piece of plastic might change our lives forever.

We still don't live together, but our relationship grows stronger every day. We're in a loving standoff—who will move or who will propose first? We spend practically every night together. He keeps stuff at my place, and I have stuff at his. Whitney came to stay with me and kind of never left, so we spend most nights at his place now. It's been magical, but we also don't want to mess up our good thing, by putting pressure about the future on it.

Until one night this month when I let Cameron slip his penis in without a condom and finish inside me.

In the middle of my cycle.

Cameron freaked out immediately.

"I didn't mean to. My pull-out game is not strong," he says. "You just feel so good..."

"It's fine," I say. "If it happens, it happens."

"You'll let me get you pregnant?" Cameron said, staring at me. I nod, and he kissed me so voraciously, we ended up having sex without a condom again. And again.

The pill always made me feel like garbage, so I stopped taking it five years ago. There's nothing holding Cameron's little swimmers back from finding a willing egg.

I freaked when I didn't get my period on the twenty-sixth day of my cycle, like I always do.

Now, we may be facing the consequences the first month we tested fate. But I'm secretly excited to find out.

Through a gap in my fingers, I see Cameron grab the pregnancy test and flip it over.

"Oh shit," he says, staring at it or at me. His eyes animate, and a deep relief washes over me. His mouth drops. He can't speak as he hands it to me.

"Oh my God," I say covering my mouth.

I sprung for the expensive test. It says "Pregnant."

"FUCK YEAH," Cameron says, picking me up, my legs wrapping around his waist. He kisses me and pushes my hair away from my face. "I love you, baby."

"I love you."

"Oh my God."

"Oh my God."

He takes me in for another deep kiss.

I sandwich his face between my hands like I'm a panini maker. "I know we were having our little competition, and I don't want you to feel like you have to ask me to marry you again or anything…"

"Oh, I will," Cameron says. "Not today because it feels reactive, but it's coming, honey. Will you say yes?"

I nod vigorously. He kisses me hard, and I melt into his arms. A baby. With Cameron. I'm so excited.

"We are going to be awesome parents," Cameron says. "This kid won the fucking jackpot. We're going to have DI babies. We're not going to have to pay for college. Fuck, this is amazing."

"I hope the kid gets your coordination."

"The kid is going to be *huge*," he says. He flings me around. "You are going to be the hottest pregnant woman."

He sets me down on my feet and touches my stomach with both of his hands. I hope our baby can sense him. Cameron looks at me. "I cannot believe I did that."

He beats his chest with a war cry, and I laugh as he picks me up and sets me down on my bed.

We are having a baby, and we'll figure everything out.

After all, it's us.

I cannot wait to do life with him. Create life with him.

The funny thing is that he was under my nose this entire time.

All I had to do was wake up and realize it.

We arrive at our Tuesday Woody Finch team meeting, hand-in-hand.

Before Cam opens the door for me, he turns to me and asks, "Are you ready?"

"Yes," I say. We decided we would tell his family this morning. Excitement prickles my skin.

I hope everyone is as excited as we are.

We walk to the communal office first to drop off my purse and hear a noise in the supply closet, where our raw materials are kept.

"Did you hear that?" Cameron asks me.

I stop what I'm doing and hear squeaking and then a deep sound.

Cam looks at me with alarm. "What if that raccoon is back?"

Ever since Olive befriended Thelma and Louise, she's become too trusting of all raccoons. She saw one outside the brewery last month, who gave her its classic, sad, glassy eyes. She let it in, and we later found it, fat and happy, sitting on a pile of grain like a king.

It took us three days to clean up, and we're still finding specks of grain in grout.

"I've been doing a lot of reading on raccoons, so let me handle this," Cameron says, pressing me back. "I will protect the mother of my unborn child."

"Thank you, my big strong man," I say, standing a few feet behind him.

A loud crash comes from the storage room, and I hear a female giggling.

"Unless a raccoon can throw its voice like that, I don't think it's a raccoon."

Cameron looks back and opens the door like he's a SWAT team member.

I shield my eyes immediately.

Reid looks back, with lipstick all over his face, and his shirt open, revealing a rather impressive set of abs. "It's not what it looks like."

Whitney, my best friend, is fixing the strap of her dress and smoothing down her skirt.

I can only see the back of my boyfriend's head, but I know he's confused.

"What the fuck, Reid? I thought you two *hated* each other."

"Well," Reid says, throwing his hands up.

"Come on, baby," I say. I push him out the door and stand there. Whitney can't look me in the eye, and Reid fumbles with his shirt buttons.

"I'm pregnant, by the way," I shout at them as I wave a big goodbye. Reid and Whitney's mouths gape open. "Reid, meeting starts in fifteen minutes."

Once the door is closed, I press my back against it. I hear them talk softly to each other and can't make out what they're saying.

Under my breath, I say, "Of course."

Maybe Whitney, my favorite romance author, is on her way to her happily ever after.

I smirk as I walk away, pressing my hand to my abdomen.

This baby and Cameron are mine.

The End

WANT MORE?

To keep up to date with Jenny and get more Cameron and Annie and the rest of the Finch family, please go to jennybuntingbooks.com to subscribe to her newsletter!

Loved *Fool's Gold*? Please consider reviewing on your favorite retailer! It helps others find and enjoy this book.

Come find Jenny on socials! Jenny is on Instagram and TikTok at @jennybuntingbooks and can be found on Facebook at Author Jenny Bunting! She also has a Facebook readers' group called Jenny Bunting's Adultish Readers. She would love to have you!

ACKNOWLEDGMENTS

Many people help an author bring a book to market and I have to say – I have the best people.

I would like to thank my beta readers: Amanda, Beth, Erica, and Goddess Divine. You all gave me such wonderful feedback and this book is stronger and more entertaining because of you. Cameron and Annie actually going on the double date was a terrible idea. Thank you for your time and attention. I appreciate you greatly.

To my editor, Sarah of Lopt & Cropt – this is our seventh title together and we work together like a well-oiled machine. Thank you for your help on this and the quick turnaround time.

To my cover designer, Kari March of Kari March Designs – thank you for coming up with this gorgeous gold cover. Your hair photoshopping skills know no bounds.

To my proofreader Horus Proofreading – thank you for catching all my little mistakes. I appreciate you.

Thank you to DC Reeves for writing *The Microbrewery Handbook*. It really helped with the creation of Woody Finch Brewery.

Jeremy and Booker – you are the best family a girl can ask for. Thank you for creating space in our life for me to chase this crazy dream.

ABOUT THE AUTHOR

Jenny Bunting started writing stories as a kid, and romance has always been her favorite. She "published" books by designing construction paper covers and still has a horde of them to this day. Jenny has had over thirty jobs, including working at a newspaper, at the mall, as a substitute teacher, and currently in insurance as a claims adjuster. She loves peanut butter, puns, exercise, reading, brunch, and IPAs. Jenny lives with her husband and their German shepherd in the suburbs of Sacramento, California.

www.ingramcontent.com/pod-product-compliance
Lightning Source LLC
Chambersburg PA
CBHW052033240626
47153CB00006B/2056